P1

MW00932421

"*Finding Zoe* is an inspiring novel about a young woman's struggle to overcome a mental illness and lead a fulfilling and productive life. It is also a moving love story and a must read for book clubs."

Mimi Latt, Author of *Ultimate Justice*

"Rosalee Jaeger's novel, *Finding Zoe,* is a fascinating read from beginning to end. Not only was I engrossed in the aspects of a gifted pianist unable to perform in public, but in Zoe's struggle to live a normal life in spite of her debilitating disease. *Finding Zoe* is a fast-reading, absorbing and ultimately inspiring novel. I couldn't put it down."

Corrinne Barkin, Concert Pianist

"A feeling of hopefulness and understanding make reading *Finding Zoe* a satisfying experience. It is a touching portrait of a young woman's struggle with mental illness, from its first manifestations in childhood to her coming to terms with it as a teacher, wife and mother."

Lili Endlich, Ph.D. MFT

"Had Zoe been referred to me during the many years I was working with children who had learning, psychological and emotional problems, I would have had little understanding of what she was experiencing or why it was happening to her and, sadly, would have been at a loss as to how to help her or her family.

Even with today's increased knowledge-base boosting the chances that mainstream psychology could be of benefit, I suspect that alternative healing methods would still be her best bet.

When you read this book, you'll accompany Zoe on her incredible journey as she struggles to grasp and understand the mysteries of her mind and to gain insight into her unusual condition. With a misunderstood and misdiagnosed illness, it's a wonder Zoe made it through her childhood, let alone into adulthood. Like me, you'll cheer her on as she searches for answers that finally guide her forward to an eventual normal life.

Although this book is fiction, it's real!"

Gilda F. Servetter, Ph.D. in Human Behavior and
Licensed MFCC and Educational Psychologist

ALSO BY ROSALEE (MANDELL) JAEGER:

Love and Other Passions

Finding Zoe

A NOVEL BY

Rosalee Jaeger

This book is a work of fiction. Names, characters, places, and
incidents are products of the author's imagination or are used fictitiously.
Any resemblance to actual events or locales or persons, living or dead,
is entirely coincidental.

Copyright © 2011 Rosalee Jaeger

All rights reserved. No part of this publication may be reproduced or
transmitted in any form or by any means electronic or mechanical,
including photocopy, recording or any information storage and retrieval
system without permission in writing from the copyright owner.

ISBN: 1453866574
ISBN-13: 9781453866573
LCCN: 2010914941

Printed in the United States of America.

Dedicated to everyone who has suffered from a debilitating illness, and to their loved ones.

Acknowledgments

I wish to thank my writing teachers for their invaluable input: among them, Allan Seager, author and instructor at University of Michigan who published more than 80 short stories in the New Yorker, Atlantic, and other periodicals; Robert Kirsch, author, instructor at UCLA, and critic for the Los Angeles Times; Megan Crane, author and instructor at UCLA; Aviva Layton, book doctor, for her critical comments; and all my teachers in junior and senior high school, who told me that one day I would be a famous author.

I also wish to thank my experts: Dr. Lily Endlich, psychoanalyst; Dr. Gilda Servettor, psychologist; Corrine Barkin, concert pianist, and Alan Jaeger, mental training consultant and author of *Getting Focused, Staying Focused*; for their invaluable help in making all aspects of my novel true and accurate.

I thank my editor, Joy Goodman, for her unrelenting and merciless eyes, and for her many suggestions.

And finally I wish to thank my husband, Marty, and my family: Stuart, Sue, Alan, Karen, Zachary, Hanna, Harrison, and Evan, for their love, support and all the riches they bring to my life.

Finding Zoe

Chapter One – Zoe

I first lost myself when I was six.

Mom was having a summer barbeque at our tiny little house in Van Nuys, California, but it was too hot and humid outside, so a bunch of people came inside and were sitting in the living room, waving newspapers as fans, since we only had a swamp cooler on our roof and it was too humid for it to work.

I had just finished eating a hot dog and came happily bouncing into the crowded room, when suddenly, I was overcome by a strange sensation. I could see all the people in the room, and I knew I was in the room, but it felt like I was looking at all of us from somewhere else. It was as if I was in a dream. Nothing seemed real.

My face turned hot, my hands began to sweat, I got this prickly numb feeling all over my body, and I began to shiver. With my heart beating a hundred miles a minute, I ran to my bedroom, lay face-down on my bed, put my hands over my ears, shut my eyes tight, and said over and over again, "Please go away, please go away, please go away."

In a few minutes, as suddenly as it had come, that frightening feeling left, and I was just me, lying in a pool of sweat, face-down on my bed, my body still trembling, my hands over my ears and my eyes shut tight. I sat up and looked around my room. My stuffed animals were sitting on my dresser waiting for me to cuddle them. My books were neatly lined up in my bookcase. My pink chenille bedspread, now moist from my sweat, was soft and warm to my touch, and my pink curtains were as still as the air. Everything was as it should be.

Still feeling a bit wobbly, with sweat still dripping from my face, I returned to the living room. Everyone was exactly where I'd left them: waving their newspapers, talking and laughing, just like before "it" happened. I grabbed a bunch of M&M's and stuffed them in my mouth, so happy that everything was fine and that I was me, and that it must have been the hot-dog I ate, because whenever I felt sick, Mom would tell me it must have been something I ate.

When I was seven, we moved to this big beautiful house in Woodland Hills that had five bedrooms and five bathrooms. Mom decided to paint each room in the house a different color. The bedrooms were shades of pink, blue, and lilac, the den was green, the living room and dining room were a pastel burgundy, and the kitchen was bright yellow. Each room had carpeting to match its color except the kitchen which had speckled yellow linoleum. No one could be bored in our house.

Our backyard was also great, with a swimming pool, a row of pomegranate trees along the back block-wall fence, lots of grass, and a guest house that my dad had built before we moved in, to use as his office.

Dad was an insurance agent and Mom was his secretary. Dad had always worked out of the house, starting with Mom and Dad's two-bedroom apartment in West Hollywood, then our tiny little house in Van Nuys, and now this corner of our humongous yard. A cement path led from the door of Dad's office, around our house to the sidewalk out front.

The first thing Mom bought after we moved into our new house was a big black baby-grand piano for the living room, and all three of us kids, my brother Andrew, two years older than me, my sister Claire, two years younger than me, and I, started taking piano lessons.

From the moment my fingers touched the keys, I knew this was what I was meant to do: play the piano. I loved the feel of the keys under my fingers. I loved the sound of each note emanating from the soundboard. I loved that I could look at black notes on white paper, and by hitting black and white keys, transform them into beautiful melodies. And I loved the fact, that the piano was such a gigantic thing, and yet I could master it, I could get it to speak through me.

I practiced all my little pieces every day until each one was perfect, and then I couldn't wait for Mrs. Blake, our piano teacher, to come back the next week so I could play for her, and get more pieces, harder pieces.

I was really happy that summer, but in September, when I started back to school, "it" happened again. There I was in my new classroom with my new teacher and a roomful of kids I had never met before, and suddenly my face turned hot, my hands began to sweat, I got this numb prickly feeling all over my body, and I began to shiver. I was too embarrassed to run from the room, although that's what I wanted to do, so I just closed my eyes, wishing it would go away, hearing my teacher's voice like an echo from a mountain top, and within a few minutes, "it" was gone, and I felt normal again. But I was afraid to open my eyes, afraid to move, afraid that it would happen again.

And it did happen again.

Isolated instances, when for no reason I would get that same feeling, as if I were in a dream, that the people around me weren't real, like I was Alice in Wonderland and had fallen down the rabbit hole.

It happened on the playground at school playing handball. The ball hit the wall and as it bounced back at me, the whole schoolyard of running, screaming kids suddenly seemed out of focus, as if I was looking at them through my dad's eyeglasses.

It happened at a birthday party, sitting around a backyard picnic table with 12 other little girls. Suddenly, it was again as if we were all in a picture in a picture book, and if someone turned the page, we would all disappear.

It seemed to happen most when I was with a lot of people or in an uncomfortable situation, but once it happened when I was home alone looking in the bathroom mirror. That might have been the scariest of all. There I was looking at my reflection, and all of a sudden, the person in the mirror wasn't me. I lost who I was.

Each time it happened, I'd get that numb tingling feeling and start to shiver, and then, I'd shut my eyes tight, touch my face and squeeze my arms, trying to make that feeling of not being me, of not being part of the real world go away. Usually, after a few minutes, it would go away. But each time it happened was more frightening than the last, and seemed to be lasting longer. At some point, I began hearing a voice within me before the feeling hit, warning me it was coming. That was almost as frightening as the attack itself. I named the voice, the Destroyer, because it was trying to destroy me.

I wanted to tell someone about this horrible thing that was happening to me, to find out if maybe it was happening to other people, too. But I was afraid to ask anyone or tell anyone, not even my mom, because I didn't want anyone to think I was abnormal, or some kind of freak. So I kept silent about it and kept my distance from all the kids at school. I had a secret, a terrible secret and I didn't want anyone to find out about it.

Maybe that's another reason I loved the piano so much. When I was playing the piano, I could think of nothing but the music.

Unfortunately, no matter how many hours I spent at the piano, there was still plenty of time to think about my problem, to try to figure out why this was happening to me. Had I done something really, really bad, and this was my punishment? Or was I just born crazy? I didn't think I was born crazy because in every other way, my life seemed pretty normal.

Andrew, Claire, and I did what most kids do: we walked to and from school each day; we all took piano lessons, except at some point Andrew gave up piano lessons for guitar lessons; Mom took the three of us to the library every two weeks where we'd load up with ten books each, although I was the only one who read all ten; she took us to museums, mostly art museums; and there was always music in our house and in our car. Mom loved classical music. Her favorites were any piano concerto, any violin concerto, or anything by Beethoven, Chopin, or Mozart. Maybe that's why they became my favorite composers.

She also loved opera, and every Saturday morning, the Metropolitan Opera with Milton Cross would be blaring through the house. But I liked it; I liked everything Mom liked, even the opera. Even before we moved into our new house, I'd lie on her bed with her and listen for awhile. She'd lie there with her eyes closed, hugging me to her chest or holding my hand, and saying every now and then, "Isn't this gorgeous?"

As for Andrew, Claire and me, of course, there was the usual fighting between us, but considering how close we were in age, I think we got along pretty well. In a way, our family was a tight little island: there were just the five of us. All our other relatives lived in Detroit, and while I missed having grandmas and grandpas, aunts, uncles, and cousins around all the time, like other kids, I still got to see them. Either they'd come to visit us, or we'd go to Detroit, to visit them.

Only it wasn't Detroit we went to, but the suburbs of Detroit. Detroit was kind of like the Westward movement, only it was the white people moving out of Detroit, and the black people moving in. In fact, my dad's family was probably the only white family left in Detroit. But my Grandpa Ralph didn't mind, because my dad's two brothers were going to be doctors and both his sisters were going to the University of Michigan.

My dad had started to go to college, but dropped out to marry my mom when he was 19 and she was 18. My mom's parents weren't happy about that, since my mom's brother was already a doctor, and my mom's parents wanted my mom to be one, too. They also weren't happy that my dad took my mom to Los Angeles, but after Andrew was born a year later, I guess they forgave my dad, because they were always nice to him.

My dad didn't seem to mind he didn't finish college, but my mom was always saying how sorry she was that she didn't go, and that she was going to make sure her children didn't make the same mistake!

By the time I was nine, I was practicing the piano two to three hours a day. I loved practicing so much I couldn't wait to get home from school and get my schoolwork done, so I could sit down at the piano, and play and play. I loved the scales, I loved *Hanon*, I loved playing all my little pieces, perfecting this one, and then going on to conquer the next one.

I whizzed through my *John Thompson's First Grade Book*, and then the *Second Grade Book*, and then the *Third Grade Book*, in what seemed like no time at all.

I thought Mom would be happy about my progress, but instead she was upset. "Zoe, I'm happy that you love to play the piano, but I don't think it's healthy for a young girl to be spending all her free time at the piano. You should be outside playing with your friends."

What friends, I thought. I didn't really have any friends, although most of the kids at school were friendly enough to me, except, of course, for the "in" girls who would only talk to each other and God. But the only kids I spent time with after school were the two girls who lived down the block: Teri Vogel and Melissa Saperstein. Both of them seemed to really like me, and didn't think I was weird because I got good grades in school and practiced the piano every day. So I guess, in a way, they were my friends.

They'd come over now and then to play with me, and invite me over to their houses. But even with them, there was this barrier between us. I had to hide who I really was, my fears, my malady, the voice that spoke to me. They certainly wouldn't want to be my friend if they knew the truth about me. Besides, I really was too busy with my homework and my practicing to spend too much time with them.

Not only was Mom upset that I was playing the piano too much, but she and my dad were both upset that Andrew was playing the guitar too much.

By now, Andrew not only had an acoustic guitar, but an electric guitar. He had begged Mom and Day night and day to get him that electric guitar and eventually they caved in. He had learned to play both guitars in like a minute, and now spent all of his time in his room making up songs and strumming away on one guitar or the other.

Fortunately for Mom and Dad, Claire wanted nothing to do with music.

Claire was not the least bit like Andrew or me. She had a zillion friends. Every day of the week, she was at a friend's house or they were at ours; and on the weekends, either she'd sleep at a friend's house, or they'd sleep at ours.

I really didn't like many of her friends. They were always making little snide remarks about Andrew and me, like, "Does your brother ever come out of his room?" or "What would your sister do without her piano?" Like we were the biggest jerks in the world.

But I didn't care. I didn't care what anyone thought, or what anyone said. I had found my niche in life. When I was playing the piano, nothing else mattered to me. I was in a different time and place, a place I loved, a place where I felt comfortable, safe and at peace.

A few months after my ninth birthday, Mom and Dad decided that Claire and I should take tennis lessons. Mom and Dad were both big into sports. They played tennis with their friends every weekend and sometimes during the week; Dad was crazy about the Dodgers and took us to a baseball game every now and then; and they both watched baseball, basketball, golf, and especially tennis—every minute of Wimbledon and the U.S. Open—on TV.

Dad was dying to get Andrew into sports. He started in on him when he was three, taking him to the tennis court and hitting tennis balls to him, taking him to the park to kick soccer balls and play catch, putting up a basketball hoop in our yard and shooting baskets with him. And every year after Andrew turned six, Dad tried to sign him up for a baseball, basketball, or soccer league, each in its season. But no matter how hard Dad tried to get Andrew to play some sport, Andrew refused to play any of them. All Andrew cared about was his music. And that was a big problem between Dad and Andrew. Sometimes I felt sorry for Andrew because he wasn't the son my dad wanted, and sometimes I felt sorry for my dad because Andrew wasn't the son he wanted. I think that's why Claire and I tried to be the best girls we could be.

So when Mom asked Claire and me to take tennis lessons, we both said, "yes."

I actually thought it would be fun to play tennis, although I was a little scared about getting out on a tennis court with a bunch of girls I didn't know. What if "it" happened? It would happen in a situation like this. Being stared at, or doing something

I might fail at. I didn't want to make a fool of myself. But I also didn't want to disappoint my mom and dad. I was totally torn about the whole thing.

On the day Mom took us to our first lesson, Claire trotted right out to where the teacher and the other girls had gathered, but I hung back with Mom.

"Go ahead," Mom said with an encouraging smile.

I smiled back, trying to embolden myself. But the last place I wanted to be right now was on this tennis court.

"Zoe, go join your sister," Mom said, this time without a smile.

I started to walk toward the teacher and the other girls, but as I approached, I felt my stomach muscles tighten, my hands go numb. If I couldn't feel my fingers, how was I going to hold a tennis racquet? I wanted to run, to hide, to be any place but here.

Mom was standing by the fence watching us. The other girls were practice-swinging. I began to shiver, my face turned hot, and my Destroyer said, "You can't do this."

I turned and ran to my mom. "I want to go home."

"Zoe," she said in her stern voice, "you can't sit at the piano all day. You need some exercise."

"But I don't feel well," I said.

She sighed. "Can we at least wait until Claire is done with her lesson?"

I was afraid that just standing there, out in the bright sunlight, with all those strange girls around, "it" would happen. I couldn't take a chance; I had to get out of there. "No, Mom. I want to go home now."

"You're impossible," Mom said. But drove me home.

Fortunately, Claire loved her lesson, and wanted to go again. Thank God for Claire, I thought. At least Mom and Dad had one normal child in their family.

In spite of my fears about taking tennis lessons, I did learn to play by playing with Claire, Dad and/or Mom. Just the two, three, or four of us on the tennis court was fine. It was the class I was afraid of. And while I was never going to be a great tennis player, I did enjoy the game, and was at least getting some exercise, which made Mom happy.

The following year, when we kids were 8, 10, and 12, Mom decided to go to college. She had been bemoaning the fact she hadn't gone to college for as long as I could remember, and now at age 31, she was going to do it.

Dad wasn't too happy about it.

She told him about her decision at lunch one Saturday afternoon in August. Mom, Dad and I were sitting around the kitchen table eating their favorite lunch: tuna salad sandwiches on whole wheat bread. Andrew was upstairs playing the guitar and Claire was at a friend's house, when Mom said, "Dan, I've decided to go to college."

Dad took a big bite of sandwich, "You mean take some classes in night school?"

"No," she said. "I mean full time, during the day."

Dad stopped chewing and looked at her with disbelief. "You've got to be kidding me."

"No, I'm serious."

He took a minute to swallow. "But you can't go during the day. You're my secretary."

"I guess you'll have to get another secretary."

"But I don't want another secretary. I want you."

"I'm sorry," she said, "but I've made up my mind."

He thought for a moment, "But what's wrong with night school?"

"It'll take me forever."

"Then what'll I do for a secretary?"

"I'll find you one."

He looked pretty upset, but I guess he knew that once Mom made up her mind, there was no changing it. "Okay, Gail," he said, "but you better find me a good one."

Frankly, I was pretty stunned myself by my mother's decision. If she went back to school, who was going to take care of us? But she arranged her schedule so that she took classes only between 9 and 3, or at night, so she could take us wherever we had to go.

Chapter Two — Piano Lessons

It was about a month after Mom started school that my piano teacher, Mrs. Blake, told my mom she thought I needed a more advanced teacher.

"Zoe's amazing," Mrs. Blake said to my mom.

"I'd rather she not be so amazing," my mom said. "All she does is practice the piano."

Which really wasn't true. I did spend my two or three hours a day practicing, but I also spent a lot of time on my homework and reading books, and I did spend some time with Teri and Missy, although we weren't as close as we could have been. And in September, I had started Hebrew School. I thought that might trigger an attack: the first day in a new setting, a new class, new kids—but it didn't. In fact, I hadn't had an attack in quite a while and was beginning to think maybe they'd gone forever. Maybe it was just a childhood disease, like measles or mumps. Maybe it would never come back. But still, I was afraid to let down my guard. Afraid that if I wasn't vigilant, it would come back.

"I have someone in mind," Mrs. Blake said. "She taught at Julliard."

"Julliard," my mom said with an exclamation point.

"Yes, Julliard," Mrs. Blake said, with the emphasis on 'Julliard'.

Mom looked pensive. "My mother's cousin went to school there."

I was wondering why I had never heard this before.

"He was a violinist," my mom said.

"Oh," Mrs. Blake said, "how exciting."

"Yes, he became a first violinist with the Boston Symphony."

"How come you never told me about him?" I asked.

"Because he died," she said.

Neither Mrs. Blake nor I seemed to know what to say to that.

"So," Mrs. Blake broke the silence, "getting back to Zoe....of course, she'll have to audition for Ms. Hockensmith. That's her name, Ms. Hockensmith."

Mom seemed lost in a dream and then suddenly snapped out of it. "But why can't you continue as her teacher?"

"I would love to," Mrs. Blake said, "but really, Zoe is at a stage where she needs someone more sophisticated than I am. I just teach beginners."

"But surely," Mom said, "you can just give her harder pieces."

Mrs. Blake smiled, and as if talking to a child, said, "You don't understand, Gail. She needs someone who knows things I don't know."

Another moment of thought on Mom's part. "Does she come to the house or do I have to take her there?"

"You'll have to take her there."

Mom looked exasperated. "This couldn't come at a worse time. I just started back to school full time."

"It's only one hour a week."

Mom grimaced. "How much does she charge?"

Even at ten, I knew that probably was not the issue. Even at ten, it was obvious to me, my mom did not want me to take lessons from a more advanced teacher.

"You'll have to ask her that," Mrs. Blake said. "I'll give you her phone number and you can call her and arrange for the audition, providing, that is, that the price is right."

Mrs. Blake wrote down a number on her card and handed it to my mother.

My mother looked at it with a furrowed brow. I knew she was unhappy, but I also believed she would call.

"Okay, then," my mom said. "But you will come next week anyway, won't you?"

"Of course," Mrs. Blake said. Then giving me a hug, "Good luck on your audition, sweetie. Don't worry, you'll do great!"

At that moment, I loved Mrs. Blake more than anyone on earth.

But even before she was out the door, I began to worry about the audition. I didn't like the sound of it, and I didn't like the idea of it. When I played the piano, it was just for me. I didn't care what anyone thought, or anyone cared. It was just my own private haven. Mrs. Blake was all right because she was there at the beginning. I felt safe with her. But now, this Ms. Hockensmith, she would be judging me. I would be naked before her. I didn't like that. Could I get through it, or would I have an attack?

Maybe I should just tell Mom to forget the whole thing, that I wanted to stay with Mrs. Blake. Except I did want to play better. I wanted to play like the people on the records: Horowitz, Serkin, Gilels, Rubinstein. I wanted to know everything they knew; I wanted to perfect my technique, to discover all the music I had not played yet: everything by Mozart, Chopin, Beethoven. I wanted to master every piano concerto. How I loved listening to them. I wanted to be the best that I could be.

I heard Mom talking to Dad. "I don't know about this new teacher. Zoe spends too much time practicing as it is."

"If she's happy, let her alone," Dad said.

"But it's not healthy for her. She's already spending three hours a day at the piano. She needs a normal life."

"Then don't get this new teacher." Dad didn't have much patience for talk like this. He just wanted to solve the problem and move on.

"I don't know what do," Mom said.

"Just let her do what she wants. At some point she'll meet some guy, get married, have babies, and that'll be the end of it."

"If she meets some guy."

"Of course, she will. She's a pretty girl. Some guy will snap her up."

"If she ever gets away from the piano long enough to meet a guy."

"You make the decision. I'm going to watch TV."

I had mixed emotions...to root for Mom or Mrs. Blake?

Mom made the call. My audition was set for four o'clock the following Tuesday. That whole day, I couldn't think of anything else. I think I may have failed my history test even though I knew all the answers. My chest was burning, and I was feeling nauseated the whole day. Was it worth it? Yes....because I wanted to study with Ms. Hockensmith. I wanted it so badly.

By the time we pulled up in front of her house, I was a nervous wreck. Why had I agreed to do this? And then this feeling of dread came over me and I heard the Destroyer's voice, "Zoe, you're an idiot. Why did you agree to do this?" And suddenly I wasn't me. I was some other person who did not know how to play the piano. Who could not realize the moment. Who definitely could not take a step out the car door, let alone play a piece.

I shrunk down in the seat, and said, "Mom, I can't do this. I want to go home."

"But Ms. Hockensmith is expecting us."

"I'm sorry, but I feel nauseous. I think I'm going to throw up."

Mom was somewhere out there...staring at me. Disbelief in her eyes. "You're sure?"

"Yes, I'm sure," I fairly yelled at her.

She sighed, got out of the car, and walked up to Ms. Hockensmith's door. I closed my eyes tightly, wishing this feeling would go away...but it would not. My hands were sweating, but my body was shivering. I needed to get out of here.

In a few minutes, Mom was back...looking pitiful, but driving. Driving me to safety.

The moment I got home, I ran up to my bedroom and shut the door, praying no one would open it. I knew my body was covered with needles, that I was hot and cold at the same time, but there was nothing I could do about it. I wasn't there. I hid under my pink bedspread, feeling helpless and hopeless. Why was this happening to me? Why couldn't I lead a normal life? What had I done wrong?

After what seemed like hours, I knew I was back, back to the real world, because I couldn't catch my breath from the tears clogging my throat.

It was three weeks later that Mrs. Blake again brought up the idea of my taking lessons from a more sophisticated teacher. This time, I went through the same anxiety I had gone through the last time Mrs. Blake had brought it up. But Mrs. Blake would not let go of it.

"Zoe," she said. "I know you want to be the best pianist you can be."

"Yes," I said. That was true.

"Well, you will never attain your dream if you stay with me. You need someone who knows more than I ever will. Please, Zoe, for me, for yourself, go see Ms. Hockensmith."

"But will I have to audition?"

"Don't think of it as an audition. Just think of it as playing a piece for your new teacher. She's a very lovely lady. She won't be critical, or insult you. She'll just be swept away by your brilliance and beg you to be her student."

"But I want you to teach me," I said, partly because I did want her, but mostly because I was afraid of that audition.

"I can't teach you anymore," Mrs. Blake said. "I wish I could."

"But if she won't take me, will you still teach me?"

"Yes," she said.

I thought it over. If I just looked at it as playing a piece for my teacher...maybe I could get through it. "All right," I said. "I'll try again."

"Good," Mrs. Blake said, giving me a hug.

"But will you still come to see me?"

"Of course," she said. "You'll always be part of my life."

So Mom called again, and made another appointment for Tuesday at 4, and again, I couldn't concentrate on anything at school the whole day, but at 4 o'clock, there I was walking up to Ms. Hockensmith's door, and I was not sweating, I was not shivering, I was not nauseated, because I told myself that if I failed the audition, Mrs. Blake would continue teaching me.

Mom rang the bell, and there she was opening the front door, Ms. Hockensmith. I liked her immediately. She was an elderly woman with plain grey hair and no makeup, who looked as nervous as I felt.

"Come in," she said in a gentle voice.

Her house was immaculate with non-descript furniture... everything seemed tan...except for the two black pianos: a baby-grand in her living room, and an upright in her dining room.

The walls were bare, but there was a black bust of Beethoven on her mantel piece.

After introductions, Ms. Hockensmith said, "Mrs. Blake spoke very highly of you, Zoe."

I'm sure I blushed. But I didn't really want small talk. I wanted to get to it. To get it over.

Perhaps she got the message because she said, "What would you like to play?"

"The Mozart D Minor Fantasia," I said.

"Fine," she said.

I sat on the black padded bench at the baby-grand. It was a Steinway. Mine at home was a Hamilton. But the keys were the same. The touch should be close. And I was here at my favorite place: the piano. As I began to play, the tension in my stomach relaxed for the first time that day. Every part of me was focused on the notes, my fingers, and the sound and beauty of the music.

When I finished, Ms. Hockensmith said, "That was very good, Zoe." Then turning to my mother, "I would very much like to have Zoe as my pupil."

Decision time for Mom. Apparently she had already agreed to the price on the phone. "Do you come to the house, or do I have to bring her here?"

I felt like she was talking about a sack of potatoes.

"I'm afraid you'll have to bring her here."

"Oh," Mom said, disappointment in her voice. Yes, it would be a burden in her life, but no more than taking Claire to tennis lessons, I thought. "All right," Mom said.

"Good. Then shall we make it every Tuesday at four?"

"I think that'll work," Mom said, still not happy.

"All right then."

We all stood, shook hands, and Ms. Hockensmith said, "See you next week, Zoe."

Walking to the car, I never felt so happy in my life. I had gotten through it. I had not had an attack, and I was going to be taking piano lessons with a teacher from Julliard!

Ms. Hockensmith was a wonderful teacher, very soft spoken, but very knowledgeable.

I discovered that the reason her house had been so bare was that she had just moved here from New York, and her paintings and knick-knacks hadn't arrived yet. But by my second lesson, the walls were adorned by framed posters from Carnegie Hall and a few landscape paintings; and books and music filled her floor to ceiling book shelves.

In a way I felt sorry for Ms. Hockensmith: she had never married or had children; she had never been famous or made a recording, although apparently she had been a great pianist. The emptiness of her home, and apparently her life, made me feel sad for her and I decided I didn't want my life to turn out as hers had.

After my lesson, if there wasn't another pupil immediately there, I would stay awhile and talk to Ms. Hockensmith about what I was studying at school, and about her musical career. She had given many recitals she told me, and had accompanied many solo instrumentalists and singers, but had never played a concerto with an orchestra, except the one at Julliard, which was still a highlight of her life.

"It's a feeling like no other," she told me, in her sweet soft voice. "One I would like you to have, Zoe."

We almost never talked about personal things, and I knew she would never think of hugging me, like Mrs. Blake had. But I could tell she liked me. I hoped as much as I liked her.

She started me on Czerny, the Bach two-part inventions, a book of Myra Hess' favorite pieces, and the Mozart sonatas. I loved each and every assignment. I could not get enough of them, especially the Mozart sonatas. How terribly beautiful each page was. I wondered at the man's genius. If only my malady would leave me alone, perhaps I could become a great pianist. I hoped I had found the cure...not to put myself in an uncomfortable position; not to get too close to anyone.

Chapter Three — Challenges

A few months before Andrew turned thirteen, he began preparing for his Bar Mitzvah. I was now in my second year of Hebrew School, and Claire would be starting next year when she turned ten.

Although Mom and Dad weren't that religious, we had always belonged to a synagogue, and Mom and Dad had always been active in the brotherhood and sisterhood—maybe because it was good for business. Still, we did go to temple on the high holidays, and Mom did make Passover dinner, and decorate the house for Hanukah, but basically that was it. We didn't light candles on Friday night or keep Kosher, or go to Friday night services. In fact, I wasn't even sure my parents believed in God. But they made sure we knew we were Jewish.

Strangely, while Andrew wasn't crazy about regular school, he actually liked Hebrew school. "There's something about those Hebrew letters," he told me. "They're kind of like music. A different language. But I like it. I like learning the sound of each, and I like the chanting. It's kind of spiritual. So why not go to Hebrew school?"

Mom and Dad were planning this humongous party for Andrew, even though it wasn't what he wanted, but they had all these friends and clients they had to invite.

"How do you feel about it all?" I asked Andrew.

"I'm just a pawn in their game of chess," he replied, and then wrote a song about it, changing it to, "I'm just a pawn in the game of life." The words went something like, "I gotta do what I gotta do, not what I wanna do, wanna do, 'cause I'm just a pawn in the game of life, I'm just a pawn in the game of life."

All four of our grandparents flew in from Detroit a few days before the Bar Mitzvah. My mom's parents stayed at a hotel, because they could afford it; my dad's parents stayed at our house because they couldn't. I liked all four of my grandparents, but they were very different from each other.

My mom's mother, Grandma Nina, was a teacher; her dad, Grandpa Jack, was a CPA. Of course, I felt closer to my mom's parents because they came out to visit us every year that we didn't go Detroit. They were both very sweet and loving, and always stylishly dressed.

Neither of my dad's parents had gone to college. His father, Grandpa Ralph, was a baker; his mother, Grandma Ruth, had gotten pregnant at 18, and spent her life raising five children in the same three-bedroom, one-bathroom house that they still lived in. Grandma Ruth was very fat and a little sloppy, and Grandpa Ralph liked to tell dirty jokes.

Yet the sad thing was that neither of my dad's parents was very nice to my dad. My dad hadn't finished college, and all they talked about was my dad's brother, the pediatrician; his other brother, the ophthalmologist; his sister getting her PHD in pharmacy; and his other sister getting her master's in psychology. Even I could feel how much these conversations hurt my dad.

My dad's parents hadn't been out to visit us since we moved into our new house, and one afternoon while I was sitting in the backyard with my dad and Grandpa Ralph, Grandpa Ralph said to my dad, "This is some house!"

"Yeah," my dad said, "it is pretty nice."

Then Grandpa Ralph turned to my dad and kind of whispered, "I guess Gail's parents helped you out with it."

My dad's face turned red and his eyes started bulging. "No, Dad," he said, "I bought it all with my own money."

Grandpa Ralph was pensive for a few moments, and then said, "Well, of course you never had to pay rent on an office and Gail was your secretary for all those years."

My dad took a deep breath. "That's true," my dad said, "but my kids didn't have to share a bedroom with their two siblings, and my kids didn't have to share a bathroom with six other people—they each have their own bathroom; and my kids live in a beautiful house in a high class neighborhood." He took a breath. "And I've probably made more money in the last three years than you made in your whole life." And with that, he got up and walked back to the house.

My grandpa looked stunned for a moment. Then he turned to me and said, "When I came to this country I was a Greenie. I was *lucky* to get a job as a baker. I had five kids to support and a wife who never worked. What does he want from me?"

I didn't know what to say to that. I was eleven. "I know, grandpa," I said. "You did the best you could." And then I stayed and listened to him tell joke after joke, until my mom called us to come in for dinner.

Aside from the incident in the backyard and the few tensions going on between my dad and his parents, I was having a really fun week. I loved having my grandparents around, having dinner together every night, and I actually enjoyed playing the piano for them, and getting lots of accolades about how brilliant I was. But as the actual day of the big event approached, I became more and more apprehensive: I was so afraid that "it" might happen.

I got through the morning services all right, but then in the evening when we were preparing to go to the party, I heard it. The voice. The Destroyer was back. It said, "You can't really do this." It said, "All those people. You know what happens to you when you're around too many people. They'll all be looking at you. You know you're not going to get through this."

"But it isn't my Bar Mitzvah," I argued with it. "No one's going to be looking at me."

"Oh, yes they are," it said. "Everyone's going to be looking at you."

My stomach started churning. "No one's going to be looking at me," I said aloud, trying to shut out the Destroyer, trying to pretend that everything was going to be okay.

I put on my pretty new pink dress, my dyed-to-match pumps with one inch heels, went into the bathroom to brush my hair and put on my lipstick, and then "it" happened. That numb prickly feeling came over my body, and I began to shiver. I closed my eyes tight because I was afraid to look in the mirror. Afraid I would not see myself. "No, no, no," I said to myself. "Please, dear God, don't let this be happening."

My mom was at the door. "Zoe, are you ready?"

I hung onto the cold hard porcelain of the sink, praying I would come back to reality. Please, dear God, let me come back. "I'm not feeling well," I said.

"But we have to leave now," she said.

"Please go without me," I said.

"Zoe, don't be ridiculous. We're not going to go without you. What's wrong? Are you nauseous? Do you have a headache?"

"Yes," I said, praying "it" would leave me, praying she would just go and leave me.

"I'll give you an Alka-Seltzer. That cures everything."

Not what I have, I thought. Then miraculously, the numbness began to fade. I opened my eyes, and it was just my face staring back at me. My face whose lips needed lipstick, and whose shiny nose needed maybe a touch of powder. I wanted to fall on my knees, to thank God. I wanted to dance, to sing. It had left me. I could go to the party.

The party was amazing. More like a wedding than a Bar Mitzvah. The theme was famous musical groups, which meant that each table's centerpiece had the name of some famous group or musician, like *The Beatles, Chicago, Aerosmith,* and Jerry Garcia. (Mom wouldn't allow *The Grateful Dead*). I thought a Bar Mitzvah should have a religious theme, but most of them now were about the Dodgers, the Rams, the Lakers, the Bruins, or the Trojans.

But the three best things about Andrew's Bar Mitzvah were: 1) all four of our grandparents were there; 2) Andrew's band was hired to play the music, with him playing his acoustic and electric guitars; and 3) I got through the party without any more problems.

After Andrew's Bar Mitzvah, things went back to normal. I was doing well in regular school and Hebrew school, Ms. Hockensmith was very happy with my progress at the piano, and Mom was still after me about having more friends and being more sociable. To make her happy, I decided I would make an effort to spend more time with Teri and Missy, and surprisingly, I found that I actually loved being with them. Maybe part of it was that they thought it was great that I was so dedicated to the piano, and would often want to sit for awhile and listen to me play.

The only blight on my happy state was that looming before me was the dreaded Bat Mitzvah. It wasn't coming up for a year, but just the thought of me standing in front of the thousands of people Mom and Dad were planning to invite, was enough to give me goose-bumps.

About six months before the event was to take place, Mom wanted me to go with her to pick out invitations....the first step on the way to Hell. I didn't know if I had the courage to confront her, but I had to try.

"Mom, I really don't want a big Bat Mitzvah."

"But why not? You worked hard. You deserve the same big celebration Andrew had."

"But I don't want the same big celebration Andrew had. I don't want anyone at my Bat Mitzvah, except our immediate family. You, Dad, Andrew, Claire, and of course, the rabbi and cantor."

"There is no way that's going to happen," she said.

"But that's what I want," I said.

"But why wouldn't you want what Andrew had?"

"Because I don't."

"But why?"

She seemed so strong, so eager, and I felt so tiny, like David against Goliath. I wanted to tell her the truth, to tell her about this horrible thing that happened to me. I wanted her to cuddle me in her arms, and tell me everything would be all right. But if I told her the truth, wouldn't that be even more disappointing to her? That I wasn't normal. That something was wrong with me. And if she found out, then everyone would find out. I couldn't let that happen. "I'm sorry, Mom," I said, "but I just don't feel comfortable in front of people."

"Well, you better get over it," she said," because you *are* going to have the same big Bar Mitzvah Andrew had."

After we argued back and forth for a few weeks, she grudgingly agreed to let me have a private service...just the rabbi, the cantor, and the five of us, but she wouldn't give up about the party, and neither would I. "What if we just go out to dinner at some fancy restaurant...just the five of us," I suggested. "Maybe at the beach."

"But what about all your friends and all my friends?" Mom replied.

"I don't want them," I said.

"But what about all our relatives from Detroit?"

I really would have liked to have the relatives from Detroit, but what if "it" happened and I wasn't able to get through my Bat Mitzvah. How embarrassing would that be? "No," I said. "I don't want our relatives from Detroit."

"But what about your grandparents?" Mom implored. "You can't expect them to fly all the way to California for your Bat Mitzvah and then not go to the service or the dinner."

Again, it was like a stab wound to my heart. Yes, of course I wanted my grandparents there, and all my aunts and uncles and cousins, and my two friends, Teri and Missy, but I was afraid. "No, Mom," I said. "I just want the five of us. Just you, Dad, Andrew and Claire." I knew I was being harsh, but I also knew that if I let my grandparents come, I'd have a fight over every other relative and friend Mom wanted to invite.

"Well then I won't invite them," Mom said. "If there's not going to be a service or a party, what's the point?"

Somehow she broke the news to my grandparents that they were not invited to my Bat Mitzvah. I felt terrible about it. How could I not have my grandparents at my Bat Mitzvah? But I just couldn't take a chance of "it" happening. I had to do whatever I could to take the pressure off me.

And it worked. I had this nice quiet Havdallah service in the evening so that none of the congregation was there, just the rabbi, the cantor, and the five of us, and then the five of us went out to a really fancy restaurant at the beach. I could tell how disappointed Mom and Dad were, but they never said a word, and I'd say, all and all, it was a really nice evening.

A year later, Mom graduated from Cal State Northridge with a 3.8 average and a B.A. in Liberal Studies. Dad wanted to throw her a big party, but surprisingly she didn't want one. That was unusual for Mom; she wanted a party for every occasion. The only thing I could figure out was that maybe she was ashamed because all her other friends had graduated from college at a normal time. Maybe she didn't want to make a big deal about it.

Whatever it was, the family did go out to a fancy restaurant at the beach, not the same one we'd gone to for my Bat Mitzvah, but a new trendy one.

As we were eating, and after Mom had downed two glasses of wine, she informed my father that she was not going back to work for him.

Dad's face turned red. "What do you mean you're not coming back to work for me?"

"I've decided I want to become a docent at the L. A. County Museum of Art."

Dad face turned a little redder, "But you know Arlene's been on overload for months now, and I was just waiting for you to be done with school, so you could come back to work for me." Arlene was the secretary Mom had hired for Dad four years ago.

"Well then," Mom said, "I guess I'll just have to hire you another secretary."

"But I don't want another secretary. I want you."

"Sorry, Dan," she said, "but I *am* going to become a docent."

Dad gave her his 'there's no use arguing with you' look, took another sip of wine, and said, "So what does it entail, this being a docent?"

"I have to go through a year of training and then I'll be able to lead tours at the Museum."

"A year of training," he said more with exasperation than understanding.

"Yes," she said.

Now he leaned his head forward, toward her face. "So tell me, after four years of college and another year of training, how much money are you going to make as a docent?"

Mom picked up the bottle of wine and poured what was left into her glass. "Nothing," she said. "It's volunteer."

Dad just about choked on that one. "So...you mean after all this time and money, you're going to make nothing?" The emphasis was on the word "nothing."

I somehow felt that Mom had planned all this... no party, just dinner out in a public place with the kids....for this confrontation.

"Money isn't everything," Mom said lightheartedly.

"Then you are never coming back to work for me?"

"No, I am not."

"But a docent at the Museum?" Dad said, not quite able to fathom it.

"It's what I want to do," she said, staring him in the eyes, daring him to challenge her.

Instead, he lifted his wine glass, and said, "To your mother. A woman who knows what she wants, and gets it."

After dinner, Mom and Dad decided that Andrew, who had just gotten his driver's license, should drive home. They'd both had too much to drink. Dad sat up front with Andrew, and told Mom to sit in the back 'with the girls'.

A year later, it was Claire's turn to be a Bat Mitzvah.

In the two years between my Bat Mitzvah and Claire's, I had had three small incidents. The first was at my friend, Teri's Bat Mitzvah, where I was dancing the Hora, and without warning, I was overcome by the feeling that the dance floor and everyone on it wasn't real. I ran off and hid in the bathroom until the feeling left me.

The next was my first day in junior high, when I was overcome with the feeling that someone had just snapped a photo of me and everyone in my class, and that I was both in and out of the photo. I squeezed my eyes tight, put my hands over my ears, and eventually the feeling left me.

The third time was when Missy's mom had dropped us off at The May Company, and Missy and I were in separate dressing rooms trying on clothes. My room was filled with blouses and sweaters and jeans and skirts, and I was trying to decide which to buy and which to leave. Suddenly I was overcome with my warm prickly feeling, and my heart starting beating so fast I couldn't catch my breath. I sat on the bench, and again squeezed my eyes tight, put my hands over my ears, and in a few minutes it passed. I pulled off whatever I was wearing, put on my own clothes, dashed out of the dressing room, called to Missy that I would meet her in the parking lot, ran down the escalator and out the front door to the parking lot, and stood breathing the fresh air, and wondering if I would ever dare go into a department store again.

Claire, unlike me, was dying to have the big bash. Maybe part of it was to make up to my parents for the party I didn't have, but most of it was because she really wanted it. She now had two zillion friends and wanted them all at her party. In fact, her friends and her looks (meaning her hair, her makeup, and her clothes) were the only things she really cared about. That and having a boyfriend. Yes, even at 12, if she wasn't with her friends, or didn't have a boyfriend, she was miserable. Perhaps in some way I was jealous of Claire. If I had to look deep, deep inside me, I would have to say that I would have liked a zillion friends, too, but as things were, I was just thankful that I had Teri and Missy. As for the boyfriend...yes, I would have liked that, too.

Of course, I began to worry from the date the Bat Mitzvah was set, up until the day it took place. And while I was a little uncomfortable all that day and all evening, wary, listening for the Destroyer's voice, worried that he would start talking to me, worried that "it" would happen, "it" didn't happen. I couldn't figure out why, except that maybe no one was going to pay any attention to me. Claire was definitely going to be the star of the show, as she always was.

The best thing about Claire's Bat Mitzvah was that all four grandparents and some of our aunts, uncles and cousins were there. The bad thing was that Mom insisted on hiring a disc-jockey, so Andrew's band only got to play when the disc-jockey was taking a break.

I think by the time I turned 15, the three of us were pretty much on our own paths: Andrew was, like on another planet with his guitars, his band, and his musician friends; Claire was Ms. Popular and the tennis player (yes, she was now totally devoted to tennis- which earned her lots of Brownie points with Mom and Dad); and I was the student and pianist.

Chapter Four — Discovery

Right after Claire's Bat Mitzvah, Miss Hockensmith informed me that she was going to be having a recital for a few of her best students, and she "particularly" wanted me to be in it. There would be 10 of us in all, each playing one piece, and it was going to take place on a Wednesday night at the Jewish Center in a room that held 50 people.

I guess she said "particularly" because I had found an excuse not to play in any of her previous recitals, but for some reason, I wanted to play in this one. Maybe it was because I loved the selection I was going to play, the first movement of Mozart's sonata in G major, and that I knew it so well. I knew it like I knew my own name. I could just sit down at the piano and play it like it was part of me.

So I was torn about this recital—upset with myself because I really wanted to do it, but worried that I couldn't do it. I kept telling myself I had nothing to worry about...it was only four pages, and the notes just flowed from my fingers...but still there were going to be all those people in the room, and what if "it" should happen, and my mind went blank, and my fingers froze. What if I had to stop in the middle of the piece and run off the stage? How humiliating would that be?

With each passing day, I became more and more tense.

To take off some of the pressure, I asked Ms. Hockensmith if I could have the sheet music in front of me, instead of playing from memory, and she said, "Of course." One less thing to worry about.

But it didn't matter how much I tried to encourage myself or build my confidence, there was the Destroyer's voice in my head telling me that if I played in the recital, "it" would happen. On the day before the recital, I knew I couldn't do it. I told my mom. "I can't play in the recital."

"Why not?" she asked, looking upset.

"I just can't."

Probably remembering our fight about my Bat Mitzvah, she said, "I know you're nervous. Everyone's nervous before performing in public. But you know that sonata so well and you play it so beautifully, you're going to do just fine."

"I don't know," I said. And then admitting, "I'm really scared."

"It's just stage fright," she said in her positive tone. "Everyone has stage fright. It's just a hurdle you have to get over." Then putting her hands on my shoulders and looking me in the eyes, "I know I haven't been very supportive of your piano playing, but I really think it would be good for you to play in this recital. You've got to get over this fear of performing in front of others. If you can you do it this one time, you'll never be frightened again."

That sounded good to me, and a reason to not cancel. Maybe she was right. Maybe if I could do this one thing, if I could get through this recital without that bad feeling taking hold of me, I could do anything.

"Even if you make a mistake," Mom said, "no one's going to notice. So stop worrying about it, and just go on up there like you own the world. You'll do fine, I promise you."

She sounded so confident...but how could she promise such a thing? It wasn't in her hands, but in mine, literally.

"Well, I'll see how I feel tomorrow," I said, regretting the words even as I spoke them. You shouldn't have agreed, my voice told me. You shouldn't have.

The next evening, we drove to the Jewish Center together, Mom, Dad, Andrew, Claire and I, and once inside, I took my seat in the front row along with the other nine pianists. But I was no sooner seated, than "it" happened. Suddenly, the stage, the piano, the room, all the people in the room seemed like a dream. I was completely detached from all of it, like I was watching a movie and I was one of the actors in it.

My face turned hot, my heart was banging so loud I thought everyone must hear it, and that prickly numb feeling came over me. I didn't know if I could stand, but I had to. I had to get out of there. I forced myself up, ran to the back of the room, then to the bathroom, into a stall, locked the door and sat down on the cold hard toilet seat, my head hanging down, my sweaty hands clutching my burning face. Mom had followed me and I heard the click clack of her high heels on the white tile floor as she entered the bathroom. My eyes were shut tight. "Zoe," she called, "are you in here?"

"Yes, Mom. But I'm sick. I'm terribly sick."

I heard the click clack approach my door. "What is it, Zoe? Are you throwing up?"

"Yes," I lied. "I'm very nauseous."

"My poor girl," she said. "Is there anything I can do?"

How I wished there was. But there was nothing anyone could do. "Yes," I said. Just tell Ms. Hockensmith I can't play."

Mom was silent for a moment, and then she said, "I should never have forced you to do this."

I opened my eyes. I was sitting on a cold hard toilet seat in a bathroom stall at the Jewish Center. I was me, and Mom was Mom and everything was all right. "It's not your fault," I said.

But she didn't hear me. She was already on her way out to tell Ms. Hockensmith, I wouldn't be playing.

I thought the ride home would be like death, but my dad was the only one who acted as if someone had died. Andrew asked if I was all right, and then Claire said how happy she was that she didn't have to sit through a bunch of boring pieces, and Mom said, "I'm so glad you're feeling better."

I promised myself that night that I would never play the piano in public again.

When I next saw Ms. Hockensmith, she told me how sorry she was that I had not been able to play. I was sitting on the padded piano bench; she was sitting on a chair beside me.

"You know, of all my students, I think you have the most talent. You may not play as well as some of the others, but you will outdistance them at some point."

At that moment, I had a flash. What if I told Miss Hockensmith the real reason I couldn't play that night? What if I told her the truth about me? And then the moment passed, and I was left feeling sad and alone.

She must have spotted how I was feeling because she said, "Don't worry, Zoe, they'll be other recitals. Even concerts maybe."

But not for me, I thought.

And then she reached over and patted my hand. She had never touched me before. "Don't give up, Zoe. There's no telling how far you can go."

I felt a tear in my eye. How sweet she was. And how I would disappoint her.

The week after my non-performance at the recital, Teri's mom called and asked if I would consider giving piano lessons to Dana. Dana was Teri's little sister.

I didn't take any time to answer that one. "Yes, I'd be glad to."

"How much do you charge?" she asked.

"I don't know," I answered. "I've never given anyone lessons before."

"Well, we'll figure it out," she said, and we made a date for the following day, right after school.

At the end of Dana's lesson, Dana's mom said, "How's three dollars a lesson?"

"Great," I said.

Three dollars was a fortune to me, but I would've done it for free, because I had so much fun teaching Dana.

It must have been fun for Dana too, because the next week I got a call from a friend of Teri's mom who wanted me to teach her daughter, and then a friend of that lady who wanted me to teach her son. It wasn't long before I had thirteen little kids to teach and was raking in the bucks. I felt that Mom and Dad were really proud of me, maybe for the first time in my life.

Andrew asked, kind of jokingly, if any of my students wanted to take guitar lessons, and I actually asked each of the parents about it, and got three students for Andrew...not my students, but their siblings.

Teaching piano was perfect for me. I was comfortable in each of the private homes I went to (they were all within walking distance), I was on a one to one with the children, surprised at how much patience I had, and I also felt I was doing something good for the world, or humanity, or the arts, by bringing music into these children's lives.

Meanwhile, Miss Hockensmith was again after me. This time to participate in a piano concerto competition being held at the Dorothy Chandler Pavilion. There would be several cash prizes and a scholarship award.

I told her right from the start that I didn't want to participate. Rather I told her, not that I didn't want to participate, but that I didn't think I could. Or make that, that I definitely could not.

"And why is that?" she asked.

I stuck to my standard response. "I just get nervous performing in front of people."

She was thoughtful. "A lot of people have that problem." Then she said, "What if we put a blindfold on you?"

It was the first humorous thing I'd ever heard her say. "I don't know. Maybe we should try it," I said.

She patted my hand – the second time she ever touched me. "We've got to do something to get you into that competition. What if we just prepare the concerto, you know, just get it to that point where it's absolutely perfect, and then, maybe, you'll want to play it."

I hesitated because I didn't think I'd want to play it under any circumstances. "What harm can it do?" she asked.

None, I thought, except one more disappointment for both of us. But she seemed so eager, I had to give it a try. "All right. Let's do it. Who knows? Maybe a miracle will happen."

"They do sometimes," she said, "if we prepare for them."

Then, again, I felt this terrible sadness for her. She was such a sweet, kind person, but so alone. What kind of life did she have... except living on other people's dreams.

If I did drum up the courage to play in the competition, it would be for her, not for me.

So we practiced and practiced, me playing the piano solo on the black baby-grand; she playing the orchestra part on the black upright in the dining room, and then the week before the competition, we did our final rehearsal, and it was one of the most thrilling experiences of my life. I wasn't playing the music; I was part of the music, and the music was part of me. Ms. Hockensmith and I were welded together in magical way, and the most beautiful music possible was all that existed. If I never achieved anything else in my life, I would always have this exquisite point in time.

After we'd played the last note, we both sat for a moment, not saying anything, not wanting to break the spell of the moment. Then Ms. Hockensmith said, "Zoe, you really must play in this competition."

I wanted to, how I wanted to do this for Ms. Hockensmith, and for all the people in the audience who could share the exhilaration that Ms. Hockensmith and I had created in her home.

"I'll see," I said, hoping, praying that I could do it.

The next day, my Destroyer started talking to me. "Yes, it was great in Ms. Hockensmith's house, I will give you that, but once you walk up on that stage with all those people in the auditorium...you're not going to remember a note. Remember what happened last time you performed...and that was just for a bunch of ordinary people and nothing was at stake. You can't do this. You really can't."

I broke the news to Ms. Hockensmith the next day on the phone...I couldn't bear to face her in person. I felt that I had stabbed her in the heart. But I had also stabbed myself.

The following year, Ms. Hockensmith began talking to me about college. "Where are you planning to go?" she asked.

"I think either UCLA or Cal State Northridge."

"Well, if you don't mind me making a suggestion....maybe you should consider Julliard. I have some influence there...but I'm sure once they've heard you play, you won't need any influence."

Julliard, I thought. How fantastic! But it would be so far away.... so far from my family and everything and everyone I'd known all my life. And I'd have to live in a dorm, and probably perform every day. Just the thought of living in a dorm frightened me, let alone the performing.

"I realize it may be out of your comfort zone," Ms. Hockensmith said, "but it's really where you belong. You are so talented, Zoe."

I was very flattered. "Thanks, Ms. Hockensmith, for thinking of me, but I just don't think I can do it. Don't get me wrong, I'd love to do it, but you know about my stage fright." I felt worse for her than for myself. She wanted this for me so badly. "I'm really sorry," I said, and then again I thought about telling her the real truth about me....why I had stage fright. Because my Destroyer wouldn't let me alone! Maybe she'd think I was crazy. I knew for sure she wouldn't take me in her arms. I knew she wasn't touchy, feely. She was just the sweetest woman alive.

She sighed. "Well, promise me you'll think about it."

"Yes," I said. "Of course I'll think about it, and I'd love to go there. I just don't think I can."

Driving home from her house that afternoon, in the little red Honda my dad had bought me for my sixteenth birthday, I had to pull over because the tears were flooding my eyes. Julliard! How I would have loved to go there. How I would have liked to meet the other musicians, to be given the best instruction, to spend all day with my music. But those things could never be, not for me. I wanted to scream out to God, why have you done this to me? What terrible thing have I done to be so cursed? Why did you give me this talent, only to thwart me at every turn? Then I comforted myself with the thought that Mom probably wouldn't let me go anyway. She wanted me to go to a normal college. I was spending too much time at the piano anyway. I dried my tears, blew my nose, and drove home.

Just before I graduated from high school, a parent of one of my students asked if I'd have a recital for my students. I thought long and hard about that one.

Since the competition I didn't play in, I'd had a good two years. I had kept a low profile, avoiding any situation that might be stressful and not doing anything that might provoke the Destroyer.

It's true, I missed all the sweet-sixteen parties I'd been invited to, not because the Destroyer was talking to me, but because I was afraid he would talk to me. It especially killed me that I couldn't go to Teri's or Missy's sweet-sixteen parties, but I knew there was no way I could get through those two elaborate affairs without an incident. Nothing seemed worth that. But at least the three of us did go out to lunch and a movie together to celebrate.

And I actually had been asked out on a date. Steven wasn't the greatest looking guy in the world, but at least he was tall and smart. I kind of hedged about saying yes for a few days, and then decided I couldn't take the chance, although it really would have been nice to go out on a date.

So this idea of having a recital for my students was kind of a momentous decision for me. I went back and forth about it, going over the pros and cons. I had already informed my students that I wouldn't be teaching piano once I graduated from high school, and had already referred them to Mrs. Blake. I was going to be working for my dad over the summer, and once I started college I would be busy enough with schoolwork and my own piano lessons. If I did have any spare time left, I wanted to branch out and try something new. So having a recital would be a nice way to say goodbye to my kids, and it would be nice for all of them to get together and meet one another, and have a little farewell party.

If I had it at my house and I wasn't performing, how bad could it be? The kids had worked hard for the past two years, and they deserved a recital.

As nervous as I was, I decided to give it a try. I arranged for the recital to take place on a Saturday afternoon at my house. I told the kids that even though they had memorized their pieces, they could have the music in front of them; I wanted to make things as easy as possible for them.

My mom borrowed bridge chairs from friends and neighbors, and was preparing punch and cookies in the kitchen, when the Destroyer appeared. "You idiot," it said. "How could you have done such a stupid thing? You know you can't do things like this. You're not normal, for God's sake. Haven't you figured that out by now?"

Oh no, oh no, I thought. My face turned hot, my hands clammy. "Please dear God," I pleaded silently, "just let me get through this afternoon. I won't put myself in a position like this ever again. I promise. Just let me get through this afternoon for the children."

But God wasn't listening to me that day. I looked at my mom, but she wasn't my mom...and she was so far away. No place where I could get to her. "Mom," I said, "I'm not feeling so well. You'll have to let the kids and the parents in, and if I can't come in, just go ahead with the recital."

"Oh no," Mom said. "What's wrong with you?"

"I just don't feel well." I couldn't stand there talking. I had to escape. I ran up the stairs to my bedroom, lay on my bed, face down, my eyes shut tight, my hands over my ears. Why was I being tortured this way? What had I done that was so evil? I opened my eyes for a second, but nothing was real. I was in a dream. My own dream, except who was I? Where was I?

I lay there listening to the children come in with their parents, and then I heard the piano playing. I thought for sure "it" would go away any minute...but it continued on and on.

And then, when Susan Cohen was playing *Country Gardens*, it left.

Just like that it left, and I was back being me. I felt my arms... they were flesh, my flesh. I felt my forehead; it was no longer hot. Slowly, I got up, looked around my room, my stuffed animals were now on a shelf on my bedroom wall, and there they sat smiling at me.

I tried to stand and my legs were sturdy under me. I went into the bathroom, washed off the sweat from my face, put on powder, lipstick, brushed my hair, and walked downstairs to the living room, praying that "it" was over, that I could get through the rest of the afternoon with no problem.

As I entered the room, I was filled with relief and pride. There were my 13 little children, all dressed up, and playing these lovely little pieces I had taught them. Everyone was so happy to see me, and little arms were reaching out to me. "Zoe, are you okay? Are you feeling better? Did you hear my piece, Zoe?" Karen asked.

"Did you hear mine?" Seth asked. They were all around me. My sweet young students.

"Yes, I heard every piece," I said, and the children all seemed very pleased. "Now, let's continue. I believe it's David's turn."

David gave me a grin as he approached our big black baby-grand with his sheet music in hand.

After the children finished playing, and after the punch and cookies, and after all of the parents telling me how much they enjoyed the recital, and what a good job I'd done, and that they hoped I was feeling better; and after the children hugging me and telling me they'd miss me, and good luck in college; and after the living room was cleaned up and the chairs folded, I decided, that I would become a school teacher. I loved teaching little kids and if I didn't have to have recitals, it would be the perfect profession for me.

A week later, on Saturday night, I had plans to go to a graduation party with Teri, Missy, and a few other wallflowers we hung out with who hadn't been invited to the Prom. Even a few of the less popular boys were coming. I was only a little worried about going to this party because it wasn't like going to the Prom with a hundred people; it was just my friends, people I saw every day in school for the last three years, people I felt comfortable with. And it was going to be at a friend's house, a house I'd been to many times. We were each going to bring something, and I had made brownies. I actually liked to bake and brownies were my specialty, along with chocolate chip cookies.

Teri and Missy were coming to pick me up at seven, and waiting at the door for them, my plate of brownies in hand, "it" happened. I'd had no warning, no voice telling me not to go. It just happened. Someone was standing in the hallway with a plate of brownies, but it wasn't me.

The prickly numbness came over me and I felt a pain in my chest right between my ribs. I prayed it would go away. Oh no, not tonight. Please not tonight, I said to myself. But I couldn't shake the feeling. It had taken hold of me. I was gone, no longer a part of this world. I was part of some other world, out there in the stars.

I didn't know what to do...go to the party and pray I would come back to reality? But the longer I stood there, the shakier I felt. I couldn't face anyone, be with anyone, not in this condition. Not when I was in a daydream. Finally I ran to the kitchen where I found my mom. I handed her the plate of brownies, and told her I wasn't feeling well and couldn't go to the party.

"What's wrong, Zoe?" she asked.

"I just feel sick," I said from somewhere out in space.

I ran up the stairs to my bedroom, shut the door and lay face down on my bed, my hands over my ears, my eyes shut tight, and prayed I would come back to reality, to this moment, to this world, but it wasn't happening. I heard the doorbell ring. I heard the voices of my friends and my mother. But who was I? Where was I?

I heard the front door close and my mother come up the stairs and knock gently on my door. "Zoe, are you all right?"

"No. Don't come in." I didn't want to tell her the truth and I didn't want to pretend.

She, nevertheless, pushed open the door. "Zoe, please tell me what's wrong so I can help you."

I didn't want to tell her what was wrong, and I knew she couldn't help me. "Please go away."

She came into the room and sat on the edge of my bed. "I'm not leaving until you tell me what's wrong."

I looked at her from somewhere in another dimension; it was all a dream, me, my mother, my friends at the door. I wanted to tell her, I wanted so badly to tell her, had always wanted to tell her, and would have told her many times if I wasn't afraid she'd think I was crazy. But at this moment, I didn't care anymore. I had to tell her. I just couldn't carry this burden all by myself anymore. I sat up. "Mom," I said, "something's wrong with me." And I began to cry. But it wasn't me crying, it was that other person, Zoe. Zoe, whom my mother took in her arms, patted her hair, held her close.

"Please, Zoe, tell me."

"It's something that's been happening to me since I was six."

"Since you were six," she said with amazement in her voice. "Tell me, what is it?"

"I don't know how to explain it. This feeling comes over me, like I'm in a dream, a horrible dream."

"I don't understand," she said, looking bewildered.

"It's hard to explain," I said. "It's like nothing in the world seems real. Not even me."

"I don't understand," she said.

I hesitated. "I think I'm going crazy," I said, and cried even harder.

My mother hugged me to her and smoothed my hair with her hand, over and over again. "Don't worry, my darling. We'll find a doctor. We'll figure this all out. Everything will be fine, you'll see."

But it wasn't fine. This time "it" didn't go away in a few seconds, or a few minutes. It went on another day, and then another, and another.

I didn't want to leave my room. I didn't want to see anyone or have them see me. It was all too scary. Would I ever come back to reality? Would I ever be normal again? If this was to be my life, I'd rather be dead.

I lay on my bed for hours. I thought about playing the piano, that had always soothed me, made me feel better, but how could I play the piano when it didn't exist; when I didn't exist. Even going to eat with my family was an ordeal. I didn't want to tell anyone, or explain anything to anyone, especially my dad.

Mom would come into my room and bring me food to eat, and every afternoon and evening she'd turn on the TV. But even that upset me. How could a person in a dream, watch other people who weren't real?

Teri and Missy came by or called almost every day, and Andrew and Claire came into my room occasionally to see how I was doing. I think they all thought I had the flu. And every now and then, my dad popped into my room to tell me not to worry, something was going around...a lot of his clients were sick. Yes, but they weren't sick with what I have, I thought. My mom wanted to tell everyone what was wrong with me, but I wouldn't let her. It was bad enough she knew I was crazy. I didn't want anyone else to know.

On the fifth day, when I was still out-of-it, my mom took me to see a psychologist.

Her name was Ms. Halliday, and she had been recommended by one of my mom's friends, who didn't know why my mom wanted her number. Ms. Halliday listened to my story, then folded her arms on her desk, and said in a kindly voice. "It sounds to me like you're suffering from depression. Maybe life is too difficult for you and you're trying to escape from reality. But there are plenty of drugs that can help you. What you need to do is see a psychiatrist who can prescribe them." She wrote down the name and phone number of an associate of hers, a psychiatrist named Dr. Harold Weinstein.

We went to see Dr. Weinstein the next day and he listened intently to what I had to say. I even dared tell him about the voice that warned me about an attack about to happen.

He then diagnosed me with acute anxiety disorder brought about by pressure situations, and gave us the great news that I would be cured by drugs. We just had to find the right one, or the right combination. He then prescribed Prozac, and told me to come back in a month.

It all made sense, except if it was only brought on by pressure situations, then why did it start when I was only six, and not in a pressure situation, or when I was alone and not in a pressure situation. But then it was logical that it did come on in pressure situations. I already knew that. That's why I had always tried to avoid them. This last attack was probably brought on by my anxiety over the piano recital and my fear of going to the graduation party, or perhaps I was apprehensive about the graduation ceremony itself: walking across that stage with all the people in the audience looking at me, or perhaps I was fearful about starting college in the fall.

And Dr. Weinstein wasn't worried about the voice. The voice was my way of preparing myself for whatever was going to happen. It was a good thing, he said. I didn't think it was a good thing. I didn't think normal people heard voices, even if they were trying to help you.

When we got home, my report card was in the mail. I had gotten all A's except for a B in P.E., even though I had missed the last week of school. That should have cheered me up, but instead it sent me into a deeper spiral with no end in sight. Down, down, down into some black abyss. Except it wasn't me. Me was gone.

This time I was so far gone that I felt nothing. I didn't know if I was hungry or thirsty. I didn't know if I was hot or cold. I didn't know if I was tired or sleepy. I didn't even know if I needed to go to the bathroom. All my feelings, all my emotions had dissolved into nothingness.

I refused to see anyone or leave the house. My mom said it was the drug that was making things worse, and we would have to try something different.

She held me in her arms and told me, "We will find a cure for you, my darling, we will. It's just a matter of time."

When we saw Dr. Weinstein the following week, he said, "Apparently, the Prozac isn't working. We'll try another drug, and if that doesn't work, another. Don't worry Zoe, we will cure this thing."

I smiled, pretending I believed him.

After a few months, and a few more failed drugs, Mom decided to switch psychiatrists. She told me, "I didn't like that Dr. Weinstein anyway, and now my friend, Peggy Meyers, says she's got a really great psychiatrist who doesn't just give you drugs, but talks to you. Doesn't that sound great?"

I nodded, pretending to agree.

Cal State Northridge, the college I had opted to go to instead of UCLA because I thought it would be less pressure, had started now, but without me. How could I go to college when I didn't even exist?

My friends, Teri and Missy, kept calling and coming by, and occasionally I would let them in for a few minutes. I found I could play-act, talk to them, tell them I had a terrible migraine headache, but most of the time, I didn't have the energy for play-acting, for pretending everything was okay, that I was normal.

In September, I saw the new psychiatrist, Dr. Berg. He had an annoying habit of clearing his throat every few minutes, and after he had listened to everything I had to say, he asked, "Have you ever been molested?"

"No," I said.

"You're sure?" he asked.

I wasn't even sure what he meant by molested, but I answered, "No."

"Not by your father, your brother, an uncle, perhaps?"

"No," I said, more adamantly.

Dr. Berg cleared his throat. "Well, then, we're going to try some different medications on you."

When my mom came back into the room, Dr. Berg told her, "We're going to try some different medications on Zoe."

"Like what?" My mom asked.

"Well, there's a huge variety we can try...anti-depressants, anti-anxiety, anti-psychotics, and stimulants. We'll try them all, one at a time, and in combination, until we come up with something that works. It's all a matter of trial and error."

My mom said, "It sounds good to me." And then looking at me, "Doesn't that sound good to you, sweetheart?"

I was motionless.

"And," Dr. Berg said to my mom, "I'd like to see every member of your family one at a time." Another clearing of his throat. "Is that all right with you?"

By now, all of my immediate family knew I had a psychological ailment, but no one knew exactly what it was. "Of course," my mother said. "Anything for my daughter."

That evening, Mom told each member of the family that he or she needed to make an appointment to see Dr. Berg about my problem. None of them were enthusiastic, Andrew kind of making a face, Claire giving her a look that said, "Do I have to?" But my dad, was the most reluctant. "I think this is ridiculous, Gail. I don't know anything about her problem, so how could anything I have to say help her?"

"The doctor thinks it will help and that's good enough for me," my mom said.

He sighed, "Okay, Gail, make an appointment for me, will you? Any morning but Wednesday"

"Of course," my mom said.

Chapter Five—
The Hirsch Family
meets with Dr. Berg
— September, 1984

Gail

Gail Hirsch's appointment with Dr. Berg was at 3 p.m. on a Wednesday afternoon. She had just come from leading a tour at the L. A. County Museum of Art.

Gail had given up most of her activities for the past few months—her bridge games, her lunches out with the girls, her Sisterhood meetings. But the two things she could not give up were her tennis games two mornings a week—she needed those to stay in shape, and for her own sanity—and her tours at the museum. It wouldn't be fair to the museum not to do her tours, and besides, she loved doing them.

If there were an emergency, God forbid, or if Zoe needed something, Dan was in his office right out the back door.

Gail settled into Dr. Berg's brown leather sofa, as he sat on his brown leather chair. There was a small table in front of the sofa on which sat a box of tissues. Gail knew she would be needing them.

"So," Dr. Berg said, "is there anything you'd like to tell me about yourself or Zoe?"

Gail immediately teared up and reached for a tissue.

"I guess I want to tell you how completely devastated I am about Zoe. I don't understand how this could be happening to her."

"Can you think of any reason this might be happening to her?"

"No. None at all. Dan and I have always been good parents to her. We always gave her lots of love and attention. And she's always been such a good girl, so talented and so smart. You know she's a pianist. She's really brilliant at it. Which I know I should be thrilled about, but actually, I don't think is such a good thing."

"And why is that?"

"Because it keeps her from leading a normal life."

"Normal in what way?"

"Well, she only has two friends and she hardly sees them. She's just too busy with her practicing, her homework, and she was giving piano lessons to 13 little kids. I mean, it's nice to play the piano, but honestly, if I had it to do over, I would never have given her piano lessons."

"So you think the piano is the reason for her problems."

"No, not at all," Gail said. "I can't think of any reason this could be happening. Except maybe that she's the middle child."

Dr. Berg cleared his throat. "So you think her problem is caused by her being a middle child?"

"Well it did put some pressure on her."

"How was that?"

"Well you know Andrew's the only boy, and Claire's so pretty and popular." She caught herself. "Not that Zoe isn't pretty. She's actually prettier than Claire. But you've seen her. She's what I would call a classic beauty, with her long black hair and green eyes, her face a perfect oval. Claire's face is oval, too, but her cheeks are puffier and her nose and lips a little fuller than Zoe's."

"So Zoe is actually prettier than Claire."

"Yes, I'd say that. But Claire has this certain something about her that attracts people. Everyone wants to be her friend.

Unfortunately, now, she's gained a lot of weight. But it isn't really her fault. She has this new friend named Judy, who thinks eating is a joke and the more you can stuff into your mouth, the funnier. She's a bad influence on Claire and if I could break up that friendship I would. In fact I've said to Claire on many occasions, 'Make new friends, but keep the old. One is silver and the other is gold.' I got a sneer for that. I must admit it was a little corny, but I was trying to make a point. Maybe not too subtle, but I'm just so worried that Claire will end up like Dan's mother."

"And how is that?"

"Dan's mother is this big fat blob, and it worries me that Claire may have inherited her genes."

The doctor was quiet for a moment and then asked, "How does Zoe get along with Claire?"

"Very well, I'd say."

"And with Andrew?"

"I'd say she adores Andrew."

"And your husband?"

Gail paused a moment. She had to think about that one. "I think everything's good between them. I guess if I have to be completely honest, perhaps Dan does favor Claire a little bit... but that's only because she plays tennis. Dan is very big on sports, and since Claire's the only one of our children who participates in sports, he does have a special place in his heart for Claire. But I don't think it affects Zoe in any way. I don't think she even realizes it."

Dr. Berg cleared his throat. "Our time is almost up," he said looking at the clock on his desk. "Is there anything else you'd like to say?"

Gail took a long time thinking about that. "I guess there is one other thing....my mother's cousin, Henry, I've never told Zoe, or any of my kids about him. He was a brilliant violinist and played first violin with the Boston Symphony." She paused.

Dr. Berg encouraged her, "And?"

"He committed suicide."

Dr. Berg was quiet for a moment. "Do you know why?"

"No one knows why. It was a hush, hush kind of thing. I tried to find out, but no one would ever tell me anything." Suddenly

Gail's eyes filled with tears and she reached for a tissue. "I keep worrying: maybe Zoe has what he had."

"I can see that would be upsetting," Dr. Berg said. Then, "I'm sorry, Gail, but our time is up. But perhaps you could make another effort to find out about Henry."

"Yes, I'll try," Gail said, and with that, she grabbed two or three more tissues and continued wiping away her tears as she left the room.

Andrew

It was on a Thursday at 4 p.m., on his way home from Pierce College, that Andrew showed up for his appointment with Dr. Berg.

He felt kind of weird about the whole thing. He had no idea what was wrong with his sister and felt uncomfortable talking to a psychiatrist. *Maybe you're afraid he'll find out something about you,* he thought. But then, what did he have to hide?

He thought Dr. Berg looked kind of nerdy, probably what a shrink is supposed to look like. Grayish brown curly hair, thick horn-rimmed glasses, and of course, a tweed sports jacket with leather elbows. What a stereotype!

Once they were both seated, Dr. Berg cleared his throat and asked, "So, is there anything you'd like to tell me?"

Andrew thought for a moment. "No, not really."

"Do you know your sister is ill?"

"Yes, but I haven't a clue as to what it is."

"How do you get along with her?"

"Great. She's really cool."

"And how is her relationship with your parents?"

"I'd say, pretty good."

"Pretty good?"

"Nah, then great."

"And what about you? Do you also have a great relationship with your parents?"

"With my mom, yeah. Not so much with my dad."

"And why is that?"

"Well it's like my dad is into sports, and I'm not. Simple as that."

"So he's disappointed you're not into sports?"

"Disappointed isn't the word. He thinks I'm a total loser."

"Just because you're not into sports?"

"And because I'm into music. Maybe he thinks I'm a sissy. But I'm not. I actually like sports. I *am* a guy. It's just music is my life. I love to hear it, I love to make it, and I love to create it. I know my dad's disappointed in me, and my mom, too, although she tries not to show it. But it's my life, not theirs."

"So you think both your parents are disappointed in you?"

"I know they are. I actually did give sports a try, each sport in each season, but it just wasn't my thing. My dad thinks it was because I wasn't trying. But maybe I wasn't trying 'cause I didn't want to play. I do have some insights. I'm not a complete dummy just because I play the guitar and write songs. In fact I wrote a song about that...not lovin' sports: *'I'm not that kind of guy...no baseball, basketball, soccer for me. I like the taut hard strings of my guitar, the loud blast of sound ringing in my ears. No baseball, basketball, soccer for me. I'm not that kind of guy.'* I never played that song for my dad. He would have gone ballistic and said, 'You never tried.'"

"So your dad is upset because you never tried?"

"No. He's upset with everything about me. I also wrote a song about that. *'I'm not you and you're not me, so let's find a place to meet in the middle, to meet in the middle, let's find a place to meet in the middle.'*"

Dr. Berg cleared his throat "And why is your mom disappointed with you?"

"I guess for the same reasons. But she likes me more than Dad...or should I say accepts me. Or should I say, likes me. My dad hates my long hair, and the stainless steel earring in my ear... although I think he's relieved that it's not in my nose or tongue.... and I've also got tattoos that I keep well hidden. If my dad knew about them, he'd really have a fit."

"And how do you feel about your dad?"

"Good question. I don't know. Sometimes he makes me sick. He's so wrapped up in making money, and kow-towing to all his clients so they won't go to Farmer's or State Farm. He's such a pussy in some ways. But then in some ways he's macho man. He lets us all know who's boss. Still, sometimes I feel sorry for him."

"And why is that?

"Because he's got three kids who are losers."

"Why do you call the three of you losers?"

"Because I'm a musician taking classes at Pierce Junior College. I'll never be a doctor, lawyer, or Indian chief. I probably won't make much money. Not what my parents dreamed of for their only son. My sister, Zoe, is a crazy mixed-up kid, and my sister, Claire, is bulimic."

"Your sister, Claire, is bulimic?"

"Yeah. Nobody knows about it, though. She thinks I don't know, but I see what's going on. I see her pigging out and then I hear her heaving in the bathroom. We've all got eyes, but we only see what we want to see. It's not a pretty picture. And yes, I did write a song about that, too. *'It's not a pretty picture in our family. It's lies, it's pretend, it's wannabees. But if no one looks, and no one sees, then how can truth ever be? If no one looks, and no one sees, then how can truth ever be? No it's not a pretty picture in our family. It's not a pretty picture in our family.'* Can I go now?"

Dr. Berg, looking at his watch, "Yes, actually our time is up."

Claire

Claire arrived at Dr. Berg's office at 5 o'clock, right after tennis practice. Her life was so busy, between school, and tennis, and home work, and her friends and her new boyfriend, Josh, that she really didn't have time to go see some shrink about Zoe. But she had no choice.

She entered Dr. Berg's office in a huff and took her seat on the brown leather sofa. She didn't really want to be here. And once she met him, she wanted to be here even less. He scared her.

"Thank you for coming today," he said, as if he knew she was doing him a big favor by being here.

"I didn't have a choice," she said in her snippiest voice.

He settled back in his chair, cleared his throat, and asked, "Is there anything you'd like to tell me?"

What was this, she asked herself. Some kind of trap? Did he know something he couldn't possibly know? Was he asking about Zoe or herself? "No," she said. "Not a thing."

"How is your relationship with your sister?"

"Fine," she said.

"So you two are friends?"

"I wouldn't exactly put it that way."

"How would you put it?"

She gave him her nastiest look. "We're fine."

"And what does that mean?"

She guessed he wasn't going to give up. But neither was she. "We're not exactly friends, but we like each other."

"So you have things in common. You do things together?"

"No, not really. She's the smart one, I'm the popular one. She plays the piano. I play tennis." And then feeling her face get hot, a rush through her veins, suddenly feeling devil-may-care, she blurted out, "But we do have one thing in common."

"And what's that?"

She didn't believe she was actually saying this. She must be nuts. "We both have a problem."

"And what's that?" he asked matter-of-factly.

She hated his holier-than-thou attitude, his aloofness. Well, she'd give him something to blow his mind. "You're a psychiatrist, right? You can't tell anyone what I tell you."

"Right," he said. "Whatever you say to me is strictly between the two of us."

"I'm bulimic," she said. And then it hit her. What a dork! Why was she telling this smug stranger her deepest darkest secret? But in a way, it felt good. Good to finally say the word to another human being. To have it out there in the world.

Dr. Berg didn't seem shocked, or even surprised. "Do your parents know about this?"

"No. No one knows. Not my parents, not my brother, not my sister, not even my best friends." She eyed the Kleenex on Dr. Berg's table. She tried to stay strong, but she felt the tears building behind her eyelids. She was going to need one any minute.

"When did this begin?"

"About six months ago," she said, surprisingly wanting to say it all, to tell him everything. "I was a little overweight and hated it, but I couldn't stop eating. I ate everything: leftover cold spaghetti from the fridge, a whole pint of ice cream, a whole bag of potato chips, 3 or 4 candy bars like it was nothing. And after I'd feel so sick, and so guilty, I'd stick my finger down my throat and throw it all up."

She paused, but Dr. Berg was waiting, so she went on. "I thought that way I could eat all I wanted and not gain weight. But I hated myself. I hated the eating and I hated the throwing up, but I couldn't stop doing it. My mom thinks it's all my friend Judy's fault, but Judy just makes it easier. We can stuff ourselves together like it's a joke. I know how much Mom hates Judy and that she blames Judy for my weight gain, but it has nothing to do with Judy." A pause. "The pathetic thing is that even with the throwing up, I'm still gaining weight. Another reason to hate myself."

Dr. Berg didn't blink or lose a moment. "So no one suspects anything?"

"No one. My mom is always after me to go on a diet and stop eating junk food. What a joke that is!"

Dr. Berg cleared his throat. "Perhaps if you told your parents, they could help you."

"No way. Maybe my mom could take it, but I know she'd end up telling my dad, and that would be curtains!"

"In what way?"

"Because if he ever finds out, he'll think I'm a total loser."

"Maybe he won't."

Now, Claire did reach for that Kleenex. "Believe me, Dr. Berg...my sister's a loser, my brother's a loser, but I'm the tennis star he always wanted. If I'm a loser too....no, doctor, I couldn't take that!"

Dr. Berg seemed stumped. He looked at his watch. "I'm sorry," he said, "but time is up. I do want to say, though, Claire, that you need help with your problem. I know a lot of good therapists who specialize in bulimia. I urge you to call one of them."

"Yeah, and how would I explain that to my parents?"

"You could just tell them that you feel you need to speak to a therapist. You don't have to tell them why."

"Yeah," Claire said. Like that was going to happen. "I'll think about it," she said, and got up to leave.

Dr. Berg stood and took her hand. "Promise me that you'll give it some thought. Bulimia is a serious disease. It can be life threatening."

"Yes," she said, "I will." She reached for another Kleenex, and as soon as the door closed behind her, she began to sob. She didn't know why. Because she had finally told someone? Because she was so ashamed? Because she knew she could never tell her parents? Not even that she needed to see a psychiatrist.

Dan

At nine a.m., on Thursday morning, Dan Hirsch arrived at Dr. Berg's office. He made it first thing in the morning, so that he could get it over with as soon as possible. The whole thing was ridiculous. There was nothing he could tell the psychiatrist that could help Zoe in any way. This was a complete waste of time.

He shook Dr. Berg's hand, and took his seat on the brown leather sofa, while Dr. Berg sat in his brown leather chair.

Oddly, now that he was here, now that he was seated, Dan began to feel a bit apprehensive.

"Dan, if I may call you that," Dr. Berg said, "is there anything you want to tell me?"

"About Zoe?"

"Yes, about Zoe. Or anything else you'd like to say."

"I really can't shed any light on Zoe's problem, and there's nothing else I'd like to say." That'll give him pause, Dan thought, very proud of himself.

"How is your relationship with her?" Dr. Berg continued without missing a beat.

"Great," Dan said.

"So, you and she get along just fine, No tension between you, no problems?"

"None whatsoever," Dan said.

"And what about your other children?"

Dan fidgeted in his chair. He didn't really want to get into anything too heavy with this man.

"Look, doctor, I think you're barking up the wrong tree. I think we're a perfectly normal family and have led a very happy life. At least that's how I see it. I love my wife, my kids, and my job. I make a good living, good enough to buy a five-bedroom house on a half acre, south of the boulevard in Woodland Hills. Good enough so my wife doesn't have to work anymore and can do whatever she damn pleases. Good enough to buy four cars, and another one for Claire as soon as she passes her driver's test. So I don't think I can shed any light on Zoe's problem."

"So, you have no problems with any of your children."

An uncomfortable feeling came over Dan. "Well, of course, there's Zoe's problem. But I certainly didn't have anything to do with that. And Claire's great. Did you know she's on the high school tennis team?"

"No, I didn't." A clearing of the throat, and then, "What about Andrew?"

Dan shifted his position on the sofa. He could feel the tension building in his chest. "Well there have been some problems with Andrew."

"And what might those be?"

Dan leaned toward Dr. Berg. "I know you met him, so you could see for yourself. He's a goddamn hippie. He's got an earring in his ear, thank God it's not in his nose or lip, he doesn't shave, I know he's got tattoos, even though he tries to hide them, and he hangs out with these low class morons." Then, more confidentially, "I wouldn't be surprised if he's on drugs."

As Dan sat back, Dr. Berg said, "He must be a disappointment to you."

"Disappointment isn't the word. When he was born, I had such high hopes for him. I got married when I was 19, and had a kid right away, and then another and another. I had to make a living, to provide for my family so I never got to finish college, but I was hoping he would finish college and make something of himself. He keeps chiding me that I want him to be a doctor or a lawyer, but he doesn't have to be that...he could be anything he wants but a goddamn musician."

"It sounds like you're pretty upset."

"You're darn right, I'm upset."

Dr. Berg cleared his throat. "Now, getting back to Zoe, is there anything in your relationship with Zoe that could have caused her any anxiety?"

Dan was insulted. How dare the doctor suggest that he could be the cause of any discomfort to Zoe. He was always a loving and caring father. "No, doctor, nothing!" he said emphatically, and got up to leave.

"Our session isn't over," Dr. Berg said.

"Well it's over as far as I'm concerned," Dan said. "I came here as I said I would. I took time out of my busy day, and frankly I resent the fact that you would think that I had anything to do with causing Zoe's problem."

Dr. Berg stood up, cleared his throat, and extended his hand, "I'm sorry if I said anything to offend you, and I do appreciate your coming in today."

Dan was so angry that he hesitated about taking the doctor's hand. But then, he was a salesman, so he took it with a smile and said, "Nice meeting you."

Chapter Six – Frankie – October, 1984

I don't know if it was the pink pill or the green pill, or the two yellows and a white, but gradually I began experiencing moments of clarity. Those moments stretched into periods of time each day when I would feel completely normal, and those periods became longer and longer as each day passed.

I began playing the piano again. It felt so wonderful, like seeing your best friend after a long absence. How thrilling to feel my fingers on the keys again, to hear the beautiful music emanating from the sounding board. I played Chopin and banged the keys as loud as I could, gaining inward strength from the power of my hands. Then I'd play my Mozart sonatas, reveling in the brilliance of Mozart's beautiful melody after beautiful melody.

I began going for walks, reading, talking on the phone to my friends, and at some point, having so many days of feeling normal, that I met Teri and Missy for lunch. I still hadn't told them what my illness really was. They believed it was mononucleosis; I was too ashamed to tell them the truth.

The day after lunch with my friends, I decided it was time to rejoin the world and that meant going to college to become a teacher. I was still nervous, still frightened that "it" might come back any moment, but I had to challenge it, I had to try to live my life as I had planned. Dr. Berg assured me that as long as I stayed away from "pressure situations" and stayed on my drug regimen, I would be all right.

It had been almost four months since I had been in the real world, and since Cal State Northridge had already started without me, I decided to try to get into Pierce, a two year community college, where my brother was going, and where there would be even less pressure than Northridge. I'd been away from the world for quite a while, and it seemed a place to get my feet wet.

Fortunately, Mr. Parsons, the person in charge of admissions, after seeing my 3.8 from high school and my 1470 SAT, allowed me to begin three classes a month late. "I'll still expect you to get all A's," he said.

And I jibed back, "I intend to."

My brother, Andrew, was great. He was so kind and caring. He drove me to school, had lunch with me most days, then drove me home. "Really, I can drive myself," I told him, but he told me, "I need the company."

My sister, Claire, was happy for me. She cried when I told her I was feeling better, and then filled me with questions, "What was it like? How did you feel? How did you hide this for so long? Why didn't you tell me sooner? Maybe I could have helped."

I never loved my siblings as much as I did that fall of 1984.

On November 6, a few weeks after I started back to Pierce, there was going to be a presidential election. In spite of how shaky I felt, kind of like a baby duck who had just stepped into the water for the first time, I decided to work on Walter Mondale's campaign. I liked Mondale, but I especially liked that he had chosen Geraldine Ferraro as his running mate. I wanted to help make history: to elect the first woman vice-president. I must have made a thousand phone calls to registered Democrats that week before the election to get them to the poles. Unfortunately my efforts were in vain: Mondale lost every state but one.

And then, in the spring of 1985, I met Frankie.

How strange life is. If I hadn't been sick (which we now called my malady), I would never have gone to Pierce, and I would never have met Frankie. It was almost too good to be true. Although I hadn't actually had a date, I did have male friends. Again, none of my friends were part of the "in" group, but for the most part they were smart, usually funny, and presentable. There was no one I would be ashamed to introduce as a friend.

But Frankie was different. He was a total fox. Not too tall, maybe 5 foot 10, but what a face. Dark, dark eyes, a smile that would melt an icicle, and shaggy black hair like the Beatles. He was like no guy I would ever aspire to. If he only knew what he was getting into, but there was no way he would ever find out from me, unless it happened again.

Frankie and I met in the cafeteria at Pierce on a Wednesday afternoon. Andrew had a class and I was eating alone, when Frankie just came over, plunked his tray down at my table and sat down. "Hi, I'm Frankie. I haven't seen you around before; you must be new."

I felt a twinge of nervousness. Could such a good looking guy be interested in me? "No," I said. "This is actually my second semester."

"What're you studying?" he asked.

"I want to be a teacher, so I'm taking all the general classes: English, American history, and economics."

"Economics!" he said.

"Yes. I needed another class, so I thought, why not?"

"It's deadly dull," he said, taking a bite of his hamburger. "I should know; I took it."

"Then why did you take it?"

"I had to take something," he said.

"What's your major?" I asked, taking a bite of my tuna salad sandwich on whole wheat bread (a taste for which is apparently hereditary), hoping the nervous feeling in my stomach would calm down.

"Baseball," he said.

I was a little taken aback because he didn't look like a baseball player. He didn't seem tall enough, and he was pretty slight, although he was muscular and did have a ruddy complexion, as if he'd just been out in the sun. "Baseball?"

"Yeah. I'm on the Pierce baseball team."

"Well, I think that's wonderful," I said, thinking of my father. Wouldn't he like that.

"It's all I want to do," he said, his straight black hair falling across his forehead, "but unfortunately you have to take these classes, and do well in them." He took another bite of his hamburger, then wiped off the drippings around his mouth with his napkin. "So what's your name?" he asked.

"Zoe," I said.

"Don't know if I ever met a 'Zoe' before," he said.

"I was named after my mother's grandmother, Zelda," I said.

"Better Zoe than Zelda," he said, and then quickly added, "No offense intended. I like the name Zoe."

"So do I," I said.

Then he said, "So, Zoe, you want to take a walk after lunch?"

"I'd love to," I said, "but I can only go 'til two. I have my English class at two."

"Okay then," he said, stuffing the last bit of his hamburger into his mouth, "let's boogie."

I took the last bite of my sandwich, gulped down the last bit of Coke from my paper cup, grabbed my book-bag and was off with Frankie.

He carried my book-bag for me, and as we walked around the campus, I finally began to relax. I felt comfortable with him and flattered that a good looking guy like him would be interested in me.

Pierce College actually had a lovely campus, low lying buildings, lots of empty space, lots of grass and walkways, and on this bright spring day, it was warm enough to wear shorts and a tee shirt. I was, however, in jeans and a green tee, which brought out the green of my eyes. He was also in jeans but in a white tee….the kind my dad wore as underwear.

He told me his last name was Felder and I said, "So you're Frankie Felder. How alliterative."

"My folks thought it was strong."

"It is," I said. "It has a nice ring to it."

"Have you ever heard of Bernstein-Felder?"

"No," I said.

"It's a production company. My dad's the Felder."

"What kind of production company?"

"Movies. Sit-coms."

I was impressed. "Anything I might have seen?"

"Yeah. *Scandal in a Small Town, Summer in Maine,* the *Do-Gooders* TV show, and a bunch of others, some that sold, some that didn't."

"How exciting," I said.

"It's just a job to him."

"And what does your mother do?"

"She's a writer."

"So she writes the screenplays and your dad produces them?"

"Something like that."

"So don't you want to go into the business?"

"My dad wants me to, but like I said, I have another career in mind."

"And your mom, what does she want you to do?"

"Become a doctor, of course."

I thought of saying, *you must be Jewish,* and then decided to say it, "You must be Jewish."

He laughed. "How did you guess?" A pause, "So tell me about you."

"Well," I said, "I want to be a teacher...oh, I told you that...and I play the piano."

"Are you good?"

"Pretty good."

"I love the piano," he said. "My mom gave me lessons for awhile, but then I got into sports and that was the end of my music career." He thought for a moment, "So where do you live?"

"At home. With my mom, dad, brother and sister."

"What does your dad do?"

"He's an insurance agent. Not very glamorous."

"It's not what you do that counts," he said. "It's who you are," and he fastened his black eyes on me.

I was a bit flustered, but went on in my breezy way. "So do you live at home?"

"Yeah, with my mom and dad. I have one sister. She's married and has two kids, but she lives in New York, so I don't see too much of her." Then turning onto a narrow pathway, "So where do you live?"

"In Woodland Hills. And you?"

"Tarzana. Up in the hills. And then, of course, we have a place at the beach, in Malibu."

"Of course," I said, a little mockingly, "doesn't everyone?"

"I didn't mean it that way."

"I know," I said.

We were approaching the building that housed my English class. I looked at my watch, almost two o'clock. "Here we are," I said, "just in time." Then holding out my hands for my book bag, "I enjoyed our walk and talk, Frankie Felder."

"Me too," Frankie said, handing over the book bag. "Say, you want to come by my practice this afternoon? It's at 4 on the baseball field."

At that moment, there was nothing I wanted more. "I'll have to leave at 5. My brother drives me."

"Okay then," he said. "See you at 4, and then maybe we can we meet in the Caf at 12 tomorrow?"

I felt a rush in my chest; he wanted to see me again. "Sure," I said, as casually as I could.

"Okay then," he said. "See you later, and tomorrow."

"Yes," I said. "See you later and tomorrow." I'd have to tell Andrew I couldn't meet him for lunch tomorrow. I had a date with the most gorgeous guy in the world.

At three, I went to the library to study, but I had a hard time concentrating. All I could think about was Frankie, his black eyes, his black hair, how comfortable I felt with him, everything we'd talked about on our walk, and the fact that he was interested in me. How lucky could a girl get?

Finally at 3:45, I gave up, and ambled out to the baseball field and took a seat in the stands. All the guys were lined up on the foul line playing catch with each other.

When Frankie looked up and saw me, he gave me a big smile. I noticed he was the smallest player on the field. Most of the guys towered above him. But he was tall enough for me. I could wear my highest high heels and not be taller than him. And wasn't that what mattered? I quipped to myself.

In a few minutes, half the guys went into the dugout and the other half went to their positions, Frankie taking second base, and the practice game began. He looked good on the field. I had seen enough baseball games on TV and in person with my dad to see that he was quick, agile, threw hard, and ran fast. If only he was good enough to be a professional, wouldn't that be something? And wouldn't my dad be in heaven!

At five it was time to meet Andrew in the parking lot. Reluctantly, I climbed down from the stands, and Frankie waved to me, mouthing the words, "See you tomorrow."

From that day forward, I saw Frankie every day. He opened up a new world to me. I felt like I had been half dead before I met him, Now, suddenly I was going places I had never dared go, doing things I had never thought of doing. I felt so normal with him and was having so much fun, I didn't have time to think of my voice or my illness; every minute of my day was packed. Frankie had a ton of energy, he was always wanting to go someplace or do something, even after he'd practiced ball all day or played a game.

"Hey, Zoe," he'd say, "put on your bikini and grab a towel, we're going to the beach." Or, "How about we grab a bite to eat, and catch a flick." He was always hungry, and his favorite eating places were: Burger King, Carl's Junior, and Taco Bell. Another one of his passions was hanging out at the mall, going in and out of stores, sometimes buying something, sometimes not; and a few times a week, we'd go to a sports-card store. He collected baseball cards and had some really valuable ones.

But his favorite place to go was Dodger Stadium. He loved the Dodgers, so anytime he didn't have a game and they were in town, we were there. I didn't have a problem going anywhere with him, except the Dodger game...too many people for me; but he always got me an aisle seat, and if I focused on the game, and Frankie, I could get through it.

My dad, as predicted, was crazy about Frankie. Frankie was his dream come true. Every time Frankie walked into the house, my dad would shake his hand and pat him on the back and they'd talk baseball. Or if there was a baseball game, tennis match, or golf tournament, going on anywhere in the world on TV, they'd watch it together. I'd usually watch for a few minutes, and then go do my homework and practice the piano, and when I came back after an hour or two, the two of them would just be chattering away, happy as could be.

Frankie also got along great with my mom, Claire, and especially Andrew. He liked going into Andrew's room and listening to Andrew play the guitar and sing his songs. "So what'd ya say, dude," Andrew asked him, "want to take some lessons? I'm cheap."

"I'd love to," Frankie told him, "but I got to take care of the old hands."

"Maybe the calluses would make you play better."

"Sorry, dude, can't take the chance."

There was only one thing Frankie didn't like, and that was studying. But that worked out okay, because I could always study and/or practice the piano while he hung out with my dad or Andrew.

Lots of times, while I was practicing the piano, he'd come into the living room and lie on my mother's burgundy sofa, close his eyes and listen to me play. He wasn't crazy about classical music, but he said the way I played it brought out emotions he'd never experienced before. At first I felt a little nervous playing in front of him. My fingers didn't feel as strong or agile as when I played for myself or Ms. Hockensmith, but after a time, I relaxed, and actually thought I played better when he was listening, as if his enjoyment of the music inspired me to give everything I had.

Three weeks after we started dating, Frankie took me over to his house in Tarzana. His parents weren't at home, they were at the Malibu house, but he wanted me to see it anyway. I thought my house was big and beautiful, until I saw his.

It was huge and perfectly decorated, completely different from my house. While my mom had painted every room in our house a different color, Frankie's mom had done the opposite. Every room matched every other, everything blended in various tones of beige and brown, even the bathrooms.

The rooms were filled with paintings, sculptures, and potted plants. His mother also had a collection of English bone-china figurines displayed in a china cabinet in the dining room, and other pieces of glass art were scattered throughout the house. A vase of fresh flowers sat on the kitchen table. I was impressed with that, because the only time we had fresh flowers in our house was if my dad remembered to get them for my mom on Valentine's Day.

After he'd taken me through the inside of the house, Frankie opened the French doors leading to the backyard, turned on the floodlights, and we walked outside. What a yard. Obviously it was designed by a landscape architect, with flowers aplenty, a huge pool, and lounges, chairs, and a metal-rimmed umbrella table the size of our dining room table, all matching in the same beiges and browns as the inside of the house. It was pretty impressive.

"This is fabulous," I said.

"If you think this is fabulous, wait until you see the Malibu house."

I can hardly wait, I thought to say, but decided not to. I didn't want him to feel obligated to take me there.

After the tour, we settled in the den with its cushy brown sofa and huge TV, and kissed for awhile, but when Frankie tried to touch my breasts, I pulled away.

"What's wrong?" he asked.

"Nothing," I said. "I've just never done this before."

"Well, maybe it's time you started," he said.

I didn't want to disappoint him, but I also felt uncomfortable about him touching my breasts. "Would it be all right if we just kiss tonight?" I asked, sheepishly.

He smiled. "Okay," he said. "But the time will come..."

"I know," I said, "but just for tonight...."

"Sure," he said, pulling me close and giving me a kiss that never seemed to end.

I liked kissing Frankie, and I liked being cuddled in his arms, but I didn't know if I would like anything else.

From that first day of going to Frankie's practice, I went to all his practices, all his home games, and some of his away games, if they weren't too far a drive. I loved sitting in the stands, in the open air, even with the sun burning through my skin. I'd try to remember to put sun block on my arms and legs, but I always wore a visor, and even then it was often too hot to sit for two or three hours watching a baseball game, sometimes unbearably so.

But I did it. I sat there, experiencing a strange combination of feeling alive and at peace, simultaneously. I was in a totally non-threatening environment. It was a time out of mind; there was nothing to do, nowhere to go, nothing to think about except the game, and how beautiful the day was, and how lucky I was to have a boyfriend like Frankie.

After a week or two, I developed a camaraderie with the other girls who were in the stands with me, who were also there to watch their boyfriends. We chatted easily about our majors, our families, what we wanted to do after graduation, and the thing we had most in common, our guys.

All of us prayed our guy would do well, but it was when he stepped up to bat, that the tension really set in: all of us crossing our fingers, our stomachs turning over, holding our breath, and then the elation if he got a hit, the dejection if he struck out. Most of us had high hopes our guy would be drafted by a four-year college, or a minor or major league team, and a lot of the talk was about our guy's future.

"A scout from the Giants was here last game just to look at Jordan," Lisa said; or "I hope so bad that Greg makes it. He'll die if he doesn't," Debbie said; or "Derek's ERA is so low, someone's bound to want him," Felicia said.

"I just hope Frankie makes it onto a four-year college team," I told them. Being on a community college team was something; but being on a real college team was something else.

And then at the second home game after the official season began, five weeks after Frankie and I started dating, I noticed a man and woman approaching, and recognized them immediately from the photos in Frankie's house. They were Frankie's mom and dad. They had brought stadium seats with them and came and sat beside me. Obviously, Frankie had shown them a photo of me because they recognized me right away.

"You must be Zoe," his mom said to me, and then, "I'm Frankie's mother." Frankie's mom appeared like her picture except she was smaller and slimmer than she looked in her photos. She had short dark hair threaded with several shades of blonde. "And this is Frankie's dad," she said pointing to the man beside her. Frankie's dad looked to be about Frankie's height, but he was not solid like Frankie. He was heavier and with a paunch, and his thinning dark hair was patched with grey. But he had a certain swagger about him, like he was "somebody."

"Nice to meet you," he said, and then ignored me the entire game as if I were a mite on the wooden stands.

But his mom spoke to me, asking me questions about what I wanted to do and why I was at Pierce, as if I should have been at a better school. Of course, it was all right for her son to be there because he was only there for baseball. I wasn't really crazy about either one of them, but at least they had introduced themselves to me. They could have totally ignored me.

"Unfortunately, we can't get to many of Frankie's games," his mom said. "We're often out of town, or busy on some project."

"I heard you're a writer," I said, trying to be friendly. "What kinds of things do you write?"

"Screenplays and TV stuff."

"How exciting," I said, with enthusiasm, because I really did think it was exciting.

"Exciting, but a lot of hard work," she said. And then sometime later, "So what does your dad do?"

"He's an insurance agent," I told her, and after seeing the look of contempt on her face, for the first time in my life, I wished my dad was a doctor or a lawyer.

"And your mother?" Said as if she expected the worst.

"My mom doesn't work anymore," and seeing the displeasure in her eyes, added, "but she's a docent at the L.A. County Museum of Art."

"Oh...LACMA," Frankie's mom said, as if it was nothing special to be a docent at the L.A. County Museum of Art.

We didn't do much more talking, except the three times Frankie got a hit, and then all three of us stood up clapping our hands and yelling, "run, run, run," and then, sitting back down, "What a great hit!"

After the game, the parents hung around long enough to congratulate Frankie on going 3 for 4, and his mom gave him a kiss, his dad a pat on the back, both his parents said 'bye' to me, and "nice meeting you," and then Frankie and I were left alone.

"So what'd you think?" Frankie asked.

"I think you got three great hits," I said.

"Thanks," he said with an embarrassed grin. "But what I meant was what did you think of my folks?"

I hesitated a moment, "I think they're very nice."

"And what do you really think?"

There was no way I was going to tell him that. "I think they're very nice," I repeated.

"Good," he said, packing up his bag. "Now, let's go get something to eat. I'm starving."

So everything was good between us, really good, except when it came to sex. As the days passed, kissing was no longer enough for Frankie. He'd take me over his house when his parents were out of town or at the Malibu house, and he'd want to fondle my breasts, he'd try to reach under my skirt or down my jeans, and he'd want me to touch him. I didn't really want to do any of those things. But he was so persistent, that finally I gave in and let him do whatever he wanted, except I wouldn't touch him or go all the way, but I would let him rub up against me until he came.

I still liked the kissing and the hugging, and I especially liked being enclosed in his arms. He felt so strong and his body was so hard that it made me feel safe, as if nothing could harm me.

But I was uncomfortable with the rest of it. Not because I was a prude, but because I felt nothing. I wanted to feel something, I yearned and prayed I would feel something, but for some reason, the minute it went past hugging and kissing, I went numb. I didn't know if it was the pills I was taking, or if I was afraid my malady would come back, or if I was born frigid, but for whatever reason, I didn't want to do anything more than kiss and hug.

As the days passed, Frankie became more and more persistent about going all the way, but I kept putting him off. I was only 18, and it was understandable, I thought, that I didn't want to take a chance on getting pregnant, or contracting a sexually transmitted disease. It was okay, I thought, to want to put off going all the way until I was married, or at least engaged.

He accepted my excuses for now, but I knew there would come a time when he would no longer accept them. Then what would I do? Tell him the truth...that I didn't enjoy it; tell him about my malady? I couldn't take a chance of either. I didn't want to lose him, so I would say nothing until I had to.

The day before school ended, Frankie received a telephone call from the baseball coach at San Diego State. He wanted Frankie to play for them.

He called me the minute he hung up the phone. "You won't believe this, Zoe. Guess who just got a call from San Diego State?"

"Oh Frankie," I said.

"Yeah, baby," he said, "they want me. They want ME!" And then he let out a howl that just about deafened me.

I held the phone away from my ear. And when he calmed down, I said, "Oh Frankie, I'm so happy for you. But you deserve it. You're the best 2nd baseman I've ever seen."

"You bet I'm gonna be. I'll be right over and we'll go someplace to celebrate."

"Where?" I asked.

"I think Carl's Junior," he said.

And that's where we went.

His parents were happy, he told me, that he would be playing baseball for San Diego State, but my parents were ecstatic, especially, my dad.

"Boy that's great, son," he said, giving Frankie a hug.

"Thanks Mr. Hirsch," Frankie said, hugging him back.

School ended and for the next three weeks, Frankie was really after me about going all the way. He was leaving in July to play in the Cape Cod League and would be gone for six weeks, and then in the fall, he would be going to San Diego State. "We're not going to have much time together," he said, "and I want all of you now."

I came up with my usual excuses, plus a new added worry to me. "What if you meet someone in Cape Cod or San Diego?"

"I'm not going to meet anyone—I'll be too busy playing baseball."

"Still it could happen."

"It's not going to happen," he said, " 'cause you're my girl."

"But it could," I persisted. And he backed off again.

I'm not sure why he put up with me. He could probably have found a hundred girls who would have gone to bed with him, but for some reason, he liked me.

So in July off he went to the Cape Cod League, while I went to work in my dad's office.

My dad had two secretaries now: Arlene, whom he'd hired when my mom started college, and Trudy, whom he'd hired when my mom graduated from college and decided to become a docent. Arlene had been with him for ten years, and Trudy for six years, but my dad was still so busy that my mom often had to go into the office to help out. So my dad and mom were both delighted to have me help out in the summer.

It was a little crowded in the office with the four of us, my dad, me, Trudy and Arlene, but Trudy and Arlene took turns going on a two week vacation, so everything worked out. I liked working for my dad, and I liked both his secretaries. They were extremely helpful and appreciative of everything I did—it was one less thing they had to do.

Frankie and I talked on the phone almost every day. He had a tough schedule; lots of practice; lots of games and he was fatigued most of the time; but having the best time of his life. I missed him terribly, but placated myself with the thought it was only six weeks, and then depressed myself by the next thought, that he'd only be home for two weeks before leaving for San Diego.

Since I had so much free time, Ms. Hockensmith loaded me up with work. In addition to the Beethoven sonatas I was working on, she added a few Chopin Etudes, and his Ballade in A flat. I loved the challenge and was thankful that I had something challenging and absorbing to do, so I wouldn't miss Frankie so much.

Ms. Hockensmith still had dreams for me, and we went at it as if I really was going to be a concert pianist. But she understood that at this time of my life, I needed to be out in the world. I wanted to complete my college education, I wanted to teach public school, and I wanted to spend time with my boyfriend. I could not devote myself to music as she wished I could. And while I didn't say anything to her about any of it, I had already decided I did not want to end up living the lonely life that she was living. I wanted to get married and have children, and aside from my malady, I wasn't sure I would want the life of a concert pianist even if I could have it.

In August, Frankie returned, more tan than ever, with a two inch growth of hair on his head, and a one inch growth of beard on his face. He looked great. When we came together, he couldn't let go of me. "How I missed you, baby," he said, holding me close, kissing my lips, my hair, my eyes.

I loved the feel of his scratchy face, his firm body pressing into mine. "I missed you, too," I told him, and then after a few soul kisses, I asked him, "So what do you want to do tonight?" I actually knew the answer to that.

His black eyes were twinkling. "Go out with you, baby," he said.

Or course he was starving, so we went to Burger King, then drove over to the Pacific Coast Highway, parked, and went for a walk on the beach, kissing and hugging the whole time. At eleven o'clock, we ended up at his parents' house in Tarzana. The house was quiet. Apparently both his parents were asleep. He kissed me inside the front door, and then led me upstairs to his bedroom. He pulled the brown comforter off his bed; then pulled me onto his beige sheets. I knew this was it. I couldn't put him off any longer. He was too happy, too upbeat, so excited to be with me, how could I down his spirits? We began kissing, and then he began caressing me, took off my bra, kissed my breasts, pulled off my shorts, and I said, "Do you have something?"

"Yes, baby, I have something," he whispered, and he stopped a moment and opened the drawer of his nightstand. I saw him pull out a package, unwrap it, and put the rubber on his erect penis, all the while I was trying to feel excited, praying I would enjoy it, that this would be the magic moment I had dreamed of, longed for, wanted so badly.

I tried. I tried so hard. I was as loving and affectionate as I could be, except of course, when he broke my hymen and I let out a little yelp, but much as I wanted to, and hard as I tried, I didn't enjoy a minute of it.

After, as he snuggled close to me, and told me how beautiful I was, what a great body I had, and how thrilling it had been for him, all I could do was hold him tight and hope it wouldn't be as painful next time, that my lack of feeling was just a temporary thing, and that in time, I would learn to enjoy it.

For the next two weeks, Frankie couldn't get enough sex. He wanted it every day, he wanted me to go on the pill; he told me it would be more pleasurable for both of us, but with all the drugs I was already taking, I didn't want to take one more. I was still not enjoying it, but I pretended I was enjoying it. I loved being close to him. I loved his body pressing into mine, the strength of it. I even loved his kisses and sometimes his caresses, but when it came to the actual act, I felt nothing. But if I closed my eyes and thought of other things, I could get through it. It was bearable. Perhaps Dr. Berg was right. Perhaps I had been molested as a child and lost all memory of it. That would explain everything.

At the end of August, he came by my house on his way to San Diego in his new red Pontiac Firebird. The trunk and back seat were loaded with suitcases, duffle bags, and baseball equipment.

We held each other tight for a long time. I was filled with a flood of sadness reaching out to the tips of my fingers and the ends of my toes. How would I get through the next nine months without him: without our trips to the beach, the movies, the mall, all his fast food restaurants, or just sitting and watching baseball games on TV with my dad. I would miss all the fun and excitement he brought to my life. I would miss that black hair, those deep black eyes, his infectious smile, his energy that energized me. And I would miss the cuddling, yes, the cuddling, being close to him, feeling his strong arms around me, feeling safe and protected, his love for me enveloping every part of my body. He made me feel precious, like the most expensive diamond in the world.

I thought again about the chance of him meeting someone in San Diego. Someone he liked more than me, someone who liked sex, who really enjoyed it. That would be the end of me. He was so attractive. It could happen. What would I do then? What would I do without him?

Finally we let go. My chest felt like it had a lead weight in it. I could barely breathe. Then one final peck on the lips, and he was in his red Firebird, revving up the motor, throwing another kiss to me, and zooming down the street and around the corner. I stood there awhile looking after him, and then turned and went inside my house to face the next nine months without Frankie.

The next week, while Frankie was playing baseball at San Diego State, I started college at Cal State University Northridge, a real college. I loved the campus, my instructors, and my classes, and was determined to get an A in every one of them. A few of my friends from high school, including Teri and Missy, were also going to CSUN (pronounced C-SUN) so, while I missed Frankie terribly, I had plenty to keep me busy. I spent time with my old friends and made some new ones, spent a lot of time on my schoolwork, and played the piano every spare minute I had.

While Ms. Hockensmith was still hoping, I had by now had given up all thoughts of ever being a concert pianist. I had made peace with the fact I would be an elementary school teacher who played the piano as a hobby. Perhaps at some time in the future, I would want to teach piano, either privately or have a class for the children at school. But for now I was content with just being a college student, and getting through each day with no problems.

Frankie and I talked on the phone every day. He seemed to be having a tough time with his batting, but hoped it would improve as he got used to the better pitching, and whenever he came in for a weekend or holiday, we'd spend most of every day together.

In June, school ended, and Frankie received the horrifying news that he was being dropped from the team. Unfortunately his batting average had dropped from the 420 it had been at Pierce, to a paltry 230. They told him that he was an excellent fielder and that they felt fortunate that he had spent the year with them, but there were some new recruits coming in and someone had to be let go. Unfortunately it was him. He was devastated. He drove home on a Thursday afternoon and came directly to my house.

"Zoe." He stood there when I opened the door, looking like a little lost boy.

I put my arms around him and held him close. When I pulled back, there were tears in his eyes.

I took him into the house, gave him a Coke, and we sat at the kitchen table talking.

"So now what are you going to do?" I asked.

"Kill myself," he said.

"No, you're not."

"That's how I feel."

"I know, but you'll find something else you want to do."

"All those years of practice…" he said. "I gave it my all, and I still wasn't good enough."

I put my hand on his. "I know," I said. "It's awful. But you're young and healthy, and you'll find something you want to do."

He was quiet for a moment, and then he said, "Let's get married."

"No," I said, automatically.

"Why not?" he asked.

"You're not serious," I said.

"Sure, I am."

"But we're so young."

"So what?"

I considered it. I did love him, but I had two big problems. One was sex, and the other was my deep dark secret. Would he still want to marry me, if he knew about either of those things?

"I do love you," I said, "but I just think we're too young."

"Your mother got married when she was 18 and you're already 20."

"I know, but I don't think I'm ready to make a commitment for the rest of my life. We need to get to know each other better." Meaning *you have to get to know me better.*

"Okay then, let's just get engaged, and we'll wait five or six years to get married."

I laughed. He could always make me laugh. The whole thing was ridiculous, but if we just got engaged, what harm could come of it? I could always break it off, or he could always break it off if things didn't work out, or if my malady came back. He looked so needy.

"Okay," I said. "Sure, why not?"

"Let's go tell your mom and dad, and then we'll go tell my mom and dad."

"Okay," I said, going along with it. It was a game, and I was one of the pieces in the game being manipulated by a hand I could not control. I thought of Andrew's song, *I'm just a pawn in the game of life.*

My mom and dad were in the office. Dad's secretaries, Trudy and Arlene, who had just left for the day, were both on overload and mom had gone to finish up a few things they'd left undone. We walked hand in hand across the yard, past the pool, the green lawn, the flowers that circled the lawn, the pomegranate trees, and into the office. Mom was typing; Dad was on the phone. Mom said, "Hi, Frankie, welcome home." She knew about his bad news but chose not to mention it.

We chatted a bit waiting for Dad to get off the phone, and when he did, Frankie said to both of them, "I've just asked your daughter to marry me and she said 'yes'. So I'd like to ask your permission to marry your daughter."

For a moment they both sat there dazed. Then they both stood up and walked to us, enfolded us in their arms, and said, "Yes, that would be great. That's wonderful. When do you plan to get married?"

It was all so surrealistic. I knew my dad was in heaven...a sports nut for a son-in-law, and I knew my mom was relieved... did this mean I would lead a normal life, that she wouldn't have to worry about me finding a man who would accept me with all my problems? I think that's what she was thinking because that's what I was thinking. This was too good to be true.

I changed my clothes from my faded jeans to my nice white shorts, and put on a pink t-shirt. Frankie liked me in pink..."it matches your eyes," he joked because of course my eyes were green, like my mom's. We drove along Malibu Canyon, on a winding, sometimes scary road that cut through the mountains, until we spotted the beautiful blue Pacific.

"It's so beautiful," I said. "I should marry you, just for this drive to your parents' house, and the house itself, of course."

"Yeah, but unfortunately, it's their house, not mine."

"Well, if you're good, maybe one day, they'll give it to you."

"We should both be so lucky."

I had been to the Malibu house a few times since I met Frankie, but as I entered that June day, I was just as impressed as the first time I had seen it. It hung over a house below which had direct access to the beach. The Felder house had an unobstructed view, but you had to walk down a long staircase of wooden steps to actually be on the sand. Still, the view was worth a million dollars...actually probably two million.

The three story house had a circular feeling to it, and the entire front was glass. They had furnished it with large overstuffed pieces, so you would kind-of sink into the sofas and chairs. So luxurious. Everything was done in shades of blue. It was very different from the Tarzana house, with its browns and beiges. That house was more formal; the Malibu house was plush and casual.

Sheila was in her office on the upper level where all the bedrooms were, and Sheldon was in his office on the lower level. We entered on the middle level, caught our breath at the magnificent view, and then Frankie shouted out, "Mom, Dad, I have something to tell you. C'mon down and up." We looked at each other and laughed.

In a few minutes, Sheila came down the circular staircase; and in another few minutes, Sheldon came up the circular staircase. Both their faces showed concern. "What is it?" each asked.

Frankie put his arm around me, "Zoe and I are engaged."

There was a blank expression on their faces for a moment, and then Sheila said, "Engaged?"

"To be married," Frankie said, and I shivered. This was not a good idea. They were clearly upset. How stupid was I to go forward on this thing with Frankie...on a whim. Of course we were both too young to get married. I hung back.

"Frankie, you're twenty years old, you have no job or profession; you haven't even finished school yet. Why are you talking about getting married?"

Frankie looked at me. "Because we love each other."

"Fine," Sheila said...apparently Sheldon had decided to let her handle the whole thing and stay out of it..."keep on loving each other, and if you're still in love after you've finished school and have a job, then fine, we'll both be very happy."

"But I am going to have a job," Frankie said. "I'm going to work for Dad."

Dad looked surprised. "You are?"

"Well, you always said you wanted me to go into the biz with you. So here I am, ready."

That was Frankie, completely impulsive.

"You know," Sheldon said, "perhaps we ought to discuss this later…I'm really in the middle of something…I have calls to make and it's getting late."

Frankie looked disappointed.

And then, it hit me, like a smack in the face…the whole scene changed…or rather the scene didn't change, except that I was no longer in it. My body was there, but I wasn't. I turned away from his parents and looked at the ocean…I saw it, the waves, the water, but I couldn't realize it. I looked to the stairway, the cushy blue sofas, Frankie's face, and Sheila's and Sheldon's, but they were as far removed from me as the man in the moon. I wanted to scream, to run away and hide, to get out of there as fast as possible. "Frankie, please take me home."

"No," Frankie said, "we're going to have this out right now. There's nothing my parents can say to me that I don't want you to hear."

"Please, Frankie," I begged, "I don't feel well."

"Okay," he said, more to his parents than to me, "but this isn't over."

We walked out the front door to the red Firebird, and I got in, and then all the way back over Malibu Canyon, my heart was racing, my body sweating, I was dizzy and nauseous, maybe from the curves, but more from my unhappiness. It had happened again; I was not over it; it was back in spades.

Frankie kept asking if I was all right, but I couldn't tell him; not now, not when his whole world had fallen in. I would tell him later; I would have to. There would be no marriage, no engagement, no normal life for me, ever.

The next morning, I woke up and lay in bed for awhile and let myself experience the devastation I felt. How stupid I was to dare to hope. The tears were streaming down my face. What about Frankie, what about school? What about the rest of my life?

My mom came in to check on me, and she immediately knew what was going on. "Zoe," she said, "are you all right?"

"No, mom," I said through my tears.

She sat on the bed beside me and put her arms around me, bent her head to mine, "Oh, Zoe, I'm so sorry." After a few minutes she began stroking my hair. "Don't worry, my darling, we'll go back to the psychiatrist, and if he can't help you, we'll find someone who can. We're going to lick this thing, honey, you'll see."

The next day we got in to see Dr. Berg. He was pleased that I had gone so long without another "episode", and decided to try a different combination of drugs. "We don't really know what the problem is, so it's kind of hit and miss with the drugs. Let's try increasing the Nardil and cutting down on the Prozac.

"Will that cure me, doctor?" I asked.

"Zoe, as I've told you previously, we just don't know. But we'll keep trying until we find something that works." He cleared his throat.

"And what if nothing works?" I replied.

"Zoe, you know how sick you were when you first came to me, and now you've gone almost two years without a problem. Something will work," he said.

My mother, sitting beside me holding my hand, asked, "Should Zoe be getting some kind of psychotherapy?"

"I don't think it's going to help since I believe this is a malfunction of her MAO inhibitors, but if you wish to seek therapy, you could see Dr. Hedge. He has a doctorate in psychology."

"I think I'd like that," my mother said.

"Fine," Dr. Berg said, looking through his rolodex. "Here we are," and he wrote down a name and phone number, and cleared his throat.

The next day we had an appointment to see Dr. Hedge, as in hedge fund or hedge hog, or hedge along the garden wall. I didn't have much faith in anyone named hedge, but Mom liked the name. She thought it was substantial....like a tree.

Dr. Hedge was an older man with a white beard and glasses and I could just discern red pimples beneath his facial hair. Perhaps that's why he grew a beard.

He heard what I had to say and made a sound like "hmmm," every so often. Finally when I finished talking, trying to explain in every way I could what I was feeling, he said, "Tell me, Zoe, I know this is a difficult question, but it must be asked. Have you ever been physically abused?"

Asked and answered by Dr. Berg, I thought. "No," I said, a bit of annoyance in my voice.

"I don't mean just sexually."

"No," I repeated, more annoyed.

"Did your parents ever hit you?"

I thought about my dad's smacks on my behind when Claire and I shared a room in Van Nuys and wouldn't go to sleep, but kept jumping on each other's bed. Should I tell him about that? Would they put my dad in jail? But I had to tell the truth. This was my psychologist…the person who could make me well. "My dad did give me a little slap on the behind a few times."

"Aha," he said in a musing tone. "And what about mentally? Did your parents yell at you or belittle you? Make you feel bad?"

I tried to think over the past. Well there were times, of course there were times when they said I wasn't trying, or I could do better, and there was their disappointment about my tennis lessons, my piano recital and my bat mitzvah. But did that count as abuse? If anyone was abused, it was Andrew. My dad sure knew how to belittle him. "No, I don't think so," I said aloud.

"What about your siblings? Did they ever hit you or belittle you?"

"No, definitely not."

"How about friends? Do you have a lot of friends?"

"A few," I replied, "but none of them ever did anything to hurt me or they wouldn't be my friend."

"Hmmmm," Dr. Hedge said. "I was thinking perhaps this was something like a split personality disorder, but there doesn't appear to be anything traumatic enough in your history to substantiate that." Then looking at me with piercing eyes. "You're sure nothing traumatic ever happened to you?"

"Well yes," I said sarcastically, "*this* happened to me. This dream-world happened to me."

"Yes," he said, almost apologetically, "but what set it off?"

"I don't know," I said. Wasn't that his job—to figure that out? Obviously, he was stymied.

When my mom came back into the room, he told her it wouldn't hurt if I continued to come to talk to him once a week, but that basically I should stay with my drug treatment. My problem appeared to be physical rather than mental or emotional.

When we left the office, my mom asked me if I'd like to talk to Dr. Hedge once a week, and I said, "No." What was the point of it? He didn't know any more than I did.

Frankie had called every day to see how I was doing, and he wanted to come over, but I was still "out of it" and not up to seeing him or anyone else, so I told my mom to tell him I had the flu and was too ill to even come to the phone.

He continued calling every day and I continued having my mom put him off. I knew that if I talked to him, I would have to tell him the truth about me and then it would be over between us. I also knew that was inevitable, but I couldn't deal with it while I was in the state I was in. Every day, I lay on my bed for hours with the TV on. I didn't want to do anything, go anywhere, talk to anyone, not even play the piano. In fact, if this was going to be my life, if I never got better, I wanted to die. I realized this wasn't the first time I thought of dying. The voice inside me echoed my thought, "It would be better to die than go on living like this."

A week later on my visit to Dr. Berg, he added an additional little white pill, and within the week I was feeling pretty spacey, spacey enough so that I wasn't afraid to talk to Frankie.

"Boy that was some flu," he said, walking into my house and giving me a big hug.

"You sure you're not contagious." Kind of a joke.

"No," I said, wondering if this was the last time I would see him, because I was going to tell him the truth. Dr. Berg had said it was nothing to be ashamed of. It was an illness like any other, and the more people I told, the better I would feel. I doubted that; I still didn't want anyone to know, but I felt I was wasting Frankie's time. I had to tell him.

We sat on adjoining cushions on my mom's burgundy sofa in the living room, and he started telling me about his job. He had started working for his dad, getting his feet wet. "You know it's kind of cool in a way…all these celebrities walking around calling me, Frankie. And it's kind of interesting. Of course I visited sets before, but somehow when you're working behind the scenes, it's all different. I actually think I might like it. You get to be with people, and try to solve problems. Only thing is I've got to wear a suit and tie. You know how I feel about that. But Dad says I'll get used to it. And the pay is probably more than I'd get as a baseball player in the minor leagues."

"Sounds great," I said.

He kept on talking while I kept thinking about what I would say, and finally he realized I wasn't listening. "What's going on, Zoe? You okay?"

"No, Frankie," I said, "I'm not okay. I've got this problem. Something I never told you about, but should have."

He turned serious. "What kind of problem?"

"It's hard to explain," I said. "I have these….episodes," I used Dr. Berg's term, "where I don't realize myself."

Frankie looked baffled. "Don't realize yourself?"

"Yes. Where I feel like I'm in a dream."

"You mean like a nightmare?"

"No, not a nightmare. It's like I'm watching my life from somewhere else. But I'm not in it."

"Holy shit," he said. "Sounds scary."

"It is," I said.

Trying to regain control, "So how often does this happen to you?"

"Not too often," I said, "and usually it only lasts a few minutes….but after I graduated high school, it went on for almost four months."

"Four months!" he said, seeming pretty shaken.

"Yes, that's why I went to Pierce instead of C-SUN. I had missed the start of my first semester at C-SUN and Pierce agreed to take me, even though it was a month late. And then I was fine until the day you took me to see your parents about our engagement."

"Well is there something they can do?"

"Yes, I'm going to a," I didn't want to say the word '*psychiatrist*', "doctor, and I'm taking some medicine."

"Jesus," he said, "I'm pretty shocked. You always seemed so normal." And then regretting his choice of words, "I mean you're still normal. You just have a problem, right?"

"Right," I said, thoroughly depressed. So this was the end of it.

"Well, it doesn't matter to me," he said, "you're still my girl."

I loved him for saying that, but I couldn't let it stand. "Oh, Frankie, you're so sweet. But I don't think you realize this could last for months, forever even, and even if it does go away, it could come back at anytime. No one even knows what it is."

"It's okay," he said. "We can deal with it."

"Oh, Frankie," I said, taking his hand, looking into his syrupy black eyes, wondering if he really meant it or if he was only saying it because he didn't have the courage to break it off. I was thinking, "Please don't leave me," but aloud I said, "Let's not make any decisions right now. Go home and think about it and we'll talk again when I'm feeling better."

"Okay," he said, "but I'm not changing my mind."

He kissed me goodbye, but I was too spaced-out to feel anything.

The next morning I regressed. And the next day I was even worse. I couldn't understand it. When he had said, "you're still my girl," that should have made me feel better. "It's just a tease," the Destroyer said. "Nothing's going to make you feel better. Forget the drugs, the doctors, even Frankie... it's definitely over with you and Frankie."

The following day, Frankie came by without notice. I heard the doorbell ring. I heard the creak on the stairs and a knock on my door.

My mother crept in. "Frankie's here. He wants to see you."

"No," I told my mom. "I can't see him. I can't see anyone." I was curled up in my bed in the fetal position. But I was really in outer space.

"Can't you see him for a minute?"

"No," I said.

I heard him at the door, "Please, Zoe, let me in."

"No," I called. I couldn't see him in this condition.

My mom walked back to my bedroom door and closed it behind her, but I heard Frankie say through the closed door, "Mrs. Hirsch, please tell Zoe that I'm going to be going to film school at NYU, and that under the circumstances, I think we shouldn't be engaged anymore."

"Okay, Frankie, I'll tell her," Mom said, and then I heard them walking down the stairs.

Soon after, my mother came back into my room and sat beside me. She began stroking my hand. "Zoe, there's something I have to tell you..."

"I heard," I said, and then turned on my side. I couldn't talk to her, I couldn't think, I couldn't feel anything. I just wanted to hide under my quilt forever and never come out. I was dead to the world, except that I knew my body was shaking from crying so hard.

Chapter Seven — Eric

By September, I was feeling better. Somehow the summers were my enemy, even though I loved the sun and the heat. But something happened every summer, it seemed. Perhaps that was when I was raped, as Dr. Hedge had suggested, or when whatever traumatic experience I was supposed to have had, happened.

I started back to school at C-SUN, and was glad to have my school work to fill my head. I still wasn't over the devastation of losing Frankie, if one can ever get over something like that, but while Frankie hadn't stuck by me, I still had my friends, and between school and practicing the piano, I was pretty busy and pretty happy. I thought a lot about Frankie, and at some point began wondering if I had truly loved him. Maybe I thought I loved him because he loved me. Perhaps that's why I hadn't enjoyed sex with him. Perhaps I was in love with love, and wanted someone to love me so badly, that I talked myself into being in love with him. Perhaps.

I went through the year with no problem, getting all A's, except in Phys Ed where I got my usual "B" (I guess I just wasn't good at sports) and that summer, still feeling healthy, again worked in my dad's office.

In the fall, Teri Vogel got engaged. She was marrying a great guy, David Smolensky, and she asked me to be her maid of honor. I was touched, honored, and saddened because, after thinking about it for a few days, I knew I couldn't do it. I couldn't walk down the aisle with all eyes upon me, because I was afraid "it" would happen.

I told her one afternoon after classes when she came over my house to help her plan her wedding. We were sitting in the living room, on my mom's burgundy sofa, drinking Cokes, listening to a tape of the Commodores, with her debating the pros and cons of various color schemes, when I finally got up the courage to interrupt her. "Teri, there's something I have to tell you," I pushed the words out. "This is really hard for me," I continued, "but I can't be your maid of honor."

She seemed surprised. "But why?" she asked.

"I just can't walk down the aisle with all eyes upon me."

"But why?" she repeated.

"I just get too nervous," I said. "I thought about this long and hard, and I'm really sorry. I really want to be your maid of honor, but I just can't do it."

She thought a moment. She knew I had a problem, but she wasn't sure exactly what that problem was. "Then can you be a bridesmaid?" she asked.

Obviously she had no idea of what my problem was, and for a moment I thought of telling her about it, but I didn't want her to think I was a nutcase. Besides, if she knew, mightn't she tell someone else? And then that someone might tell someone else, and pretty soon, everyone would know. After all, if I couldn't keep it a secret, how could I expect anyone else to. No, I couldn't risk it. "I'm sorry," I said, "but I can't do that either. But I'll do anything else I can to help with the wedding."

Teri was thinking again, probably deciding if she should probe further, or just let it go.

"Well, how about paying for the wedding?" she asked with a straight face.

"I do have some money saved from when I gave piano lessons," I answered, equally straight-faced.

"I don't think it'll be enough."

"I could ask my parents for a loan."

"How about if you just go with me to pick out a dress, and maybe sit at a table and give out the place cards?"

"Yes, I'm good at that."

"And you will come to my bridal shower?"

"Definitely," I said, although I knew that I might not be able to.

We both sipped our Cokes, feeling comfortable with one another as we always did, and let the voice of Lionel Ritchie take over the room.

The following week, Teri picked me up to go look at dresses. She was driving her brother's hand-me-down Toyota Camry with already 150,000 miles on it, and as we turned onto Ventura Blvd, I asked her, "So how do you feel about changing your name from Vogel to Smolensky?"

"It could be worse," Teri said, stopping at a red light. "It could be Schmuck."

We both laughed. "Or it could be Smokensky," I said.

"Or it could be "Smolenofsky," she said.

As we drove along, we kept coming up with more names and giggling at each one. And then as we pulled up in front of *Brides are Us*, she parked and said, "You know David has a friend. No, you don't know, but he does."

"And what's *his* name?" I asked.

"Simoneau."

"Is that the first name or the last?"

"The last, silly," she said, pulling her keys out of the ignition.

"Or it could be the first and the last," I said. "You know, Simon Oh."

"Yes, it could be that, or it could be Simonize," she said.

We giggled again. "Or it could be Simon says," I added.

"So do you want to go out with him?" she asked.

"What's his first name?"

"Eric," she said.

"Eric Simoneau," I said. "Okay."

As we emerged from the car, we were both excited about impending events...finding a dress for Teri and perhaps a man for me.

The following Saturday night, Teri, David, Eric and I went on a double date. Boy, was I happy. Eric Simoneau was in his first year of law school at UCLA, tall, probably six-two, with curly blond-brown hair, black rimmed glasses, and he liked classical music and opera. You don't find a guy like that every day. He seemed to like me too, especially after Teri told him that I was a marvelous pianist and had a 4.0 average.

I corrected the last, "Not quite," I said. "I did get that B in Phys Ed."

He smiled. "But are you a marvelous pianist?"

"I should be, with all the practicing I do."

"I'll take that as a 'yes'" he said. And I let it stand.

We went to dinner and to see the movie, *Moonstruck*, which put us all in a great mood, especially Eric and me because we both loved the opera scenes.

Since I was the last one picked up, I was the first one dropped off. Eric walked me to the door. "Can I call you?" he asked.

"Sure," I said. "My phone number's easy. Do you want me to write it down or can you remember it?"

"I'll remember it," he said.

"It's 888-1468."

"Got it," he said. "I'll call you."

There was no kiss, and no kiss on the cheek, but that was all right with me.

He did call, and after going to Teri and David's wedding together, having a wonderful time, eating, drinking and dancing almost every dance together, we started seeing each other almost every day.

Eric was the opposite of Frankie, and maybe that was part of his appeal. He may not have been as much fun or as exciting, but at this point in my life, I wanted someone steady and reliable. Someone I could count on to be there for me. His quiet aura made me feel peaceful.

Eric, unlike Frankie, was a student. He was like me. We were both passionate about doing well in school. Good grades were everything to us, but especially to him because he would have to pass the bar at some point. We were both content to spend hours at the library together studying. Or we'd sit out on a bench on the UCLA campus, holding hands, discussing his classes, my classes, current events like Halley's Comet and the hole in the ozone, and philosophical subjects like: 1) Should we abolish capital punishment? 2) Is there an afterlife? 3) Is there a God, and if so, what form does he, she or it take?

Eric's dad had been raised Catholic; his mother was a Unitarian, so Eric had been brought up with no religion, except a Christmas tree at Christmas-time. It didn't bother me that Eric wasn't Jewish; and it didn't bother him that I was.

If we weren't at the library, we'd usually go over my house and study together, and then he'd take a break and lie on the sofa listening to me play the piano. After my parents went to sleep, we'd go into the den, turn off the lights, and lie on the burgundy carpet listening to our favorite music, like Cesar Frank's Symphony in D minor, or a Rachmaninoff piano concerto, and kiss and caress each other.

But we never went all the way. He would have, but like Frankie, I kept putting him off. He knew about Frankie, but not that Frankie and I had been engaged because I didn't consider an engagement of a day a real engagement; and I didn't tell him that Frankie and I had gone all the way because I was afraid he wouldn't want me if he knew I wasn't a virgin. I didn't want him to think I was a slut, or spoiled goods, so I just told him I wanted to save myself for my husband. And he accepted it. I hated deceiving him, but I didn't really want to go all the way, afraid that, again, I would feel nothing.

And then I had my other big secret. I wanted to tell him about both, but I was frightened he would leave me, like Frankie had, if he found out.

So I was carrying around all these burdens, and as the weeks and months went by, they became harder and harder to carry. I debated back and forth, should I tell him one, or the other, or both, or neither. It began to invade my thinking and now and then a voice would say, *tell him, tell him, tell him.* But I didn't have the courage.

And then, he proposed. We'd come out of the UCLA library when it closed, and the campus was pretty deserted. It was a hot evening in April, but a cool breeze was coming in from the ocean.

We decided to sit awhile on a metal bench near the library, and he picked up my hand and said, "Zo, (I loved when he called me 'Zo') you know I'll be taking the bar in August, and then going to work for my uncle's law firm in September, and you'll be starting teaching, so I think we should get married the week after the bar exam."

Said so sweetly, so matter-of-factly, that I almost missed the words. "Married," I said, almost a question.

"Yes," and he turned to face me, "Will you marry me?"

Oh joy, oh devastation. My whole body was pulsating with elation and terror. He wanted to marry me! The perfect man and he wanted to marry me! But he didn't know my deep dark secret. Secrets, I corrected myself. I felt the tears gathering behind my eyelids because the reality of it was that I couldn't marry him. Not unless he knew, and then he probably wouldn't want to marry me. "I can't marry you," I said simply.

He seemed surprised. "Why not?"

"Because there are things you don't know about me," I said.

What could there possibly be that I don't know about you, his hazel eyes wondered. "Then tell me," he said.

I didn't know where to begin. "I'm a liar," I said.

A liar," he said, almost laughing.

"It's true," I said.

"And what have you lied about?" he asked.

I began to sweat even though I actually felt cold. There was no escaping it now. The choice had been made for me. I had to tell him everything. "You're not going to like this….but first of all I'm not a virgin. I did have sex with Frankie."

He dropped my hand. "Then why….."

He didn't have to finish the sentence. I knew what he was asking. "I was just afraid that if you found out I wasn't a virgin, you would think less of me, or wouldn't want me altogether." Which was true, but left out the fact that I hadn't enjoyed sex with Frankie and I was afraid I wouldn't enjoy sex with him.

He again picked up my hand. "I'm not a virgin; why do you have to be one?"

I breathed audibly. One hurdle over; one to go. "And there's something else."

He waited.

I tried to think of the right words to use. "I have this malady," I said.

"What kind of malady?"

"It's hard to explain. I go into this dreamlike state, but it's not really a dream, it's a nightmare."

He seemed bewildered. "You mean you have nightmares?" Like it wasn't any big deal.

"No," I said, frustrated that I couldn't describe it properly. "It's like I'll enter a room, but feel I'm not really there."

"And how often does this happen?"

"It's unpredictable. It's happened several times in my life. At first it only lasted a few minutes, but when I graduated from high school, it lasted almost four months, and then when Frankie and I broke up, it came on again, and lasted almost three months."

"I'm still not sure what happens to you, but it sounds awful," he said.

"It hasn't happened now for over two years, and my psychiatrist said it may never happen again, that it may just be an adolescent disease that I can grow out of. But still I don't know. I've also been on a lot of drugs, but my doctor is cutting down on them because I'm doing so well."

"That's good," he said. And then paused a moment. "Anything else?"

"No," I said, feeling totally relieved, totally free of stress. How wonderful to get it all out, to not have to pretend and lie. Whatever would happen now, I was ready for it.

"Well if this disease or whatever you have hasn't happened for over two years, maybe it'll never happen again…and it sounds like it comes and goes, so even if it comes, eventually it'll go. I love you, Zo. You're the perfect woman for me. And I'm not a coward and I'm not afraid. I love you and want to marry you. No one knows what life has in store…maybe I'll become ill. Would you stand by me?"

"Of course," I said, my insides filling with happiness and gratitude and the tears spilling out of my eyes.

"Then, will you marry me?"

How much I loved him. And how lucky I felt. How could such a wonderful perfect man want to marry me? "Yes," I said. "Yes." And we kissed.

We told my parents that night that we were engaged, and they were both ecstatic. Eric was not the sports-person my dad would have liked, but he was solid, going to be a lawyer, and his father was a doctor. My mother was happy for the same reasons, but also, like with Frankie, relieved that I had found someone who would love me and take care of me "for as long as we both shall live". I thought the fact that Eric wasn't Jewish might have been an issue, but it wasn't.

The next night we went over to Eric's house to tell his parents that we were engaged. I had, by now, spent a lot of time with both of them, and I liked them. His dad, Edward Simoneau was not as tall or as slim as Eric, and his hair wasn't curly blonde-brown, but straight, brown and starting to grey. He did have Eric's hazel eyes, however, and Eric's prominent nose and full lips. Edward specialized in internal medicine and was as quiet, thoughtful and serious as a doctor should be, but always friendly to me.

Eric's mom, Heather, was more like a hippie. She wore long colored skirts, and unkempt hair. Not that it wasn't clean. I knew she washed it daily, but there it was, with no order, no style, just a bunch of brownish-blonde frizz. But I liked her. In a way, she was like me, off in a dream world somewhere. She always seemed distracted and disorganized as her home was. She was not one for neatness.

The Simoneau family lived in a large home on a street that seemed more suburban than urban. Huge branches hung over the road, reminding me of a painting by a French impressionist of a French country road. There were no sidewalks, but most of the homes had tailored lawns. Not, however, the Simoneaus. Theirs was the kind of lawn most neighbors abhor. It was mowed each week by their gardener, but the shrubs were overgrown, and all kinds of foreign plants flourished like weeds in no particular order.

The inside of the house was much like the outside. Two huge brown leather sofas took up most of the living room, and an enormous oak dining table filled the dining room. The furniture seemed of good quality, but every surface was covered with papers, books, magazines, pencils, pens, notepads. Yes, Heather was an English teacher and apparently a profuse reader, to say nothing of the papers she had to correct. But Edward was easy-going and did not seem to mind the clutter in the house, which again, was clean…they had a cleaning lady once a week, but would have sent both my mom and dad into a hissy fit.

When we told Eric's parents that we were getting married, both Edward and Heather hugged me, and Heather said, "I want to make you an engagement party. You know, a big blow-out here at the house. Invite all our family and friends, and of course all your family and friends." The last part spoken to me.

"That'll be great," I said, a tinge of fear rising in my chest. I wanted to get married, but I didn't think I could handle a big blow-out.

Heather continued, "I'll call your mom and dad and see what's a good date for them."

Our two parents had not yet met, and I wondered if Heather would clean up all her stuff for the party, or just let people put their drinks and food on top of her books and papers.

"Sounds good," I said, trying to assure myself that nothing bad was going to happen, that I would not have an attack, and then corrected myself, an episode.

But as the date got closer and the invitations went out, my Destroyer started talking more and more about the dangers of this party. I tried to quiet it, I tried not to listen, but it was relentless. "You know, Zoe, this is the exact kind of thing that brings it on. You know how it came on before the piano recital, and before the graduation party. You know how it came on when you and Frankie told his parents you were engaged. The thing you don't need in your life is a big party where you'll be the center of attention, where you'll have to perform, where you'll have to be charming, and where everyone will be looking at you."

"No!" I yelled at my voice. "I don't have to be anything but myself. Eric and his parents love me just the way I am."

"But will they love you when you have to run from the room, when they realize what a sick girl you are, that you're never going to be well, that your illness is going to keep coming back. Do you think Eric wants to spend the rest of his life with someone who is mentally ill?"

"But the doctor says I may never have another episode. That it was just a childhood disease. That I'm going to be well from now on."

"And if you believe that, then I have a bridge I want to sell you. And what about the wedding? How will you get through that? And managing a house? And having kids? Face it Zoe, you will never be able to do any of those things."

I fought it, I did. I did everything I could think of to do. I kept myself busy; I wouldn't allow myself to think. I bought a new dress, black low-cut, and black pumps, and my mom bought me a silver and gold braided necklace and earrings. I set a date at the hairdresser for 10 a.m. Saturday morning, but when I awoke the Friday morning before the party, I knew all was lost. I looked around my room; everything was where it should be, but I wasn't there. I was hovering somewhere outside the picture. I ran to the kitchen to tell my mom.

"I can't go," I said.

She took one look at me and knew. Like the day I walked in from the Malibu house. She knew. She got up from the kitchen table where she was drinking her coffee and reading the newspaper, and came and put her arms around me. "Oh, Zoe, I'm so sorry."

I began to cry, "Oh, Mom, what am I going to do? I can't go to the party. I can't get married. I can't live like this."

I was just sobbing away, unable and not wanting to stop. How could this have happened to me? Why? What did I do wrong? What did I do to deserve this….this torture.

Mom held me for a long time, caressing my hair, speaking to me in soft tones…"It's going to be all right. It's going to pass like it always does. You'll see. I think we should see another doctor. Someone's bound to be able to help us. Maybe we've just been going to the wrong doctors. There must be some doctor out there who can help us. We just have to find him."

Finally I calmed down and Mom said, "What if you go to the party?"

I looked at her like she was the crazy one. "I can't go, Mom. Not when I feel like this."

"But no one would know. You could just play-act. Pretend."

"No, Mom, I can't." And I turned away and headed back to my bedroom. I knew how distraught my mom was, how much she had been looking forward to this party. Oh God, I thought, how this could be happening to me again?

Mom followed me. "I'm sorry, Zoe. I should never have suggested such a thing. Of course you can't go." She caught up to me as I climbed into bed. "Maybe you'll feel better tomorrow, but if you don't, I'll call Heather and tell her you're ill."

Heather...how I hated doing this to Heather...and Edward, and my mom and dad, and Eric. Poor Eric. Of course I should never have said I would marry him. Perhaps I would never come out of this. Perhaps I would feel this way the rest of my life. How could I ever have children? What if an attack came while I was a mother? How could I care for a child? How could I even be a wife, run a household, get a job? It was all too overwhelming to think about. I would have to break it off with him at once. Immediately. Before tomorrow. I couldn't go through another rejection like with Frankie.

Heather took the news very well, and went forward with the party anyway. "I've already got the food and drink, so we'll just all get together and celebrate the engagement, even though Zoe can't be here. I'm sure she'll like that."

Eric stayed for awhile at the party and then came over to see me. We talked and cried and he kissed and caressed the body that did not belong to me, and I told him I couldn't marry him, and he said, "We'll see."

He was busy studying for finals, taking a review class for the bar, studying for the bar, but still he came to see me almost every day, even if it was just for a few minutes, hoping each time he saw me that I would be feeling better. But my malady went on for weeks.

My mom contacted my teachers and they all assured her that as soon as I was well, they were sure I'd be able to catch up, and Mom found me a new therapist, a psychologist again. I was going to continue on with Dr. Berg, my psychiatrist, who immediately put me on a new drug regimen, but Mom thought it would be good for me to have someone to talk to.

Boy, did she choose the wrong psychologist. Miss Summers believed in a different approach. She said nothing, just listened. Sometimes we would sit there for the whole hour and not say one word. What could I say to her? I already knew I wasn't molested, I'd had no traumatic events in my life to trigger this thing, and my psychiatrist had already said it was not mental or psychological, but physical. So why the hell was I wasting my dad's hard-earned money talking to someone who never talked. Mom didn't care. She had heard good things about this therapist and wanted to give it a try.

Finally, after two months of sitting in Miss Summers' office and saying nothing, my malady left.

"Obviously," Eric said, "it has to be physical. Since you didn't say anything to Miss Summers, it has to be that the new drugs Dr. Berg put you on are working."

"Or it could be that Miss Summers' therapy worked," I said sarcastically.

"Right," Eric said with a snicker. And then he said, "I feel comfortable now that we should go ahead with the wedding. We just have to make sure you stay on the right medication."

I was so grateful, I wept. "Oh Eric," I said, "you're a saint. No one else in this whole world would put up with me."

"I love you, Zo" he said.

"But enough to go through all the bad stuff that might happen?"

"Nothing's going to happen. We're just going to make sure you stay on your drugs."

"So you don't mind marrying a druggie?"

"You're the perfect girl for me."

He had told me that a hundred times, along with how pretty I was, what a great body I had, how smart I was, what a great pianist I was, how much he liked my sense of humor, and how much he loved going to my house. Maybe that was the biggest reason he wanted to marry me, he wanted a home as neat and orderly as my mother's; maybe he was just rebelling against his mother. But with all the wonderful things he told me, there was still the problem of sex. After we became engaged, there was no longer any reason not to go all the way.

We'd kiss and hug and then he'd enter me, and I tried to feel something, I tried my hardest, but it just wasn't there. He knew something was wrong—I wasn't that good an actress—but we attributed it to the fact that I was on all these drugs, and we both believed that in time, all would we well. We loved each other and that was all that mattered.

Still, I worried about my lack of sexual feelings and decided to ask Dr. Berg about it at my next appointment.

"What is wrong with me?" I asked. "When it comes to sex, I feel nothing. That can't be normal."

"It's a tough one," he said. "There could be any number of reasons why you're not enjoying it. Some physical, some psychological."

"Could it be the drugs I'm taking?"

"Yes, some of the drugs definitely have an affect on the libido."

"Then what do I do about it?" I asked.

"I guess at this stage, it's a choice: being healthy or being sexual."

"Maybe my fiancé would prefer the latter."

"We can try cutting down on the Lithium."

"Do we dare?" I asked.

He cleared his throat, "It's up to you."

"I'll think about it," I said, and then pondered, "Was it worth it? To stop taking my drugs, on the chance it might make me sexual? I had to say 'no'. Nothing was worth it. Even losing Eric.

When I told Heather and Edward about the real reason I hadn't been able to come to the engagement party, they both seemed very concerned. Especially Edward, the physician. "Let me look into this," he said. "Maybe I can find out something that will help you."

"I would really appreciate that," I said.

The next night, Eric told me that his parents had had a sit-down with him. They loved me, they thought I was terrific, but he should seriously consider did he want to spend the rest of his life taking care of a sick person? Whatever I had may not ever be cured. And what about children? Would I be able to care for them? And what if I went into a seizure and never came out.

(I had not used the word 'seizure' but I guess they thought it was more forceful than 'episode'.)

I couldn't hate them for what they said. I understood. I would feel the same way about my child and I'm sure if Claire or Andrew were marrying someone with my problem, my mom and dad would tell them the same thing.

But Eric reassured them that all would be well, and that we were going to proceed with the wedding.

Chapter Eight – Getting Married

We planned the wedding for August 20, 1988. Eric would be finished with the bar exam by then, and I would be finished with the two summer school classes I was taking to make up for the two classes I missed by starting my first semester at Pierce. We decided to have a small wedding and be married by the rabbi at my synagogue. Heather was upset about that. Not about the rabbi or the synagogue, but that it was going to be a small wedding. She confronted Eric. "You're our only child. This is our only chance to have a wedding and I want everyone in the world to come."

"Sorry, mom," Eric told her, obviously thinking he didn't want a repeat of the engagement party episode. "We're going to do whatever Zoe is comfortable with."

What a sweet darling man. No wonder I loved him so much.

Heather agreed to the private ceremony (shades of my bat mitzvah)…just our immediate families—there was no way I could walk down an aisle with hundreds of people staring at me—and I agreed to a party at the Marriott for a hundred people. Heather and my mom could each invite 48 people, and I was inviting Teri and David Smolensky, and Missy and her husband, Albert Kahane.

We served appetizers, dinner, and a wedding cake for dessert, and hired Andrew to get a band together for dancing. Andrew agreed to keep the music soft and sweet, except for the few rock and roll numbers that were a necessity at any wedding.

Eric and I loved to dance. For me it was the best of all possible worlds, holding each other close, moving to the music, and the music itself, especially since it was my brother leading the band.

My grandparents were the only relatives from Detroit who came in for the wedding, which in a way was a blessing for my mom. It meant she could invite more of her friends to my wedding. And while my mom's mom, Grandma Nina, looked great, and was out on the dance floor, dancing up a storm, my dad's mom, Grandma Ruth, had gotten so fat and unsteady on her feet that she could barely walk.

Through all of the planning for the wedding, the Destroyer had been speaking to me a lot. Telling me that I could never get through all of this. Even if there weren't hundreds of people staring at me, I would still have to walk down the aisle. And the party, that was going to be a real stressor. How could I get through that? It was coming, the Destroyer said. Better end it now and forever. Give up your life; it's never going to be normal.

But I kept pushing it down. I tried not to think about it, and I kept myself so busy and occupied every day that at night, I fell into bed exhausted. That and the pink and purple pills did their job. The wedding went off without a hitch.

I was overjoyed. Finally, finally, we had found the right combination of pills. It was physical. It wasn't my fault. God bless Dr. Berg and the pink and purple pills.

The first thing Eric and I bought for our new apartment was, of course, a piano, a used walnut Fischer upright. Eric thought we should get a new snazzy-looking Japanese spinet, but the sound was too light. I needed a piano that could not only speak, but shatter the speed of sound.

Then we bought a bed, a sofa, a kitchen table, and all the basics we would need to start our life together.

In September, Eric started work at his uncle's law office, and I started teaching third grade at Porter Valley Elementary School.

I couldn't have imagined how much I would love teaching. I loved everything about it, decorating my bulletin boards, writing on the blackboard, the smell of chalk on my fingers, the camerderie between myself and the other teachers, the little desks and little chairs, the books and papers, and pencils and paints, and the children....the sweet adorable children, each with a definite personality, definite likes and dislikes, eagerness to learn, open to new ideas, and so smart.

I could talk to them as if they were adults. They understood abstract concepts; they understood the subtle meanings of what I told them and what they read, and they were sensitive to the feelings of the other children and adults. They were also surprisingly affectionate, most of them hugging me each afternoon when they left the classroom.

I could not believe how lucky I was that I got to interact with these fascinating human beings every day, that I got to teach them things they didn't know, that I got to know them almost as well as their parents, that I got to help mold their lives.

Every day, I came home with scads of papers to correct and lots of planning to do for the next day. I was totally consumed and that was good because it didn't give me time to think about anything else. Fortunately, Eric was as busy as I was.

As for Ms. Hockensmith, I was still seeing her, but only once a month. My life was now too busy to spend hours at the piano, and since I was not going to become a concert pianist, my piano playing became more like maintenance than climbing to greater heights. I knew Ms. Hockensmith was disappointed in me; and I was disappointed in myself. But what choice did I have?

I would have felt even more guilty about "abandoning" Ms. Hockensmith, but six months before my wedding, she had rescued a dog from the dog pound, an Alaskan Malamute named Kiska. He was a large, beautiful dog, with grey and white bristly hair, and he stayed in the kitchen or out in the backyard when Ms. Hockensmith's students were there. But she would let him come into the living room when I was there. I told her I liked Kiska and his presence didn't bother me one bit. While I was playing, he'd lie by the tan sofa, often with his tail wrapped around his nose or face, but the minute I stood up, he'd come over and ask me to pet him. Which I did happily.

When summer came, Eric and I decided to buy a house. The real estate market was on a down-turn in L.A., and the price of houses had fallen. Now was the time to buy.

We found a lovely two-story house in Sherman Oaks, not too far from the Sherman Oaks Park. It had three bedrooms and a den, a large living room, a small dining room, and a large family room attached to a roomy kitchen. We loved the neighborhood and the house, and while it was more expensive than we intended, as long as we both were working, we could afford it.

Chapter Nine — Zoe and Eric

In January, 19 months after Eric and I got married, I began to think about having a baby. Amazingly, I had gone the entire 19 months with only a few incidents of feeling on the brink of disaster, but never actually losing myself.

Eric was spending more and more time at his job, and I was spending all my spare time playing the piano, preparing for my class and correcting papers. Papers were piled to the ceiling in our den...but that was the only place. I kept a neat house like my mother, nothing like Heather.

By this time, we had purchased most of our furniture. I liked the country look, so in the living room we had a flowered print sectional sofa in pinks, purples, and greens with lots of throw pillows, and baskets filled with dried flowers, which I planned to supplement with vases of real flowers when our roses came in. For the kitchen, we bought a butcher block table and ladder-back chairs with flowered print cushions; and in the family room was a coup de grace, a purple sofa and matching easy chair—I loved purple and Eric liked it too.

Since we were running out of money, it was either a dining room set or a baby-grand piano. I chose the piano, a brown walnut Baldwin. Way too expensive, but once I tried playing on it, no other piano measured up. Eric was a good sport about it, and I thanked God again for sending him to me. We did not, however, sell the upright. We put it in the dining room, just in case one day, our children would want to play a piano concerto, and then I could play the orchestra part with them, as Ms. Hockensmith had done with me.

So everything was going well; perfect, in fact, so that again I was hoping that maybe I was over my affliction. Maybe it would never come back. Maybe I could realize my dream to have a baby.

I asked Dr. Berg about it.

"As you know, everything passes through the placenta. You'll have to cut out all the medication until the baby is born."

Here we go again. To have the baby or not to have the baby. Things had been going so well, did I dare disturb the universe? Maybe I was intended to have a happy life, after all. Maybe I was over whatever it was I had. I did want a baby so badly. I did want four babies.

I considered it for a few months to see if my voice was going to talk me out of it. But my voice was silent. And so, I decided, it was a message from heaven. If the thought of having the baby did not summon the voice of the Destroyer, then perhaps I could have the baby without any problems. I had to try, I thought, and stopped taking my birth control pills, my anti-anxiety pills, my anti-depressants, my anti-psychotics, and my stimulants.

Within two months, I was pregnant.

How joyful those first few months were. How much I loved having a baby growing inside of me. I already loved the baby more than anything or anyone in my life. I swore I would be a good mom, that I would stay healthy and take care of my baby. I was glowing. Everyone said so. Eric was thrilled. My mom and dad were thrilled. Heather and Edward were thrilled. It was the happy ending to the fairy tale: me without drugs, me feeling normal, and me pregnant.

Until my eighth month when the Destroyer came back. The Destroyer started talking softly to me just before I fell asleep at night. "You know a lot of things could go wrong with this baby. It could be born like you, with all your problems. You think it isn't hereditary, but if it is physical then you got it from someone, and are now passing it on to someone…your baby. A lot of bad things can happen during delivery. You know the baby can be strangulated."

"No," I said trying to shut out my thoughts. "Nothing bad is going to happen. The doctor says everything is perfect and I'm going to have a nice healthy baby. No one in my family has ever had what I have. No one's ever even heard of anyone having what I have."

But with each passing day, the voice became louder.

School ended and I had nothing to occupy my time or my brain. I was just kind-of waiting for the baby to be born. I was a ripe field for bad thoughts and they kept coming.

"You know you're pretty selfish," the Destroyer was saying. "How dare you bring a baby into this world in your condition. You must be insane to be doing such a thing."

"No, no," I cried, "don't do this to me. Don't sabotage my baby. Go away. Leave me alone."

"You know you're not going to get through this. You know you're going to have an episode. It's coming any day now. They may have to take the baby away from you. Maybe your mom will raise it, or Heather. She won't notice a bigger mess in the house. Eric will leave you for sure now. Maybe they'll put you in an institution."

I tried to fight it, tried my hardest, tried not to let it get to me, but in the end, it won. The Destroyer destroyed me.

I went into a trance, but tried to hide it from everyone. I had tried play-acting before, but now I was doing it in spades. Nobody could tell that I wasn't myself, that I wasn't even there. I had the 'puppet me' talking and laughing as if it really was me. Nobody had a suspicion, except Mom. She kept asking me, "Are you all right?"

"Yes, I'm fine."

And then the next day, "Are you all right?"

"Yes, I'm fine."

And then the next time she saw me, "Are you up to buying some stuff for the baby?"

"No, Mom. I'm feeling kind of tired."

"Are you sure you're all right?"

"Yes, Mom. I'm fine."

My girlfriends wanted to make me a baby shower, but I told them that in the Jewish religion it's bad luck to buy things for a baby before it's born. Anyway, I had plenty of stuff already. My mom had bought us a crib and mattress. Heather had bought us the dresser to match the crib and a changing table. My mom had bought a layette for the baby, and Heather had bought some cute little yellow outfits. We didn't know what sex the baby was going to be. Eric and I both did not want to know until its birth, so Heather was treading the fence.

Finally, the day arrived, and in my trance, feeling the pain, but knowing it wasn't real, Eric drove me to the hospital and stayed with me until he was kicked out of the delivery room, and there, our baby, our daughter, Molly Simoneau, named after my mother's grandmother, was born.

I was in a daze the entire time in the hospital and driving home, but I was so thankful that my baby was healthy, that nothing had gone wrong, that the Destroyer was wrong about everything, that it didn't even matter that I was out-of-it.

I went through the motions of being a good mom, of feeding my baby day and night (I could not breast-feed because Dr. Berg put me back on my medication the day after delivery), and changing my baby's diapers, and bathing her, and holding her and kissing her and caressing her. I felt that everything in my life, everything I had gone through was worth it to have this tiny, innocent, sweet, adorable person in my life. I didn't know I could love anything as much as I loved this little girl. I hoped and prayed every day that when I awoke in the morning, I would feel better.

And then when Molly was three weeks old, it happened. I was still a little fuzzy, but I knew I was on the path back, that I could be a good mom, and I would be.

Eric had gone through the whole time, knowing that I wasn't feeling well, but pretty much ignoring it. My mom knew but didn't show it, just pretended that I was fine, that all was fine. And Heather, who absolutely went wild over the baby didn't suspect a thing. She thought I was perfectly normal in every way. Probably if she didn't think I was normal, she would have had another talk with Eric like the one she had with him before we were married. But she was always nice to me, and I still liked her even knowing she had tried to talk Eric out of marrying me.

By the time Molly was six weeks old, I felt perfectly normal. The pills had done their job, and I really believed that as long as I stayed on the pills, everything was going to be fine.

In September, I returned to teaching. Much as I wanted to stay home with Molly, I decided it would be better for me to go back to teaching for three reasons: 1) being at home left me too much time to think, 2) I loved teaching, and 3) being at home left me too much time to think.

We hired a nanny, Hortensia, for four days a week, and my mom agreed to take care of Molly every Friday, and be a backup if Hortensia couldn't come any day for any reason.

Hortensia had been recommended by my friend, Teri Small. Yes, the Smolenskys had changed their name to "Small." Teri had used Hortensia for the first two years of her baby daughter's life and told me she was the best! Hortensia, from El Salvador, a tiny little thing with a ton of energy, spoke perfect English, drove a car, and was a loving, caring person, so I completely trusted her with my baby.

It seemed, at last, that I had the perfect life: a husband, a home, a beautiful baby, and a great job. I was completely happy and at peace.

Therefore, at the end of the year, when Eric suggested we have another baby, I agreed.

Again, I got pregnant almost immediately, and that is when all hell broke loose.

With this pregnancy, the Destroyer did not wait long to attack. It was only my third month; I had only been off my medication for five months, when it started attacking me non-stop. There was not a moment of my waking hours when it was not there, whether standing in front of my class explaining a math or reading concept, or diapering Molly, bathing her, or taking her for a walk. It was always there. "You idiot," it said, "why did you have to mess with success. You were doing so well with the pills, and now they're gone...for another six months. You were lucky to get away last time, but you're not going to get away this time. This time, they're going to have to take two babies away from you instead of one because you are going to enter never-never land

and never get out. You dope. You idiot. You know you have this problem…you know it's coming back and yet you went ahead with this outrageous plan, based on what? Hope? Well, this time, it's not going to work. So say goodbye to your husband, your home, and your two babies. Your life is over."

I was completely disconnected, as far from reality as I'd ever been. I tried going through the motions, and I was doing pretty well at play acting, at pretending that everything was okay, but at some point, it became impossible. How could I interact with all my darling children at school or with my sweet adorable baby at home when I was floating above their heads, when I was in an alternate universe, when I was watching myself from somewhere else, not able to realize the moment? And a baby was growing inside me.

I took a leave of absence from my school; I kept Hortensia coming each day; and I hid in my bedroom most of the day, unable to interact with anyone. But I had company; the Destroyer was with me every moment, telling me this was the end of my life. There was nothing more to live for because I was never coming out of this state. I lay on my bed, putting my hands on my belly, feeling the life within me and crying. Crying for this baby, for the hand fate had dealt me, for Molly growing up without a mom, for Eric, poor poor Eric; he was warned but did not heed the warning, and for my mom and dad. They didn't deserve this. They had done nothing wrong. But neither had I.

Mom came every Friday and as often as she could on the other days, even though Hortensia was there. She'd hold my hand, put her fingers through my hair, ask me a million times if there was anything she could do, but of course, she knew there was nothing she could do.

"As soon as you have the baby, and are back on your medication, you'll see, everything's going to be back to normal. It's only being off the drugs that is doing this to you."

I wanted to believe her. I tried to believe her, but the voice inside me, said, "What do you expect her to say? She's your mom. But she doesn't know anything. I know everything. And I'm telling you, you're finished."

Chapter Ten — Another Visit to Dr. Berg's Office — May, 1993

Gail

I don't know why I came to see you today, except that I needed to talk to someone.

My heart is broken. Of course, my heart is broken. How could this have happened to us? To Zoe? What did she do to deserve such misery? She's always been such a good girl, a nice girl, a smart girl. I can't find any joy in my life anymore. I go through the motions. I still play tennis and bridge, and do my tours at the museum, and go out with friends and pretend to be having fun, but there is this black cloud hanging over me.

None of our clients or friends know about Zoe. We've kept it a secret all these years. It's not that I'm ashamed of my daughter. I just don't want anyone to think she's not normal for her sake. I don't want people looking at her as if there's something wrong with her mentally. Although you seem to think it's biological, still, other people wouldn't see it that way. And they'd feel sorry for me. Poor Gail, with a psychotic daughter. They wouldn't treat me the same, and it would be there behind every word they uttered, their pity. I couldn't take that. Better keep it a secret.

I don't know what's going to happen now. And that worries me. What's going to happen after the baby is born? What if she doesn't return to reality? I guess I could give up being a docent at the museum; I could give up tennis and bridge, and just be a mom to my grandchildren. I'm not that old; I still have energy. I could do it. I would keep Hortensia, though. I couldn't do it alone, not raise two little children by myself.

And then I think about Andrew and Claire. Well, at least with Claire, we didn't do anything wrong. She's turned out just fine. Thank God. Not that I don't love Andrew with all my heart, but he is a disappointment in a way, especially for Dan. He's 28, and still no job. No real job. Just doing his music now and then and selling handbags.

Oh yes, selling handbags at all the office buildings along Ventura Boulevard. They're knock-offs of expensive handbags and he just goes from office to office trying to sell them to the secretaries. They're actually pretty authentic looking. I couldn't tell if they were real or not. But then again, I would never spend that kind of money on a real designer bag. But I bought a Louis Vuitton from Andrew. It's the least I can do.

He doesn't like taking money from me, but every now and then I insist on giving him a hundred or two. I don't know how he'd survive otherwise. He lives in this horrible house with three other guys, so I guess his rent is pretty low, but then again, how much money can he make from an occasional gig and selling knock-off handbags?

I tell you, sometimes when I think about my life, I can get depressed, so I try not to think about it. I just try to get through each day as best I can. I mean, what mother could have a daughter in Zoe's condition and not get depressed? I just have to keep trying to be there for her, to help her in any way I can, and to pray that after the baby's born, the drugs will kick in and things will be back to normal.

I've talked to the rest of my family and they've all made appointments to see you. They all say they don't need to talk to you, but I think they all must be affected in some way. I think it'll be good for them to talk to you.

Dan

My wife insisted that I come to see you. I don't know what good this is going to do. Yes, of course I'm upset. What father wouldn't be? To see your child suffering as mine is? To see her hiding in her room, totally depressed. I don't even understand really what her disease is. I know you think it's biological. What does that mean? If it's biological then why can't you fix it? With all those drugs out there, why can't you find one that will fix it?

You don't say much, do you?

Anyway, that's about all I have to say.

Andrew

I guess we have a pretty mixed up family...with my sister and her illness and my other sister and her illness, and me, 28 and still no real job. No wonder my mom wants us all to see a shrink.

But basically, I'm doing all right. My band has a new singer and she's really rad, and we've been playing a lot of gigs, little hole in the wall places, but still it's exposure. That's what we need, exposure. Just one guy with an "in" to like us and we'll be on our way. It could happen.

I sat in with Eddie Vedder and Pearl Jam at a gig before anyone knew who they were, and now look where they are. Of course they didn't play my kind of music, so even if they asked me I wouldn't have joined the band, so I don't have any regrets about it. You just have to be lucky, you just have to be heard by the right people, and that's what we're trying to do. Just get out there.

And then I have this other gig, just me, playing guitar on Friday and Saturday nights at a really fancy restaurant on Ventura Boulevard. I'm not making much money, but I don't need much. Fortunately, the guy who owns the house I'm living in doesn't much care if I miss a month or two. We have a great set-up there.

Me and my two friends. He's got a pool table and a pool, so what else do I need, except his house is kind of a dump.

And then I sell purses, door to door, or office to office to be more exact, and make a few bucks there. And every now and then, I get a donation from my mom. So I'm living pretty well. Only thing is, I met this girl. She's a real fox, and she likes me a lot. She's really creative. She's a hairdresser. Only thing is if I wanted to marry her, I'd have to get serious about a job. I guess I'm not ready for that yet. I'm still hoping that one right guy will come along because what I really want is to make music night and day.

Claire

So here we are again, talking about Zoe. Not that I don't feel sorry for her. I do, I really do. I love my sister and I would never want anything bad to happen to her. But I've got my own problems, and I'm suffering, too. But of course I still haven't told anyone about my problem, not anyone, not even my best friends and especially not my mom or dad. I'd never tell my dad, not in a million years.

So here I am suffering under this terrible burden and all my mom thinks about is Zoe. But of course, that's my fault. If I told her, I know she'd be sympathetic. So why don't I tell her? I can't. I just can't. I'm so ashamed of myself, and my mom and dad think I'm so perfect. And then there's my brother. They think he's a total loser, so if I told them the truth about me, that would make three out of three. I don't know if they could handle that.

The crazy thing is that with all my eating and throwing up, I'm still gaining weight and my mom's on my back all the time. She keeps telling me about this diet and that diet and all it takes is a little will power. "Maybe if you just cut down on your portions," or "Maybe you should join weight watchers." She hasn't a clue.

In a way, I'm glad I'm talking to you. Maybe I should see a shrink. But how could I get the money? You know I'm in my last year of law school, even with all this eating and throwing up, and not even liking school. Isn't that a crack-up? I didn't really want to go to law school, but what was I going to do? I finished college and there wasn't anything I wanted to do. I didn't want a menial job and I knew my dad really, really wanted me to do something great, so I decided to go to law school. The only thing that worries me is passing the bar. You better bet I'm going to work my butt off so I pass it the first time. I'll die if I have to take it twice.

I guess my time is up, but I think it helped me talking to you. Maybe you should give me the name of a shrink. Maybe I can get enough money to go see him or her. God knows, I need to talk to someone.

Chapter Eleven — Answers

As soon as my baby girl, Sophie, named after Eric's mother's grandmother, was born, I immediately went back on my drugs.

Things were really tough at home for awhile. My mom was there most days, and Hortensia was there most days, Andrew dropped by a lot, and Claire—even though she was studying for the bar—came whenever she could. Then Heather would stop in and might spend hours helping out, and, of course, Eric was home every evening and on the weekends.

I seemed incapable of doing anything. I loved looking at the baby, and I loved having Molly climb on me, or cuddle with me, but I was no help at all. I felt horrible about it. I felt useless, an added burden to all these wonderful people taking care of me.

A month passed, and another, and Dr. Berg tried this drug and that, and various combinations of drugs, but nothing was working, and Mom decided I should see another psychologist. Mom had met someone at a party who told Mom about her daughter who seemed to have a problem similar to mine. The woman had given Mom the name of her daughter's psychologist and Mom made an appointment.

We went to see Dr. Halpern when Sophie was four months old.

Dr. Lauretta Halpern had a lovely office on the second floor of a new building on Ventura Boulevard in Encino. She was an attractive middle-aged woman with a PHD in psychology, and I immediately liked her.

I told her my story, and she said, "Zoe, it appears that none of your doctors have told you that you have all the characteristic symptoms of a little known but psychologically recognized disease, and this disease is called depersonalization disorder. And not only do you have this disease, but lots of other people have this same disease."

I was shocked by her news. Shocked and relieved, and in some perverse way, happy. I had a disease. A real disease with a name: depersonalization disorder. And I wasn't the only person in the world who had this disease. Lot's of other people had it. I wasn't a freak; I wasn't crazy; I just had an illness like any other illness.

And then the anger set in. Anger that of all the doctors I'd been to see, not one, not even Dr. Berg, who'd been treating me for nine years, knew about this disease, and hadn't made the effort to find out about it.

I asked, "Where does this disease come from?"

Dr. Halpern explained, "We don't really know the cause. It seems to be brought about by some life threatening danger, but it could also be a malfunction in the brain. Depersonalization disorder hasn't been studied widely, so its cause and occurrence in the population are still unknown. But whatever the underlying cause, it seems to be brought about by anxiety or stress, which in turn leads to worry about becoming depersonalized, which in turns leads to becoming depersonalized, which in turn leads to depression. It's a vicious cycle."

I listened carefully to every word she said, and then, trembling, I dared to ask the life and death question. "Is there a cure for this disease?"

Dr. Halpern hesitated. "I know of patients who have gotten better, but in the sense of: is there some magic drug, or magic therapy that will make it go away forever? I don't know of any."

All of my relief at knowing I had an actual disease, and I was not alone, evaporated.

"But what I would say," Dr. Halpern continued, "is that we can try a combination of therapy and drugs, and hopefully, you will get better."

"But not completely," I said.

"I can't promise that, no," Dr. Halpern said.

So here I was, back to my worst fears.

Mom must have noticed because she said, "But this is wonderful news, Zoe. It means you're not crazy. And there is hope that you will get well. It's always been a periodic thing, and you always come back sooner or later. Maybe with Dr. Halpern's help, we will find the right drug, or drugs."

I had heard all of this before except the part that I wasn't crazy. Well that was comforting.

Dr. Halpern said, "I will be contacting Dr. Berg today and find out exactly what you've been on and what you're on now, and then together we can discuss if we should make any changes. In addition, I'd like you to start therapy with me as soon as possible." She perused her calendar. "I'm completely booked tomorrow, but how about Thursday at 10 o'clock?"

"That'll be fine," Mom said without consulting me. She was my caretaker and my driver, and if 10 o'clock was okay for her, it was okay for me.

"Ten o'clock, then," Dr. Halpern said walking us to the door and taking my hand. "You might try looking this up on the internet if you have a computer."

"I will," I said, looking forward to Thursday.

As soon as I got home, I went to Google and typed in "depersonalization" and there were 3000 hits. I couldn't believe it. Dr. Halpern was right; there were a lot of other people out there in the world with the same disease I had. I immediately started feeling better.

I hit on the first person, then the second, then the third. I couldn't believe what I was reading...all these people out there who were suffering as I was. Who experienced the exact same feelings I did...who were as frustrated and depressed, and dysfunctional as I was. It was as if the whole world had opened up to me. I wasn't a freak; I hadn't done anything wrong; I just had a disease, perhaps incurable, but nothing I had done wrong.

I sat at the computer reading until I couldn't keep my eyes open. I heard my baby crying. Sophie. How little I knew of her; how little I had given her. I went to her crib, lifted her up, held her close to me. "I'm coming back, Sophie, my love. I'm coming back to you."

At my next appointment with Dr. Berg, in spite of my depersonalization, in spite of my depression, amid my tears, and blowing my nose every two seconds, I let him have it. "How could you not know about depersonalization disorder?"

"I never heard the term," he said.

"Well there's 3000 hits on the internet," I said, as sarcastically as possible. "Maybe you should look it up."

"I have heard of dissociative behavior, but no one knows what causes that or how to cure it. All we can do is treat the symptoms."

"But still," I said, "you're a psychoanalyst. You should know about these things."

"I'll look it up as soon as you leave," he said.

"And talk to Dr. Halpern. She's going to call you."

"I've already talked to Dr. Halpern," he said.

"And?"

"We're thinking of making some changes in your medication. I'll call you as soon as we've made our final determination." And he cleared his throat.

A month after my first visit to Dr. Halpern, the depersonalization left me. Talking to her didn't seem like it was helping, but maybe it was. There was nothing new I could say to her, but I did tell her about my Destroyer. I told her all the things it had said to me. Everything, no matter how painful. She listened, and commented, and told me I had to learn to shut it out. To keep my mind occupied so it could not enter. I told her I had tried to do that, but it didn't work, and she told me to keep trying. And to avoid stress because that was the catalyst that seemed to start the whole cycle. I told her subconsciously or consciously I knew that because I had tried to avoid stress my whole life.

Dr. Berg had called a few days after his talk with Dr. Halpern, and had put me on a new regimen of pills, and whatever did it, I came back.

It was already October, and I didn't think I should return to teaching. I now had two little girls, and I was afraid I wouldn't be able to handle the pressure of trying to take care of my little girls and teaching, so I told Hortensia I would only be using her as needed, and since Eric had moved up a bit in his firm and gotten a nice increase in his salary, I decided to become a full time stay-at-home mom.

Since Eric was working so many hours, and I wasn't, it fell to me to do everything around the house. But I welcomed it; I believed it was one way to keep the Destroyer at bay. Just keep my mind occupied and not let any thoughts of the Destroyer come in.

It was amazing how busy I was. But I guess anyone who's had two kids under three will understand. There was taking care of them and the house, and the shopping and cooking, and getting together with friends and their little kids, and washing clothes, and running errands, and paying bills. And I still tried to get in at least an hour of practicing every day. Practicing for what, I didn't know. But it was a form of relaxation for me. A way to get away from all my responsibilities, to do something just for myself; to be at one with the music.

I was only seeing Ms. Hockensmith occasionally now...there was no need to see her more often than that, but I went to see Dr. Halpern every week. And then after a few months, I didn't feel talking to her was helping, so I stopped going. I did continue seeing Dr. Berg every month because he was the one in charge of my pills, and the few times I felt an episode coming on, Dr. Berg, in consultation with Dr. Halpern, re-arranged my medication, and I got through them without losing myself.

And then the summer came—the summer—my nemesis, and I had two episodes. The first occurred when I took Molly to a birthday party at an indoor gym and there were all these children running around and so many parents and so much noise, that I freaked out. I looked around at all the chaos and suddenly I wasn't there. I got a Coke, drank it, went to the door, opened it, breathed the fresh air, focused on the sky, then Molly, then the sky, then Molly, all the while trying to block out the sights and sounds of the cacophony surrounding me, and within five or ten minutes I was back.

The second episode happened when I went to the park with Teri, Missy, a few of their friends I hadn't met before, and all of our kids. By now, Teri, Missy and I each had two kids, but unfortunately, Missy's second child, a boy named Timmy, had been diagnosed with Autism. I felt so bad for her. It was bad enough having my disease, but to me there was nothing worse than having a child who was handicapped in any way. The remarkable thing was that none of the other children were mean to Timmy, or teased him in any way; it was as if they understood that Timmy had a problem, and they seemed, in fact, over-solicitous to him. Especially Molly.

All of the moms sitting on adjoining benches were chatting away and all of the kids were playing in the sand box when suddenly it happened. Suddenly it felt as if I'd just stepped off a merry-go-round, and everything was still spinning. How could this be happening, I asked myself. I wasn't under any pressure, unless you consider being with the few women I had just met, pressure. There didn't seem to be any logical reason for this happening at this moment, but happening it was, and without any warning from my Destroyer. I pretended everything was all right, waited a few minutes praying it would go away, and when it didn't, I got my girls out of the sand, to the car, into their car-seats, drove home, put them down for their naps, and called my mom to come over.

Happily, by the next day, I was feeling pretty normal.

Eric never knew about either of these episodes. Fortunately, they were quick, but still unsettling. Unsettling enough so that in September, I decided I had better go back to teaching. I had always done well while teaching, and much as I hated leaving my little ones, I decided it was better for them to have a healthy mom who worked, than a basket case who stayed at home. Luckily, Hortensia hadn't taken a permanent job and was delighted to come back to us.

Chapter Twelve —
Andrew in Love —
May, 1995

Andrew was in love and getting married. Her name was Amy Peterson. She was tall and gangly, about two inches taller than Andrew which made her about six feet tall, and she was a born-again Christian, but you'd never know it; she was so much fun, so upbeat and lively, and she had a purple streak in her blonde hair, tattoos on her neck and upper arms, and at least six earrings in each ear.

Claire and I instantly loved her and she adored Andrew. Amid giggles and embarrassment, they showed us the tattoos they had done on their backsides: his of a hair-dryer; hers of a guitar.

Amy wanted Andrew to become a hairdresser so they could spend more time together. She thought it'd be the perfect job for him. He'd get to be creative, women adored him, and he could work part-time and still do his music. Being a hairdresser was just something he could do until he was discovered.

Mom and Dad weren't happy about the upcoming marriage, and it wasn't because Amy wasn't Jewish. They would have preferred him to marry a Jewish girl, if he could find one who'd want to marry an unemployed musician, but they couldn't very well object to Andrew marrying someone who wasn't Jewish, when they had so full-heartedly accepted Eric, even though that was a whole other set of circumstances.

No, the reason they objected to Amy was because she was a hairdresser and came from a poor family. They were hoping Andrew would marry a professional or at least a college graduate from at least a middle class family. On more than one occasion, I heard Dad say, "How are they going to survive?" And I'm sure Mom was thinking, "With a little help from me."

I knew Mom was giving Andrew money every now and then, but I also knew she hadn't told my dad about it. I guess selling purses on Ventura Boulevard and playing a few gigs a month just wasn't cutting it.

On Father's Day, Mom invited all her kids and grandkids over for swimming and barbeque. Andrew brought Amy and Claire brought Ted, a man she'd been dating for a couple of months, who was 19 years older than her. We were all sitting around the redwood table in the backyard, Eric, the girls and I in our wet swimsuits, eating hot dogs, hamburgers, salad, beans, and corn, and drinking wine and Cokes, when Andrew turned to Dad and said, "Dad, I wonder if you could loan me some money."

Knowing what I knew, I was startled to hear Andrew ask Dad for money.

"What for?" Dad asked, biting into a fat kosher hot dog covered with mustard, ketchup, relish and onions.

"I want to go to beauty school," Andrew answered.

Dad couldn't believe his ears. "Beauty school," he spat out.

"I want to become a hairdresser," Andrew said with a proud smile at Amy as if he'd just won a Grammy.

She grabbed his hand under the table and gave it a squeeze.

Dad took a swallow, then pointed his hot dog at Andrew, and spoke in an exasperated tone, "Of all the things you could be in this world, how could you choose to be a hair-dresser?"

Everyone at the table turned quiet except for my little girls who were poking each other with ears of corn and giggling.

"Because I like it and I'm good at it," Andrew said.

Dad did a little shake of his head, "Well, I don't get it and I don't think it's a fit profession for a man." Code-words for

"Another disappointment from my son." And then he took another bite of his hot dog.

All of us, except my girls, held our breath, wondering what was coming next.

But Mom stepped in to save the day. "Well, I think it's wonderful that you want to be a hairdresser, and of course, we'll loan you the money."

Andrew turned to Mom, "Thanks, Mom. I promise I'll pay it back as soon as I start working."

"Don't worry about it," Mom said. And then to everyone. "Now who wants another piece of corn? I got it fresh from the corn stand this morning and it's absolutely fabulous."

Within a few months, Andrew had completed beauty school and was working beside Amy, getting more and more customers every day. Apparently it *was* a good job for a man, contrary to what Dad may have thought. And it was perfect for Andrew, as Amy had predicted. It was creative and he could arrange his hours so that he could spend as much time as he wanted on his music; he could wear anything he wanted to work, the more outrageous the better, and he was good at it. So good, in fact, that by the time of the wedding he had already paid back all the money my parents had loaned him. But that was probably a drop in the bucket to what the wedding must have cost them.

Amy's parents wanted a tiny wedding in a church, and then a tiny reception after with nuts, wedding cake and champagne, but Mom and Dad had other ideas. Andrew was their only son; they had a lot of family, friends and clients they wanted to invite, so they offered to pay for the entire wedding if Amy's parents would agree to have the wedding at a synagogue and make it a fancy wedding with a sit-down dinner, a band, and the whole shebang. It was important to Dad to make a big show for his clients, and while my parents weren't that religious, they did not want their son married in a church and they specifically did not want the name Jesus mentioned during the ceremony.

Amy's parents went along with it…all of it, because I guess they did want that big wedding for their daughter and were willing to sell Jesus to get it.

The wedding was scheduled to take place on January 6, 1996, and Andrew and Amy asked Claire and me to be bridesmaids.

I considered it for awhile. The last two years had gone well for me. Even the last summer passed by with only a few weeks of feeling depersonalized. And January was a good month for me. I usually felt fine. But the more I thought about it, walking down the aisle in front of those hordes of people, I decided I could not take the chance. It wasn't as if I was the only person to consider. There were my girls. I couldn't do anything that might endanger my ability to be a good mom to them. Although it broke my heart, it was obvious that I could not be a bridesmaid.

When I told Andrew and Amy about my decision, they were disappointed, but understood. Claire, meanwhile, was all excited about being a bridesmaid, even though she'd already been a bridesmaid 14 times and a maid of honor five times, including my wedding.

I went with her for her final fitting. Unfortunately, she had gained some weight since she last tried on the gown, and they were going to have to let it out a bit.

"I'm so fat," Claire said to me, while looking at herself in a mirror, turning this way and that.

"You're not fat," I said, "just a few pounds overweight." It seemed this conversation had been taking place since we were teen-agers. Her weight seemed to go up and down, and she was always complaining about it, even when she was in a thin stage.

"You look absolutely beautiful," I said.

"No, I don't," she insisted. Look at these thighs and my butt." And then turning to look at herself in the full length mirror, and patting herself, "If I could only cut off a few inches of my thighs and my butt."

"No one's going to see your thighs or your butt in your flowing burgundy gown." Amy had chosen the color scheme of burgundy and black. The bridesmaids, my mother, and Amy's mother would be wearing burgundy gowns, much to my mother's liking since that was her favorite color, and the men would be wearing black tuxedoes with burgundy cummerbunds and ties.

"I know," she said, in a disgusted tone, "but still I hate them."

Although Claire was a little overweight, she was still beautiful. She didn't know I envied her. She was so clever and confident and had so many friends, and now she was a lawyer in a prestigious law firm, where she was working day and night and making tons of money. At least Mom and Dad had one kid who was a total success.

The only thing missing in Claire's life was the right man. She had had a few long term relationships, but none of the guys were right for her. She seemed to intentionally pick the wrong guys. Guys who wouldn't make a commitment, or were married, or treated her badly. I couldn't understand how she could stay with a guy who didn't call when he was supposed to, or always be late, or cancel a date at the last minute. She never had the kind of support I had from Eric. She told me, from time to time, that she envied me. Well, yes of course, I did have a great husband and two great kids, and I didn't blame her for envying me for those things, but I also had this terrible disease.

"Don't envy me," I'd tell her. "You're beautiful and healthy and you'll find someone soon who deserves you."

"From your lips to God's ear," she'd say.

The wedding was fantastic, held at an imposing synagogue on Ventura Boulevard in Encino. (Wasn't the best of everything on Ventura Boulevard in Encino?) The sanctuary was decorated with red roses lining the aisle and adorning the chupa and the bema. Almost everyone was dressed in a tuxedo or gown. I would never have imagined Andrew getting married in a setting like this, and wearing a tuxedo. He even shaved the stubble on his face and removed his earring for the occasion.

I was in heaven because my two little girls, Molly and Sophie were the flower girls. How adorable they looked in their long burgundy gowns, and how seriously they took their jobs of throwing rose petals on the white runner that covered the aisle. I was overcome with joy as was Eric. He loved our girls as much as I did.

Mom, Dad and Claire seemed as elated as I felt. Claire brought her latest beau to the wedding—a good-looking guy she'd met only a month ago, and as for Mom and Dad, you'd never know they'd ever been disappointed in Andrew, not as Dad in his tuxedo, and Mom in her burgundy gown, proudly escorted Andrew down the aisle.

It was an incredible evening, topped by Andrew sitting in with his band every chance he got.

Back at home, after we put the girls to bed, Eric, who'd had too much to drink, wanted to make love. Our love life still wasn't that great. I was still unable to feel anything, and while I tried faking it, Eric had long ago figured out that it was a fake. Even so, I thought things were okay between us. We seemed to be having sex often enough, Eric always had an orgasm, and he never complained. But this night, for some unexplained reason, he got annoyed with me.

"You know, it's no fun making love to an ice cube."

"I'm sorry, Eric, I'm trying my best."

"After all the shrinks you've seen, you're still not enjoying it, are you?"

"I'm sorry, Eric. I don't know what's wrong with me, unless it's all the drugs I'm taking. Dr. Berg said they do affect my libido. But I love you, I love being close to you, I love your kisses, but it's as if I'm dead down there."

"Are you sure you weren't molested by someone?"

"Of course, I'm sure."

"Am I doing something wrong?"

What was I to say to that? I'd only experienced sex with two men, and felt nothing with either one of them. How would I know if he was doing something wrong? "Of course not," I said.

"Well, I've got a hard-on that won't quit, so just lie back and enjoy it the best you can."

I let him ride me as hard as he could, and when he was finished, cuddled his sweating body in my arms as I reminisced about my girls walking down the aisle, and everything else that happened at Andrew's wedding.

Chapter Thirteen —
Zoe —
June 21, 2000

It was the first Monday of summer vacation.

I got my daughters, Molly now nine, and Sophie now seven, ready for camp. I made each of them a peanut butter and jelly sandwich, walked them outside to the sidewalk, waited for the bus to arrive, kissed them goodbye, waved to them through the bus window, went upstairs to my bedroom, and still in my robe and slippers entered my walk-in closet to hide until 5 o'clock when my girls would be coming back from camp. I lay on the soft beige carpeting in the closet, surrounded by my pants and Eric's, my blouses, his shirts, our shoes lined up neatly on shoe racks, and then spent the rest of the day in hiding.

My malady had come back on Friday, the last day of school, and the Destroyer hadn't stopped talking since then. It kept telling me that this time I was never going to come out of it; that it would go on forever, that I would be removed from reality for the rest of my life, that I would never be normal again, that I wouldn't be able to take care of my girls, that Eric would leave me and take my girls with him. I couldn't take that. I couldn't take living without my girls...I would rather die than lose my girls.

And then it suggested, maybe that would be a good thing...for me to die. It would be easy, just an overdose of pills. I had plenty of those, and then I could have peace, and not suffer through this again. I could do it when I went to bed at night, and then it would be Eric who discovered me in the morning, and my girls wouldn't have to see me dead.

I tried my hardest not to listen to the Destroyer, as Dr. Halpern had told me, but there seemed no way to stop it. I told it that I would never kill myself, that I would never leave my girls, but it went on and on.

Still, difficult as the day was, through all eight of those hours I spent trying to shut out my voice, I knew that things weren't really that bad, because I kept looking at my watch to make sure I would be out in front of the house to meet the girls when they came home from camp.

Ten minutes before the bus was to arrive, I walked outside to wait for them, and at 5 o'clock, the camp bus pulled up, the doors opened, and there were my two darling daughters.

They emerged from the bus with their lunch boxes and back packs, looking exhausted and tattered, just as they should look after a day of sun, swimming, and playing in the outdoors. They both ran to me, embraced me, and were chattering about what happened today at camp, as I led them into the house. "Are you hungry?" I asked.

"No," they replied, collapsing on the purple sofa in our family room. "Can we watch TV?"

"Of course," I said, relieved that they would make no demands on me. I turned on the TV and sank into the matching purple easy chair…just to be in their presence, just to see them.

The past four years had been increasingly difficult for me. The school years passed without a problem, but every summer, my malady would reappear, and it seemed as if the Destroyer was gaining power. Not only were my episodes lasting longer, but I was believing each time that I would never return to reality.

I dreaded the summers, and Dr. Berg told me I was creating a self-fulfilling prophecy. If I didn't think about it, it wouldn't happen. Easier said than done. It seemed the harder I tried not to think about it, the harder it was not to think about it. In any case, I knew I was in for another season of torture.

Eric didn't get home until eleven that night, which was not unusual, especially since he had called at seven to tell me he might be late.

"How'd everything go?" I asked when he entered the house.

"Brutal," he said, pushing his black-rimmed glasses higher on his nose. "I had to go over a thousand interrogatories and admissions."

"I guess that was pretty tedious," I said.

"It was," he said. "But at least they're done." He seemed distracted, preoccupied. Perhaps still going over those interrogatories and admissions in his mind. He set his briefcase on the floor beside the butcher block table in the kitchen, settled on the purple sofa, and asked, "How're the girls?"

"They really loved their first day at camp," I said.

"Good," he said. And then as an afterthought, "And how was your day?"

Should I tell him the truth? Drop another burden on his already burdened day? I could probably go on for days before he'd notice, with the girls going to camp every day, but it was too heavy for me to carry alone. "It's back," I said.

He sighed, closed his eyes for a moment, probably remembering his mother's admonition about not marrying me, and said, "I'm sorry to hear that."

"Me too." I wanted to go to him, crumple in his arms, have him hold me. But he seemed too far away. Too far for me to reach him.

"What shall we do?" he asked.

"Well, the girls are in camp every day. I think I can manage."

"Are you sure?"

"I think so," I said.

"Well, you'll let me know if you need any help. Now, I'm really exhausted. I've got to go to bed."

"Yes," I said, "of course."

And he left me sitting there alone, somewhere not in his world and not in the real world, wondering how I would get through tomorrow.

The summer passed and I made it through, as usual, with a little help from my mom, Hortensia, Heather, Andrew, Amy, Claire and Dr. Berg. By the time the girls started back to school, I was back to my normal self, back to my new third-grade class, and relieved that the summer was over. It was still a mystery to me.

Why did my depersonalization come back every summer? Why did it leave every fall? Was it coincidence or something about summer vacation that frightened me? I didn't know and Dr. Berg didn't know. One would think I would be happy to have the time off, to be with my daughters. It didn't make any sense to me. But then, nothing about my illness made any sense to me.

A few months into the new semester, one of my teacher friends, Caitlin Cooper, told me she was going to take a yoga class. "Come with me," she said. "It'll be fun."

I thought about it: yoga meant to me stretching and relaxing. I needed both, so I told her I would come.

"It's every Wednesday night," she said. "I hope that's okay."

"I don't know," I said, "nights are tough for me. You know my husband's out so much."

"Well, I hear this guy is great and it's a beginner's class. Why don't you try it once and then worry about it."

"Okay," I decided. If Eric wasn't going to be home, I could probably get my mom or Heather or Hortensia to come over. "Wednesday night."

"Good. I'll call and tell them we're coming."

As it turned out, Eric was not going to be home early that night, but Mom was available, and happy to come over.

Since Caitlin and I lived in opposite directions, we drove separately and met at the Zen Studio, not on Ventura Boulevard in Encino, but on Riverside Drive in Studio City. I liked the place the minute I stepped inside.

It was dimly lit, sparsely furnished, a waterfall over rocks, three dark red chairs, a stack of mats on one side, a Chinese screen on the other, the smell of incense in the air, and in front of us wearing a white t-shirt, jeans and sandals, a man about my age, with long, tousled, blond hair, warm brown eyes, and a welcoming smile on his face. He greeted us all, several women, a few men, as we entered with a hand shake, and a "Glad to see you", "Welcome back," or, "Hi, I'm Doug Ladea. Nice to meet you."

He had each of us get a mat, but told us we'd all have to buy our own mats if we decided to continue, and then he began giving us instructions. We bent our bodies this way and that, holding poses here and there. Sometimes I could do it, sometimes I couldn't, but his voice was always encouraging, always accepting. "It's all right if you can't do it. Just do the best you can. If anything starts to hurt, stop and wait for the next stretch."

Finally, he had us all lie on our mats, face up, arms at our sides, palms up, each leg close to the other, and spoke to us in a gentle voice, "Allow your mind to quiet...there is nothing to think about except enjoying this moment. You are in a safe, peaceful and nurturing place. Just enjoy this space you are in."

Then he put on some quiet music and we lay there until he spoke again, telling us to notice how quiet our mind was, how in tune we were with our body, how refreshed we felt.

When he finished with, "Goodnight and have a wonderful peaceful evening," I felt more at peace, I think, than I had ever felt in my life. It would be worth coming back, just for these last final minutes.

When I said goodnight, Doug took my hand in his. "It was nice to meet you, Zoe," he said. "I hope you'll be back."

And just looking into his eyes, feeling my hand in his, I felt comforted. "Yes," I said, "I will definitely be back."

"We have a schedule of classes over there," he said, pointing to a small table near the door. "If some other time is more convenient for you..."

"No," I said, "Wednesday nights are fine."

He smiled and I smiled and I walked out the door with Caitlin. "Caitlin, thank you so much for taking me. That was wonderful."

"And you did pretty well," she said, "for a mother of two who never exercises."

"Yes, I really enjoyed it."

"So it's a be-back?"

"As long as I can get Eric to come home early. Or my mom or Heather, or Hortensia to come over."

We walked in silence for awhile, and Caitlin said, "Eric sure does work long hours."

I was pretty close to Caitlin. We ate lunch together every day and had a lot in common, both being teachers of third grade at the same school. I had not told her about my affliction, so she thought I was just your average, normal person. But I had talked about Eric, my girls, my parents, my in-laws, my sister, brother, and Amy, so in a way, she knew me pretty well, including the fact that Eric was so busy at work, I hardly saw him. "He's just very successful. Can't complain about that."

"No, I guess not," Caitlin said. Her husband was a physicist, working on some secret project with the government. Even she wasn't sure exactly what he was working on, but it had something to do with nuclear weapons. She was two years older than me, and also had two children: a boy, 10, and a girl, seven. We had even gotten together as families, and the kids got along really well. Her seven-year-old, Samantha, and my seven-year-old, Sophie, loved each other; and her son, Nicolas, 10, didn't mind hanging out with my nine-year-old Molly, so the kids were fine. Her husband, Bob, the nuclear physicist, and Eric didn't seem to have much in common, but they muddled through each barbeque, or sit-down dinner without any problems. Fortunately we were all Democrats, and all voting for Al Gore, so even with the election coming up in November, we didn't have anything to fight about.

When Eric got home that night, I was already in bed, and he didn't even ask me how the yoga class went. Apparently he forgot I had even gone, or it wasn't very important to him.

"How'd your evening go?" I asked.

"I'm snowed under with paper work, but I made a big dent in it tonight. Which is good news for you," he said, crawling in beside me, "because I'm making lots of money for us."

"I'm glad," I said, kissing his cheek and then turning over to go to sleep. I had to be up at 5:30 a.m., and this was no time for chit chat.

I bought myself a mat, and the following Wednesday, I got my mom to baby-sit again, and the following week, Heather, and the week after that, my mom, and the following week, Hortensia. By now, I was really into yoga. I was getting better at my stretches and poses, and in general, feeling more calm and healthier. I felt the classes were really helping me. I talked to Doug about it after my fifth class. Caitlin couldn't get a sitter that night, so I went alone.

"I'm glad you're feeling that way," Doug said, in his calm, quiet way.

The other students had already left and he was turning off the music.

"I haven't really done anything athletic for years," I said, "except chase my girls around and play games on the playground every now and then with my third-graders."

"Well, I believe in exercise," Doug said.

"Obviously," I said referring to how muscular he was. "You must work out," I said.

"Not at a gym," he said. "But I do run three miles every morning, and I do play tennis and golf, but basically I do a lot of stretching."

"I played a little tennis growing up," I said, "but that's about as athletic as I ever got, much to my dad's disappointment."

"Say," he said, "would you like to get a cup of tea?"

I had no reason to rush home, I thought, and I really liked being with Doug. Just being in his presence had a calming effect on me. "Yes, I would," I said.

He turned off the fountain, the incense burner, the lights, locked the outside door, and we dropped my mat in the trunk of my car, and walked down the street aways to a cute little place called Tessie's Teahouse. "They have some good teas here," he said, "or you could have coffee, if you like."

"No, tea is fine."

We both ordered herbal teas, and sat at a little round table with our white Styrofoam cups in our hands, and talked.

"So tell me about you," he said.

And I told him about my life so far, the basics: that I had wanted to be a concert pianist, but that didn't work out, that I went to Pierce College and CSUN, that I got married at age 23, that my husband was a lawyer and worked all kinds of crazy hours, that I taught third grade and loved it, and about the stars in my life, my two little girls, Molly and Sophie. I did not tell him about my illness, although there was something about him that made me feel I could.

And then I asked about him.

"Not much to tell," he said. "I also went to CSUN, but probably a few years before you, and didn't know what I wanted to be. There was one thing I knew I didn't want to be: cooped up behind a desk all day. So that let out a lot of professions. I would have liked to have been a professional tennis player or golfer, but unfortunately there were two problems with that. First of all, and most important, I wasn't good enough. But even if I was, I don't know if I could have tied myself up with practicing eight hours a day, every day."

I smiled at him. "I suppose if you were good enough, you would have."

He smiled back, "Yes, I suppose you're right. But I wasn't, so moot point."

"So, what did you do?"

"I became a pool man."

"A pool man," I said, with a touch of sarcasm.

"Yeah," he said, "go ahead and laugh. But it was perfectly suited to me. I could make my own hours, I could be outdoors, and it was good exercise."

"Sounds perfect," I said.

We sipped our teas, me liking him more and more by the minute. "So what kind of name is Ladea?" I asked.

"It's Romanian," he said. "There's actually a famous sculptor named Ladea—no relation."

"Then you're Romanian."

"My dad is, yes, but I was born in this country."

"So how did you get into yoga?"

"Took a class, same as you. And the first time I tried it, I was hooked. So I decided to make it my life's work. I'm also into meditation, and I think you'd like that."

"I already have a pretty busy schedule," I said.

"Yes," he said, "but the thing about meditation is that it actually gives you more time."

"How's that?" I asked, genuinely bewildered.

"Because you discover that if you can take forty minutes out of your day, every day, to meditate, you can do anything."

We had each finished our tea. I looked at my watch: ten o'clock, way past the time Hortensia expected me. "On that note," I said, "I've got to go. My babysitter will be worried about me."

He stood up. "I'll walk you back to your car."

As I drove home, I thought about Doug Ladea. How much I liked him. How excited I felt being with him. How young he made me feel, like a teenager on a date. When had I last felt that? That I was a person, not someone's wife, mom, or teacher. And I felt normal…like a non-afflicted person. He hadn't mentioned that he was married or that he had kids. But what difference did it really make? I was happily married with two children, and I had an incurable illness. Even if I were free, why would he want me? Why would any man want me? I was just thankful to have Eric, no matter how many hours he worked.

The next day at lunch, Caitlin and I sitting in a corner of the teacher's lunchroom, I told Caitlin how much I liked Doug.

"What woman doesn't like Doug?" she said. "You think we go there for the yoga?"

I laughed. "Caitlin, you're a riot." And then suddenly I felt very close to her, and wanted to confide in her, to let her know who I truly was, but not here in the lunch room where someone might walk over and interrupt us, or someone might overhear what I was saying. "Caitlin, would you mind taking a walk with me?"

She looked at me quizzically. "Not at all." We gathered our paper bags and napkins, tossed them into the trash can, and walked out onto the playground And there amid the kids running helter-skelter, the clatter of voices from kids, teachers, and aides, the balls whizzing past us in the air and on the ground, and an occasional scream or bump, I told her. I told her about my malady, my affliction, my depersonalization. And I think she understood. She didn't pity me; she just listened and was my friend.

The next Wednesday night that Caitlin couldn't make the class, Doug and I went for tea again, and I asked him if he was married.

"No," he said, "I've never married."

He seemed sad, as if there was more he wanted to say, so I waited.

"I was engaged once. I was 27. Her name was Nicole. Nicole Sullivan."

"What happened?" I asked.

"She died in an auto accident."

I was stunned. "Oh, how terrible," I said.

He was in a reverie. "It was the day of her bridal shower. She was a beautiful girl, blonde, full of life, energy, sweet, kind. I was crazy about her. That day, she went to the beauty shop to get her hair done, and I went to buy flowers. I was to show up at the end of the shower her friends were giving for her…with flowers, so I was sitting at home, watching the clock. I was to leave at two to get there. She had hugged and kissed me goodbye that morning, so excited about the coming day, about our coming life together, and then at twelve, I got a phone call from her mother. I'll never forget those words or anything else about that day. Her mother said, 'Where's Nicole? She hasn't shown up at the party yet.'

"'She's at the beauty shop,' I told her.

"And then she said, 'I called there and they said she left an hour ago.'

"I began to feel uneasy, 'What shall we do?' I asked.

"'I don't know,' her mother said, and I could hear it in her voice…the same fear that I was feeling.

"Within the hour, the police showed up at her mother's house and told her father that there had been an accident….a drunk driver had run into Nicole's car and broke her neck. She died instantly." He paused. His eyes were dark; he seemed drained. "I brought the flowers to her funeral. The ones I had bought for her bridal shower. They had been beautiful, like her, and now they were as dead as she was." He didn't speak for a few moments, and then he said, "I've never gotten over it; I don't think I ever will."

"No," I said, quietly, "I don't think you ever get over something like that."

"Her parents used to be devout Catholics, and now they're atheists."

"And what about you?"

"I was brought up Methodist, but now I don't believe in any God. But I do believe in a collective unconscious."

"And that means…"

"That we're all connected somehow. Spiritually."

"But isn't that just another form of God?"

"I guess if you define it that way. But it's not a human form, or a thinking deity who sees all and knows all. It's just a feeling."

I wondered if I should ask, and decided to. "Do you ever feel Nicole's presence?"

"Yes," he said. "All the time."

We sat for several minutes not talking and then he said, "I'm sorry to have burdened you with all this. I haven't talked about it for years."

"It's good to talk about it," I said.

He smiled, "You sound like a therapist I once knew."

"Believe me," I said, "I've seen so many therapists, I think I could be one."

"Why?" he asked.

"Why?" I answered, not sure of his question.

"Why have you seen so many therapists?"

Why indeed. I didn't feel it was fair to burden him with my problems at this moment. "You know, problems."

He understood I didn't want to talk about it. "Well, we've finished our tea, and it's getting late, so…."

"Time to go," I said standing up. When he stood, I felt the urge to hug him, so I did. It was a sweet moment, the two of us with our own tragedies, coming together. Like the collective unconscious.

He walked me to my car. "See you next Wednesday," he said.

As the weeks went on, I continued with my yoga class, and whenever Caitlin couldn't make it, I would go to tea with Doug. We never talked about Nicole again, but I felt her presence always with us.

I never told him about my "problem" either. Perhaps because I was feeling well, and didn't want to curse myself by talking about my malady, or perhaps because I didn't want him to think there was anything wrong with me, that I wasn't normal. Perhaps because I was living in some fantasy that there was this attraction between us; that he might actually care for me romantically and that knowing the truth about me would end it all. So I remained light and gay and did not tell him my deep, dark secret.

When we were together, we'd talk about movies and books (he was an avid reader and I tried to read a book a month) so we had that in common, and I told him about my day at school, or my children, or what piano pieces I was currently working on. We talked about the state of the world (of course he was a pacifist and had worked on Jimmy Carter's Habitat for Humanity, actually going out and building houses in various parts of the United States) and there were moments...moments of feeling so close to him, that I wanted to tell him about my affliction, but I didn't.

I guess I should have seen it coming. I think everyone, Caitlin, Teri, Missy, my sister, brother, Amy, my mom and dad, and probably even Hortensia suspected it, but everyone was hoping it wasn't true. The obvious.

It was the first week in June, school was ending in two weeks, and my feeling of dread was already sending tentacles into the bottom of my belly.

Eric could not have picked a worse time. He knew that June was bad for me. He knew that school would be ending and that I would probably become depersonalized the day after it ended. He knew it and yet he went ahead anyway.

It had been a typical June day, cloudy and cool in the morning, sunny and warm in the afternoon, then cool again at night. I'd just put the girls to bed after our usual after-dinner routine. First, the girls took turns practicing the piano for about half an hour. I had begun giving them lessons when Molly was seven and Sophie was five. I didn't put any pressure on them; it was just another fun thing to do. And while they both seemed to enjoy playing the piano, neither showed any special talent.

At 8 o'clock, I gave them their baths, and then they took turns reading to me. I took them to the library every two weeks to get 10 books each, as my mother had done with me. Molly was an excellent reader, and Sophie was beginning to be. Then I tucked them into bed, kissing each several times, and finally went into the family room to be with Eric.

Eric had actually come home early that night, in time to eat dinner with me and the girls. I had made spaghetti, the girls loved spaghetti, and fortunately there was enough for Eric—I always made extra food if there was a chance he might be home for dinner.

After dinner, he stretched out on the purple sofa in the family room to watch his favorite channels: the stock market, various pundits on CNN, Fox, or MNBC, and sure enough when I entered the room, there was his favorite, Bill O'Reilly spouting off about the Democrats opposition to President Bush's tax cuts. I should have been suspicious of something bad, because when I entered the room he turned off O'Reilly, and asked me to come sit beside him.

"Zoe," he said, using his formal mode of address to me, "I have something I need to tell you."

I was beginning to feel lightheaded, as if I didn't really want to hear what he had to say. I thought again of offering him some chocolate chip cookies the girls and I had baked when they came home from school that day. But his inevitable words came in spite of all my willing them not to.

"I have fallen in love with another woman."

Suddenly the room turned cold and I began to shiver. *Oh no,* I thought, *not that. Not that. That is not what I want to hear.* And then as the cold grabbed my heart, I faced the truth. It was my fault. It was all my fault. What man would want a woman with my malady? I was just lucky he had stayed with me all these years… that he even married me. And then there was the sex. It seemed we didn't have it anymore and I had just ignored that fact. Just lived in my little cocoon thinking it wasn't important, or thinking that it didn't matter to him anymore, or that I was lucky not to have to put up with it anymore, or not thinking about it at all. How silly and stupid I was…how in denial all these years. I wasn't getting anything that I didn't deserve. And then I thought about my girls, Molly and Sophie, what I had done to them, driving their father away. It was, after all, completely my fault.

I did not visibly react to Eric. I did not shout at him, or cry, or throw anything at him, but I was furious with him. No matter how much I blamed myself, I could not help this burning anger building within me. "So now what?"

"I plan to move out tomorrow…just my own personal things. I'm going to let you stay in the house because I think that's best for the girls, and I will visit them, and once I'm settled I'll want them to come visit me, if that's all right with you."

All right with me, my brain screamed at him. *Nothing's all right with me. Including my health. Don't you know, you dummy, that in a few hours or a few days, I'm going to be depersonalized?*

"Okay," I said aloud and stood up. I wanted to be out of his sight, out of his presence as soon as possible.

"I'm really sorry, Zo," he said, now using his affectionate name for me. I guessed the formalities were over. "It had nothing to do with you. I think you're a wonderful person, and I still care for you….but…."

I turned my back on him and hurried up the stairs. I didn't want to hear his 'buts', I didn't want to hear his compliments, justifications, or explanations; and when I got to my room, I shut the door, took a pillow, went into the bathroom, locked the door, and screamed as loud as I dared into the pillow.

The next day when I came home from school, Eric's clothes, his toiletries, and all his coats and sweaters from the front closet were gone. He was gone forever. How much did I hate him? It would be impossible to estimate. I hated him as much as any person could hate another, but I hated myself, too. I took full blame for this, but still I could not help hating him.

I went to my beautiful baby-grand and began playing Chopin's Prelude in E-Minor, because it was the saddest piece of music I knew, sadder even than the funeral march. And when I finished playing, I stretched out my arms, and lay my head on the black and white keys, but I would not allow myself to cry. In a few minutes it would be time to pick up my girls from their after-school program, and I did not want them to see that their mommy had been crying.

The next afternoon, I was served with divorce papers. It was Thursday and I was seasoning a chicken to put in the oven to bake, while the girls were sitting at the butcher block table in the kitchen doing their homework. The doorbell rang and when I called through the door, "Who is it?" A man's voice replied, "I have a package from your husband, Eric Simoneau." I opened the door cautiously and saw a middle-aged man with a large tan envelope in his hand. "Are you Zoe Simoneau?" he asked. "Yes," I said. He handed me the envelope with the words, "You are served," and turned and walked down the concrete walkway to his waiting car.

It was then that I turned on cartoons for the girls, walked upstairs to my bedroom, shut the door, and called my mom and dad to tell them that Eric was divorcing me.

They didn't take the news well. They couldn't believe that Eric had done this to their daughter. "He's a bum, that's what he is," Dad said. "And to think I took him into my heart, I loved him like a son, and this is what he does to my daughter!" Dad was very upset.

I think Mom was more worried about me than concerned about Eric. "I think I hate him more for telling you when he did, than for what he did," she said.

"Mom, he had to tell me some time. There's never a good time."

"But he knows what happens as soon as school ends. Why did he have to tell you now?"

"But what if he told me in the middle of the semester, when I was feeling good, and then I had an attack, and it ruined the rest of the year. That would be worse. Maybe he thought I was going to get depersonalized anyway so this was the best time."

Mom considered it for a moment. "I still hate him," she said, "and I'll never forgive him."

Later that night, after the girls had gone to bed, Andrew called to tell me how sorry he was and was there anything he could do to help me.

"Maybe come by and spend some time with the children," I said. "I think it's going to be a bad summer."

Then Claire called. "The dirty rotten bastard." And I thought, all these years of me thinking what poor choices Claire had made in men. Had I made an even worse choice?

"Claire," I said, "I need your help. What should I do about the divorce papers?"

"Well, you're going to have to hire an attorney. I'm no expert in family law, but I think you have to answer in 30 days."

"Then who should I call?"

"I think Steve Fein." Steve Fein was a long-time friend of my parents, and a specialist in family law.

"Yes, I like Steve," I said.

"I've heard good things about him and being a friend of the family, I think he'll fight even harder for you."

"That's exactly what I need. Someone to fight for me."

"You've got a lot of people in that department," Claire said.

Tears came to my eyes. "Thanks, sis. You've always been there for me." And then I began to cry, sobbing uncontrollably as all the pent-up emotions of the last two days came spilling out of my eyes, my heart, my soul.

"Everything's going to be all right," Claire said. "You'll see."

When I could finally speak, I said, "I love you, Claire."

And she said, "I love you, Zoe."

On Monday after school, I dropped off my papers with Steve Fein's secretary, and made an appointment to see him the following Monday. I prayed I would be able to keep the appointment.

I got through those last few days of school in a mild haze, got out the report cards, attended the parties, the meetings, cleaned up my room, went out with the other teachers for our yearly end-of-school lunch, pretending that everything was okay, that I was okay, and then the morning after the last day of school, I woke up completely gone.

Mom was waiting for my call, and came over immediately to take care of the girls. They were signed up for summer camp, but it wouldn't be starting for a week. When she had them dressed, fed and watching a Disney movie, she came into my room.

"How are you feeling, honey?"

I started to cry. "I don't know how many more times I can go through this," I said.

Mom cuddled me in her arms, and ran her fingers through my hair as she always did. "Everything's going to be okay, like it always is. You'll have a few tough weeks, but then you're going to recover and go back to teaching, go back to your life. It happens every year; it'll happen this year."

But every year I had a husband who loved me and helped me, and this year I wouldn't. My Destroyer told me that this year would be different, that I would never recover. And I knew my Destroyer was right. It was just too difficult, the struggle, managing everything myself, a divorce to look forward to. I couldn't face the nightmare that lay ahead. Perhaps I didn't want to come back from unreality. "This time will be different, Mom." By now, I had a shorthand with Mom. She knew me so well...she even knew what my Destroyer was saying.

"We're going to get a new therapist," Mom said, as she always did. "Someone who specializes in depersonalization. I scrolled through the website and found one psychiatrist who appears to specialize in depersonalization, but she's in New York. I tried calling her, but got an answering machine, so I e-mailed her and told her all about you and asked her to please get back to me immediately to let me know if she knows anyone out here who can help you. If there isn't anyone out here, we'll go to New York."

"Thank you, Mom, thank you, but I feel so bad about being such a burden on you."

"Honey, you're a mom just like me. Is there anything you wouldn't do for your daughters?"

"No, Mom," I said.

"Well, there's nothing I won't do for my daughter."

We hugged again and next thing I knew, Molly and Sophie were in my bed and the four of us were hugging and tickling each other, and Molly and Sophie were giggling as if this was the best time they could ever have.

Claire called Steve and told him to get a continuance. There was no way I could do anything about the divorce until I got over this terrible flu I had. She told him she thought it was mononucleosis.

The following Monday, the girls started camp, and while Mom, Claire, Andrew and Amy came over whenever they could, I was on a downhill spiral. My Destroyer would not quit talking and it was hard to hear anything or filter anything through its voice. I gave up. I was utterly incapable of doing anything and spent most of my time planning my death. I had been through this many times before and already knew it would be an overdose of pills, but I had to figure out what pills, and how many and how to get them and how to get them inside me and when to do it so that my girls wouldn't be home and who should find me and should I tell someone I was going to do it so they could get my body out of the house before the girls could see it, but then, they would try to stop me. It was complicated and needed a lot of thought and planning which I felt incapable of doing.

Chapter Fourteen – Claire

On a Sunday night, two weeks after the girls started camp, it was Claire's turn to stay with Zoe. Eric had picked them up from camp on Friday afternoon and was supposed to return them to Zoe on Sunday evening, but he didn't show up. Instead he called. Claire answered the phone and after they exchanged hellos, Eric said, "I just wanted to let you know that considering Zoe's condition, I've decided to keep the girls until she's feeling better."

"What do you mean 'keep the girls'?" Claire asked.

"I mean that they are gong to live with me until Zoe is feeling better."

"But you can't do that."

"I can and I will. Let's face it, Claire, Zoe at the present time is unable to physically or mentally take care of them." And then with a sneer in his voice. "I know what's going on there."

Claire chose to ignore his remark and continued on, single-mindedly, to achieve her goal. "I don't think you can do this without the court's permission."

"I can if my children's well-being is at risk."

"How is it at risk?"

"Because," he said, "their mother is out of her mind."

Claire shivered. How could she ever have liked this man? "My sister has an illness. An illness that comes and goes, but she is certainly not a threat either mentally or physically to her children."

145

"Tell me honestly, Claire," Eric said, apparently continuing on single-mindedly with his own goal, "do you really think Zoe is not harming the children mentally? Do you really think it's healthy for them to be living with Zoe in her current condition?"

Claire didn't know what to say to that, but she knew she could not lose this fight. "Zoe has seen to it that her children are well cared for. Someone is always in the house with them."

"You haven't answered my question," he said.

It was the battle of the lawyers, and unfortunately, he was going to win. "What is not mentally healthy for them, is to be taken from their mother," Claire said.

"Claire, you're a bright girl. Do the right thing. For your nieces' sake, let them stay with me. Just until Zoe is feeling better."

Claire's heart was palpitating, beating so fast she thought she might faint. Her face turned hot as if she was embarrassed. He had said the wrong words or the right words, *do what's best for your nieces.* But what was best for her sister? How much pain could Zoe stand? "I don't know," Claire said. "Let me think about it."

"I'm preparing a document for her to sign, giving me temporary physical and legal custody. Please convince her to sign it. It'll be better for her, too. She'll have one less thing to worry about."

"I don't know," Claire said, feeling that she was in a vise that was closing tighter and tighter around her chest.

"I'm going to come by tomorrow to get the girls' things, and I've already notified the camp that I'll be dropping them off and picking them up until further notice."

"You've thought of everything," Claire said.

"I have to," Eric said. "I'm their father."

Claire hung up the phone feeling as detached from reality as she thought Zoe must feel. How was she going to tell her sister about this?

She entered Zoe's room. Zoe was sitting on a chair at her window, looking down at the sidewalk. Probably waiting the return of her daughters. She turned to Claire. "Who was on the phone?"

"Eric."

She saw her sister's look turn to consternation. "Is everything all right?"

"Yes, everything's fine."

Claire sat on the bed. "Zoe, I know you're not going to like what I have to say, but actually I think it's for the best."

"What is it, Claire?" Zoe seemed agitated.

"Eric's decided to keep the girls for awhile at his house."

"His house? His house? What do you mean his house?"

"Just for a week or two. Just until you're feeling better."

"No," Zoe said. "Oh no, I don't want that. I want them here with me."

"I know, Zoe, I know. But I actually think it's a good idea," Claire said with as much cheer as she could muster. And then quoting Eric, "This way you'll have one less thing to worry about. One less burden."

"Having my girls with me is not a burden," said as if she'd been insulted.

Claire touched Zoe's hand. "Yes, Zoe, it is," she said.

Claire saw the light go out of Zoe's eyes, and then, Zoe collapsed in sobs. "What's the use of living?" Zoe said.

Claire took her sister in her arms and rubbed her back, feeling total frustration. There had to be some cure for Zoe's disease. There had to be. And then she thought of herself, all her years of eating and throwing up, and not telling anyone about it. But at least she'd been able to do something about it. Two years ago, she had started seeing Emily Kaufman, a therapist recommended by Dr. Berg, who specialized in eating disorders. Then five weeks ago, at Emily's urging, she had joined Overeaters Anonymous.

Over the past two years, and especially the last five weeks, she had found out a lot about herself: that binging and purging was a method of control, that her life was governed by "shoulds" instead of "wants": she *should* be smart, beautiful and popular; she *should* play tennis, she *should* be a lawyer, she *should* be the person her father wanted, the person her mother was.

Both her therapist and the OA members were adamant that she must tell her family, especially her parents, about her problem, or she might never be able to overcome it. It was part of the 12 step program to come out of the closet. But that was one thing Claire hadn't been able to do, yet.

"It'll be all right," she told Zoe. "You'll get them back as soon as you're feeling better. That's all you have to think about is getting better."

Zoe spoke through her sobbing, "You don't understand. You don't understand any of it."

"No," Claire said, "I don't understand all of it. But maybe I do understand more than you think."

Claire slept over that night, and the next morning decided she'd been a fool. Wasn't it worth anything to be rid of her own disease? Poor Zoe had no recourse, but Claire did. No matter what the consequences, at her first opportunity, she was going to tell her family everything. All of them.

A week later, Gail asked Claire and Andrew if they could come over one night to discuss Zoe's situation. Gail was beside herself. Zoe had been bad before, but never this bad. Apparently this thing with Eric and the kids was pushing her over the edge.

They all agreed to meet Tuesday night at eight, and Gail arranged for Hortensia to stay with Zoe that evening. Both Andrew and Claire arrived on time, just after Gail finished loading her dinner dishes into the dishwasher.

Each one took his or her usual chair at the kitchen table, including Dan, while Gail put out some cookies she had bought at Bea's Bakery that day, and offered each of them a cup of coffee. Dan was the only one who wanted coffee, so she poured him a cup, added one Sweet and Low, a bit of milk, carried it over to him, and sat down and started talking.

"As you know, I'm very concerned about Zoe." And then she started to cry. Could she get the words out?

Claire came and sat in Zoe's chair beside her mother, and rubbed her back, as Claire had so often rubbed Zoe's back. "We know, Mom," Claire said. "We know."

"But what can we do about it?" Andrew asked.

Gail blew her nose, took another tissue from the pocket of her pants, dabbed at her eyes, and spoke in a shaky voice, "I've been thinking about it, and I'm wondering if we should put her in a place...someplace she can get 24 hour care."

"Well I'm against that," Andrew said with no hesitation. "She's not crazy. You can't lock her up."

"Besides," Claire said, "I think it'll just make it harder for her to get back to her normal life."

"I agree," Dan said. "I think it'll be like it always is. September will come around and she'll be fine."

"You never have taken this seriously enough," Gail said to her husband with an edge to her voice.

"Of course, I'm taking it serious," Dan said. "Don't you think I'm as upset as you are? It's just that I know what always happens."

"Yes, but this time is different," Gail said. "She even told me so. It's Eric leaving, and now taking the children from her. And that bitch, Heather, I think she's behind the whole thing. Why would he want the girls full time when he's with his new beloved?"

"Maybe he loves them," Claire said, "and thinks they'll be better off."

"Now, you sound like Heather," Gail said.

"Mom, I only want to do what's best for Zoe," Claire said.

"Yes, but what is that?" Gail asked.

They were all silent for a minute or two, each trying to figure out a solution to an unsolvable problem.

"I still haven't heard from that psychiatrist in New York," Gail said. "You'd think someone who specializes in depersonalization would be anxious to help someone who's so bad off."

"I've been on that web-site," Claire said. "It's really sad...but most people do seem to go in and out, so I'm sure Zoe will get better. It's just a question of when."

Gail glared at her daughter. "I don't think you realize how utterly miserable your sister is, or what bad shape she's in."

"I do, Mom, I do," Claire said. "I just don't know how we can help her and I do not want to put her in a .....(struggling for the word) ...place."

Again silence.

Then Claire said, "Maybe I could find her another therapist. Maybe the therapist I'm going to knows of someone."

All eyes were upon her. "You're going to a therapist?" Gail asked.

"Yes," Claire replied to her mother, somewhat sheepishly. She looked around the table; Andrew had a knowing look in his eye, but her dad and mom looked as startled as if she'd just announced that she was pregnant.

"Whatever for?" Gail asked.

Well, here goes, Claire thought, the shit is going to hit the fan and the cat's coming out of the bag. "I'm bulimic," she said simply.

Well of course Andrew knew, Claire could tell by looking at him. All these years he knew and said nothing. Was that kind of him, or mean, she wondered. Her dad's face was stone, and her mom looked dazed and confused as if she'd just awaken from a coma.

"What exactly is that?" her mom asked.

"It's where you eat too much and then throw up." As soon as she said the words, she was sorry. What terrible timing. What a terrible thing to do to her parents when they were already so devastated about Zoe. She should have waited until Zoe was better. But there would always be an excuse, she told herself.

"Is that what you do?" her mom asked, obviously hoping for a negative answer.

"Yes," Claire replied, feeling that she'd just committed murder.

Her mother took a moment, possibly to pull herself together, and then asked, "How long has this been going on?"

Ah, the cruelest question of all. "Since I was sixteen."

He mother turned pale; her father didn't seem to be listening.

"Sixteen," her mother gasped. "All this time, and you never told us?"

"I'm sorry, Mom," Claire said. "I couldn't."

"But why? Didn't you trust us? Didn't you think we could handle it? Didn't you think we could help you?"

Claire looked at her dad. She recognized the look. The same look she had seen on his face so many times when Andrew had disappointed him. "I'm so sorry, Mom, but I just couldn't."

Gail was quiet for a moment. "Is there anything I... we can do to help?"

Now that she had opened Pandora's box, the words came gushing out. "I've been seeing a therapist, and a few weeks ago I joined a group called Overeaters Anonymous. As a matter of fact I have a meeting tonight. And I've now told my family which my therapist has been after me to do for years. So I think I'm doing everything I can do, to get better."

Gail was still pondering, "So all these years of me telling you how to eat, what to eat...it didn't matter, did it?"

"No, Mom. I have an eating disorder. Nothing would help."

Gail was quiet again. "Was it that Judy?"

"No, Mom. It wasn't Judy. It was something I decided to do all by myself."

"But why?"

"That's what I'm trying to find out." She looked to her dad, feeling a sharp pain in her chest, a flutter in her stomach. It was as if he heard nothing, didn't want to hear anything. But she couldn't let it rest. She had gone this far; she was going all the way. "So, Dad," she squeezed the words out, "what do you think?"

He was sitting as still and inscrutable as the sphinx, "I think I'd like another cup of coffee."

Claire felt the humiliation creep into her pores. All she had done all her life to please her father, the tennis, her becoming a lawyer...all of it meant nothing now. In his eyes, she was a zero. "I'm sorry, Dad," she said.

"It's okay," he said, his eyes focused on the China cup in front of him. "As long as you're getting help."

And suddenly, a feeling of sorrow came over her. Not for herself, but for her dad. How sad that none of her dad's children had turned out the way he wanted.

Gail got up from the table to get Dan his cup of coffee. "Anyone else?" she asked. Andrew said he'd take a cup, and then Gail said, "I guess we haven't solved anything about Zoe."

So it was back to Zoe. Claire got up from the table. "Well, you three hash it out; I've got to go to my meeting."

"You mean just like that, you're leaving?" Gail asked.

"As I told you, I have a meeting tonight."

"Well, can't you skip it this once? I specifically called this meeting tonight because your sister is in a crisis and we have to do something to help her now, today, this minute."

Claire couldn't help it, she was fuming. "You know what Mom, all my life it's been about Zoe. Well tonight I have a meeting that's going to help me. And I'm not going to give it up for more talk about Zoe. This one night I got up the courage to tell you all about me, about my problem, and now it's back to Zoe. I've had enough. I'm leaving."

"But Zoe's in so much pain, has been in so much pain, has suffered all her life with this affliction," Gail said.

"Well, I've suffered, too, Mom. I've been in a lot of pain, too, Mom," Claire said. "And I know it may sound harsh and cruel, but I've done everything I could for Zoe all my life, and now I'm going to do something for me. I'm going to my meeting."

Claire got up and stormed out of the house without hugging or kissing anyone goodbye, unlocked the door of her car, got in, and sitting before the steering wheel, keys in hand, she burst into tears. Was it because she had gotten so out of control, was it because she felt sorry for herself, anger toward all of them, embarrassment, shame, or relief that now they knew. She waited until she got it all out, and then she grabbed a handful of tissues, wiped her eyes, blew her nose, put the keys in the ignition, and drove off to attend her meeting of Overeater's Anonymous.

After Claire left the house in a huff, Gail said to Dan and Andrew, "I'm stunned."

Andrew said, "Stunned that Claire's bulimic or that she got so angry?"

"Both," Gail said.

"Well I've known for years that Claire was bulimic," Andrew said.

"You did?!" Gail said, first surprised, then upset. "Then why didn't you tell me?"

"It wasn't my place."

"Even if it's a serious disease?" Gail asked, with some anger in her voice.

"It still wasn't my place. She had to work it out for herself."

"I think you made a big mistake not telling me," Gail said.

"Well, it wouldn't be my first one," Andrew said, standing up. "As for Claire blowing up, I don't blame her. Maybe somebody beside me should have noticed she has a problem. As for Zoe, my opinion is don't put her in a home. If you do, she may never come out. And now, I've got to get home to my pregnant wife." Amy was expecting their first child in just three months. "See you soon," Andrew said, and went around the table, kissed his mother and father on the cheek and was out the door.

"Give Amy my love," Gail called after him.

Gail sat for a moment, trying to gather her thoughts, trying to stay calm, and then got up, poured herself a cup of coffee, poured a few drops of milk into it, stirred it with a spoon, sat down and said to Dan, "I'm totally flabbergasted."

"You and me, both," Dan said.

"So what do you think about all this?" she asked.

"I agree with Andrew. We shouldn't put Zoe in any kind of facility. We should leave her at home." He sipped his coffee.

"And what about Claire?"

He put his cup down. "I guess I'm still in shock about Claire."

"I know what you mean," Gail said. Then, focusing on Dan's deep brown eyes, she asked, "Should we have known about it? Should we have noticed?"

"Absolutely not," Dan said. "Who could ever think such a thing was happening? Who could even imagine such a thing... eating and throwing up? It's disgusting."

"It is disgusting," Gail said, "but still I feel guilty. I'm her mom. I should have noticed."

"You were too busy with Zoe to notice much else."

"That's one of the reasons I feel so guilty about Claire."

"It's not your fault. None of it is your fault."

"Maybe not," Gail said, "but I still can't help feeling guilty." And then noticing that Dan looked more distraught than she had ever seen him. "You look a little down," she said.

"Who wouldn't be down?" Dan asked. "Finding out that the daughter you thought was so perfect, is doing this horrible thing."

And Gail waited sensing that Dan had more to say.

"It isn't just Claire," he continued. "It's all of them, Zoe, Andrew, and now Claire. Where did we go wrong?"

"I know," Gail said. "I feel the same way you do. It's not how I envisioned our children would turn out." A pause, "But I don't think it's anything we did wrong. We tried our hardest. We tried to be good parents. It's just how things turned out."

And then another thought entered Gail's mind. She put her hand on Dan's and asked, "And have I ignored you, too?"

"No," he said, bringing her hand to his mouth and kissing it. "You've always been the perfect wife to me."

"And you, the perfect husband to me."

And they both sat silently holding hands, each feeling the other person's burden, and their own.

Chapter Fifteen— Doug

One afternoon in early August, the phone rang at Zoe's home and Gail, who was spending most of her time at Zoe's, answered it.

"Hello," a male voice said, "is Zoe in?"

"Who's calling?" Gail asked.

"My name is Doug Ladea. I'm her yoga instructor."

"Oh yes," Gail said. "She's spoken so highly of you. She really enjoyed her yoga classes."

"I'm glad to hear that. So, can I speak to her?"

"I'm sorry," Gail said, "but she can't come to the phone right now."

"Yes, her friend, Caitlin, told me she wasn't well, but I was wondering if there was anything I could do."

Gail didn't know whether to laugh or cry. They had been to the best doctors in L.A. for years and now this guy pipes up and wants to know if there was anything he could do. It was laughable if it wasn't so sad. "That's very sweet of you, but I'm afraid there isn't anything you can do."

"Can I come and see her?"

"I don't think so," Gail said.

He paused a moment. "Could you ask her if she'd like to see me?"

Now Gail paused, "Not right now. Maybe sometime later."

Another hesitation. "Is this her mother?"

"Yes, it is."

"And your name is…."

Should she answer her last name or first? "Gail."

"Well, Gail, Caitlin didn't tell me the exact nature of Zoe's illness, but she did tell me that Zoe's been on a ton of medication for years for something psychological. I'm not a doctor or anything like that, but I care for Zoe, and I think I might be able to help."

"Are you a psychologist?" Gail asked.

"Not even close. But I am a student of far Eastern methodology."

"And what does that mean?"

"That I believe in alternative methods of healing."

"Like?"

"Meditation."

Gail wanted to harrumph. "I don't think meditation is going to cure my girl."

"Could we give it a chance?"

Now, Gail hesitated a really long time. What was the point of hooking her daughter up with her yoga instructor? He could be a charlatan, a quack. On the other hand, how could it hurt her? Maybe a new approach with someone she knew and liked could help. Gail was skeptical, but the psychiatrist in New York wasn't really an expert in depersonalization and couldn't recommend anyone who was, and Zoe was declining before her eyes. "All right," she said, surprising herself. "But what I would like to do is meet you first." And, she was thinking, talk to Caitlin about this guy before she gave out Zoe's home address.

"Fine," Doug Ladea said. "I own the Zen Studio in Studio City on Riverside Drive. When would you like to come by?"

"I can come by tonight," Gail said. "How's seven?"

"Seven is perfect," Doug said, and gave her his address.

As soon as Gail hung up the phone, she called Caitlin, who called her back within the hour and testified to the fact that Doug was completely trustworthy. Next, Gail called Claire and told her about her conversation with Doug. "Can you go with me tonight to meet him?"

"It sounds like you're grasping at straws," Claire said. "Do you really believe that some mystical guru can help Zoe?"

Gail sighed. "At this point, I'm ready to try anything. Please come with me."

After a moment of debating, Claire said, "Okay. I'll pick you up at 6:30."

In spite of her skepticism, Claire hung up the phone feeling somewhat hopeful. She believed in alternative methods. She, herself, had made more progress in two months with Overeaters Anonymous than in two years of therapy. She had been attending her weekly meetings faithfully. Yes, standing up at each meeting and saying, "Hi, I'm Claire and I'm bulimic." And she had a sponsor whom she called frequently, another poor soul afflicted with her disease, but who had kept it under control for years.

In the past few weeks, Claire had experienced a few stretches of time where she did not binge and purge. But she always felt on the edge. She was still not sure she could ever get past her need for food, her feeling that she was fat. She was still worrying that she could never fill that hole within her that would only be placated by food; that no matter how much food she stuffed down her throat, it would never be enough.

Why? She asked herself a million times a day? Why had she turned to food? What was it about eating she could not resist? Even though she now understood some of her problems, why couldn't she control her eating?

Maybe if her mom had been fat instead of slim, or if her mother was ugly, unpopular, stupid, things would have been different. Perhaps if her mother hadn't gone back to college, gotten a degree, become a docent at the L.A. County Museum…maybe she wouldn't need so much food. She had been over all this with her therapist, and the members of her O.A. group, and everyone had told her she must stop dwelling on the past, and only think of today, this moment, and all the things she had accomplished.

She was a lawyer, with a ton of friends; she was attractive and successful. She had a man, Phil Mazursky, a fantastic man, totally in love with her, even though he was married, but she knew it was only a matter of time until he left his wife for her. Then why the hell couldn't she lick this thing, fill that hole and move on with her life? Perhaps if Phil left his wife and married her. Perhaps that would do it. Perhaps if she and Phil had a child together. Maybe that would do it. Maybe then she would feel whole, full, and at peace.

She picked up her mother at 6:30, and as they walked into the Zen Studio ten minutes early, Claire immediately felt a sense of tranquility. As an attractive man, presumably the guru, came walking toward them, Claire decided, without him saying a word, that maybe he wasn't a quack after all.

"You must be Gail," he said to Claire's mom, holding out his hand to her. "I'm Doug Ladea."

"Yes," Gail said, taking his hand, "and this is my other daughter, Claire."

He took Claire's hand, "Nice to meet you, Claire."

Both women were mesmerized by Doug, but he didn't seem to notice. "Come, sit down," he said, motioning them to the three red chairs.

"So, what is it you propose to do with Zoe?" Gail asked, after they were seated.

"Teach her to meditate, to relax. I don't really know what her problem is, but it sounds like it's related to tension and anxiety. I think I can help with that."

"She's depressed," Gail said bluntly.

"For any specific reason?" Doug asked

"Because she's depersonalized," Gail said, knowing he would have no idea what that meant.

"Which means?" Doug asked.

"It's hard to explain," Gail said. "But what she tells us is that she goes into a state of unreality, removed from her body. She can't realize herself or anything else."

"Sounds horrible," Doug said.

Gail's eyes began to tear. "It is horrible."

The three of them sat quietly for a moment. Then Doug said, "Well, I don't mean to sound egotistical, but I think my approach might help. I'd like to give it a try."

Gail wiped at her eyes with a tissue, she was never without them, and turned to Claire. "What do you think?"

Claire turned to Doug, "Do you own this place?"

"Yes, I do."

He had to have some stability if he owned a yoga studio, Claire thought. And he seemed sincere, and probably wasn't a con artist...although wasn't that the staple of a con artist...not to appear to be one...but on the other hand, there wasn't much he could con Zoe out of, especially if she was unable to go back to work. "How much would you charge for your services?"

Doug gave her an embarrassed smile, as if he'd never thought of such a thing. "I wouldn't charge anything," he said.

Claire looked at her mother, her mother looked at her. "Okay," Claire said, "let's give it a shot."

Driving home in the car," Gail said, "I feel better already."

Claire looked at her sideways, "Don't get your hopes up, Mom."

"But he seemed like such a nice young man."

"Yes, he did," Claire said. "But even if he's the nicest guy in the world, he still may not be able to help Zoe."

"Well, we can only hope," Gail said.

"That we can," Claire said, thinking that even if he didn't help Zoe, she was glad she had met him.

The two women, mother and daughter, drove along in silence for awhile, and then Gail asked, "How are you doing?" They hadn't discussed Claire's bulimia in the three weeks since that Tuesday night in Gail's kitchen.

Claire answered, "I'm doing okay."

"You'll let me know if there's anything I can do," Gail said.

"Of course," Claire said, suddenly feeling very comfortable with her mother, realizing that somehow in the last hour they spent together, this barrier that had been between them all these years, had vanished.

Doug came to see Zoe the next day at one o'clock. She had gotten up to shower in the morning, put on white shorts and a red and white striped t-shirt, and then went back to bed. She knew Doug was coming, but even that was not enough to rouse her from her state of drowsiness. She knew part of it was a side effect of the drugs she was on, this lethargy, but she didn't want to be awake anyway. It was too painful.

She was dozing as he entered the room. Her mom was standing in the doorway. "Look Zoe, Doug is here," her mom said, and then turned and walked away.

Doug came over and sat on a bridge chair placed beside Zoe's bed. He was amazed by how terrible she looked. She seemed lifeless and limp as a cloth doll. "Hi, Zoe," he said.

"Hi, Doug," she said viewing him from outer space. She would have to gather all her energy to try to make him feel comfortable.

"Zoe, I know you're not feeling well, and I know you don't really want company, so don't feel you have to entertain me. I've just come to teach you some techniques that might make you feel better."

Hah, she thought, better men than you have tried and failed.

"All we're going to do," Doug said, "is breathe."

Breathe, she thought. Maybe he's the one who's crazy.

"Try to get comfortable," he said, and then leaning over, "let's put another pillow under your head...and looking around the room, "tomorrow I'll have another pillow for under your knees. Now," hc said, after adjusting the pillow under her head and sitting back down on the chair at her bedside, "we're just going to breathe. I want you to breathe through your nose, and do you know where your diaphragm is?"

"Yes," she said.

"We're going to take deep breaths in through your nose and then all the way down to your diaphragm, hold it there while I count to three, and then exhale through your nose. Okay?"

"Yes," she said, relieved that she didn't have to talk to him. All she had to do was breathe, which she did anyway.

"Okay. Take in all the air you can through your nose, send it down to your diaphragm, feel your diaphragm expand, hold it one, two, three. Now let it out slowly through your nose. Now, let's do it again, take a long, deep breath in through your nose, send it down to your diaphragm, hold it there, one, two, three. Now bring it slowly up and out through your nose. Now again..."

Doug sat by her bed for twenty minutes talking her through the breathing, and then put his hand on hers. "You don't have to think about anything," he said, "but if you like, you can try breathing like we just did for 20 minutes later. Okay?"

"Okay," she said.

"I'll be back tomorrow," he said, "same time, and we'll breathe again. Okay?"

"Okay," she said.

After he left, tears came to Zoe's eyes. How kind of him to come, and how pleasant it was not to have to play-act or say anything, or try to act normal. He expected nothing from her except to breathe, and that she could do. Her voice tried to tell her lots of terrible things: that he wouldn't be back, that nothing he did could help, that she was pathetic, but still, when the room got dark that night, she did her breathing.

The next afternoon, Doug was there again at one o'clock, and asked her mom for an extra pillow, which he put under Zoe's knees after he propped her head up with two pillows. Then he sat beside her bed, talking her through the breathing as he had done the day before.

He came every day for the next two weeks, and all they did was breathe together.

At the start of the third week, after breathing together, he asked Zoe how she was feeling.

"I think I'm feeling a little better," she said.

"Better how?"

"Maybe a little more relaxed, a little wider awake."

"You know, Zoe, I don't really understand your illness. Would you mind explaining it to me?"

She had told it so many times, to so many people, and yet it was still difficult to explain. "I just get this feeling…it's come over me on and off since I was a child, that I'm removed from reality. I can see the whole scene, everything that's happening, but I'm not a part of it."

"That sounds really frightening."

"And then I get depressed."

"It's no wonder. It sounds terrible."

"It is. It's worse than terrible. I can't live my life; I can't do anything. And I've tried everything, and nothing helps. I'll be all right for a while, and then boom, it's there again."

"I can see why you want to stay in your bedroom," Doug said.

"At first, Mom and Dad and my sister and brother tried to make me leave. But now, they've all given up."

"Is there anything else you want to tell me?" he asked.

She thought about her voice, the Destroyer. "Yes," she said. She knew if she told him about that he'd really think she was nuts. But if he was going to help her, she had to be honest with him. "I have this voice inside me that keeps chattering away. I can't stop it no matter how hard I try."

"And what does this voice tell you?"

"All kinds of terrible things."

"Like?"

She sighed. Did she have the strength to go through it all? "Terrible things," she said.

"Just tell me one or two," he said.

"It tells me I'm never going to get better. It tells me I'm going to lose my children." If only she were part of the real world, she would begin sobbing now. In fact, there were tears escaping her eyes.

"One more thing?"

"Yes. It tells me to kill myself."

Doug was silent, thinking. "Let's try something," he said. "Instead of trying to stop the voice, let it say what it wants, like a thought that comes to you and then passes through."

"How do I do that?"

"Just don't fight it. Let it say what it wants, and then it's over."

"No, it won't be over. It'll just keep talking."

"Let it talk, but don't pay attention to it. Just like you're listening to the radio."

"I don't understand and I don't think I can do it."

"Okay," he said, "okay." Then thinking again. "Is the voice there, now?"

"Yes," she said. "It's always there."

"Okay then, tell me what it's saying."

"You really want to hear?"

"Yes. I want to hear it all."

"Okay," she said, wondering where all this was going. "It's saying that you're a quack, that you can't cure me, no one can. And

I'm a loser for listening to you. That all this breathing is a bunch of bull, and that I'm never going to be normal. I'm never going to get my girls back. Eric is going to get full custody, and I'm just going to spend the rest of my life in this bed, a burden to my family. So I may as well kill myself now and save everyone a lot of trouble and problems. Besides, my girls will be better off without me. Eric's mother is ten times a better mother than I'll ever be." She paused.

"Anything else?"

"Yes. I just have to find a way to end it. We've already decided on the pills. I just have to figure out what kind and how many and how to get them. Maybe I can dupe you into getting them for me, or Claire might do it. She'll understand why I want to die and she'll probably be glad to be rid of me. I've been such a burden on her life. And everyone else in my family. May as well get it over with so everyone can go back to their normal lives."

"Anything else?"

Zoe was silent for a moment. And so was the voice. She had said it all.

"No," she said. "That's it for now. But it'll be back."

"Yes, it will," Doug said, "but if you just let it go on and on and don't really listen to it, it will lose its power."

"I don't think so," Zoe said.

"Not immediately," Doug said, "but eventually."

"I'll try," Zoe said.

"No, don't try. Just let it happen. Don't try, don't fight it, just let it say whatever it wants and the words will pass through, like the wind in the trees."

"Okay," Zoe said.

He stood up, leaned over, kissed her forehead and said, "Keep breathing, and I'll see you tomorrow. Same time."

As he walked out the door, Zoe thought, how strange, but she was looking forward to seeing him tomorrow. And she realized, she had been looking forward to seeing him every day once she believed he would come. She did not usually look forward to anything when she was in this state. She just wanted to be left alone. So this was a good sign; a sign that she might be returning to life.

The next day, after breathing together, Doug, again, asked her to recite everything the voice was saying, and she told him, "It's saying that this whole thing is a joke. That you're putting on a good show, but it won't last. You're going to get tired of this whole thing and then you're going to abandon me. I shouldn't get my hopes up. What could a little deep breathing do to cure my illness? No, it is all going to come to nothing. I will never get the girls back. I'm just going to spend the rest of my life in this room. I will never have the courage to leave it, to go out into the world. What use am I to my children or my family? I'm only causing all of them pain, and now I'm wasting Doug's time besides. No, I have to end the torture to myself and everyone around me as soon as possible. The pills, I have to figure out the pills. I have to get those pills, and then I will have peace."

"Anything else?"

"Yes. This whole thing is a waste of time. Tell him to go and never come back. You can't depend on him. He'll desert you eventually."

"Anything else?"

She waited a minute. "Not at this moment."

"Okay then. Anything else you want to say to me?"

"Just thank you. I don't know what I did to deserve all your time and patience."

"It's simple," he said. "I like you."

"How can you like me in this condition?"

"Because what you're in, is just a condition. It isn't you."

"But what is it about me you like?"

"It's nothing that can be explained. Why does anyone like another person?"

"I don't know," she said.

"Neither do I," he said. "Let's just call it chemistry."

She thought a moment. "Some doctors believe it's chemistry that's making me ill."

"Maybe it is, but maybe it isn't. Let's just go with the 'isn't' for now and see what happens." He leaned over and kissed her forehead. "See you tomorrow."

"Yes, tomorrow," she said, disappointed that he was leaving, already looking forward to tomorrow.

At the end of the month, Zoe knew things were better. The voice kept talking but she wasn't fighting it. Just letting the words pass through like the wind in the trees. And her energy was returning. She ventured downstairs at some point every day to play the piano. The notes were like foreign strangers to her; not because she had forgotten how to play, but because she wasn't sure it was she who was playing. But still she persisted, trying to focus not on her fingers but on reading the notes, on the written music.

On Doug's thirtieth visit, he found Zoe sitting on the chair in her bedroom, fully dressed. "I want to go outside," she said.

"You mean out of the bedroom?" he asked.

"No, I mean outside."

"Shall we breathe first?"

"No, after. I don't want to lose my nerve."

"Okay, outside it is."

They walked down the stairs, past Gail sitting on the pink, purple, green flowered living room sofa reading a book and looking up amazed, and then out the front door. For a moment, Zoe recoiled. She was not used to the sun or the heat.

Doug closed the front door behind her and she took careful steps, like a baby learning to walk, down the concrete pathway leading to the sidewalk. She decided to walk to the left because there was a steep incline at the end of her street to the right. She wanted to make this first exploration outside as easy as possible.

Doug walked along beside her past the tan house next door, with its expansive lawn and tropical plants, past the dark pink adobe house with a bed of flowers in the middle of the lawn, past the white house with green shutters at the corner with its perfectly trimmed hedges and blue and pink hydrangeas. How good the sun felt, the hot air, and Zoe realized she had been living in air-conditioning for days, and that she had been cold at times.

They crossed the street, waiting for a black SUV to cross in front of them.

"How are you doing?" Doug asked.

"It feels good to be out."

"It's a hot day," Doug said.

"I know, but I like it."

They walked past several more houses on the next block, all with well kept lawns, some with extensive landscaping, others simply done, some with lots of flowers, some with just shrubs. Zoe knew the inside layout of every house they passed. There were only four floor-plans in her tract, and while the outsides might have some variation, she knew the exact layout of the inside.

"So how do you like our new president?" Doug asked, as if they were two ordinary people out for a walk.

"I don't like him at all."

"So you voted for Gore?" Doug asked.

"Yes, and I think he really won the election," she said.

"Because...?" he asked.

"Because he really won Florida and if he won Florida, he won the election."

"I'm not much into politics," Doug said, "but I think you're right."

"I used to love politics," she said.

"You did? Then what happened?"

I disappeared, she said to herself. "I still do love it," she said, "when I'm present."

He took her hand, and it was almost too much. To be out in the sun and the warmth walking beside this man she adored.... how sad that she couldn't be part of it.

He chose not to say the obvious, that "someday you will be present," but said instead, "Did you ever work for anyone?"

"Yes," she said, "I worked for Walter Mondale. Partially because he had a woman running-mate. I thought that it would be neat to have a woman as vice-president."

"And was it fun?"

"If you call only winning one state fun."

He laughed. "What I should have said was, did you enjoy working on the campaign?"

"Yes, I did. I made phone calls, a thousand phone calls, but it was all in vain. I was invited to go to the party at the Biltmore Hotel the night of the election, but I chose not to."

"Why?"

"Because I knew it was going to be a big crowd, and as you know, I don't like big crowds. Besides, I had just gotten over a three month episode, and I couldn't take any chances."

They had come to the end of the block and were re-tracing their steps back to her house.

"I guess there's a lot I don't know about you," he said.

"But you know more than any other person in my life."

"Yes," he said. "I suppose I do."

Gail was waiting outside the front door for them as they approached the house. She noticed that Doug was holding Zoe's hand, and wondered if something romantic was going on between them. But how could there be? Zoe was incapable of feeling anything but fear.

"Hi, honey. Did you have a good walk?" Gail asked.

Zoe filled with resentment. Why was her mother waiting for her and talking to her as if she were a child. "Yes, fine."

Doug walked Zoe up to her room where they did their deep breathing together, and then did some stretches together, and then he asked her if there was anything she wanted to tell him, and she said, "My voice was very quiet during our walk, but now it's saying that one walk does not a healthy person make. That I'm going to just crawl into my bed and go back to being as far away as before Doug entered my life."

"Anything else?" he asked.

She blushed. "I'm really afraid to say this."

"Say it anyway," he said.

"It's saying don't get your hopes up about Doug. He would never want a girl like you."

He hesitated a moment. "Anything else?"

She thought a moment. "No, that's all."

"Okay," he said. "I'll see you tomorrow. Same time."

As he got to the door, she said, "I think I'll go downstairs and spend some time with my mother."

"Okay," he said. "I'll walk you down."

The next afternoon when Doug arrived, Gail was waiting for him.

"How are things going?" she asked.

"Things are going well," he said.

"You know, I can't thank you enough for all the time you're spending with Zoe and how much you're helping her. She was actually downstairs playing the piano most of the afternoon and evening yesterday. I think she's feeling better."

"I hope so," Doug said.

"Don't you see it?" Gail asked.

"It's not my place to make judgments," Doug said.

"But surely you see that she's getting better."

"As I said, I'm not making any judgments."

Gail felt a bit frustrated, but she wasn't going to pick an argument with the person who was helping her daughter. "Whatever you say, Doug."

That afternoon, Zoe and Doug went for a walk, and then every day for the next week, and on the following Monday, she told him, "I think I'd like a Whopper." She'd been dreaming about a big fat hamburger with cheese dripping down the sides.

"Sure," he said. So he drove her over to the closest Burger King and then asked, "Do you want to go inside, or sit in the car?"

"I think I'd like to go inside."

At two in the afternoon, the place was empty, except for an elderly couple over in the corner.

She stood at the counter ordering with him, and then let him pick up her hamburger and diet Coke and bring it to their table. As she bit into the Whopper, she actually tasted all the flavors, the beef, the mustard, ketchup, pickles and cheese. How delicious it was.

"How is it?" he asked, drinking from his large ice water. He didn't drink any carbonated beverages, or any with sugar or caffeine. She knew this when she ordered her diet Coke, but much as she wanted to please him, at this moment she wanted to indulge herself more.

"Delicious," she said.

He smiled the happiest smile she had ever seen on him. "I'm so glad," he said.

The next afternoon, after their breathing and taking their walk, Doug told her that he wouldn't be coming over every day anymore.

They were standing in her bedroom, near the door as he was about to leave.

She was dismayed. "But why?"

"I just think it would be best for you. But the days I don't come, we'll talk on the phone so you can tell me all your thoughts."

"But I need you," she said. "I can't do without you."

"Yes," he said, "I think you can."

"Oh, Doug," she said, putting her arms around him, "I don't think you understand. I'm in love with you."

"No," he said, "what you're feeling isn't love. Maybe gratitude."

"No," she said, "it's love."

He was holding her now, "I do love you, Zoe, and I will always love you, but not in that way. It's kind of like we're doctor and patient, and patients always fall in love with their doctors. You know that. It's called transference. But it's not real love."

"Yes it is," she said, laying her head against his chest.

"I'll tell you what," Doug said, stroking her hair, "when you call me tomorrow, you can tell me all about it."

She smiled and let go of him. "I'd like to tell you now."

"You already did," he said with a grin. "And now, here's the plan..."

He told her that she should call him every three hours, starting at nine in the morning, and ending at nine at night...or later if she wished, to tell him whatever she wanted to tell him. Then he kissed her on the cheek and was walking out the door, when she asked, "When will I see you again?"

"I think Thursday at one. Is that okay?"

"I guess it'll have to be," she said.

"Talk to you tomorrow," he said, and he was out the door and down the stairs.

Chapter Sixteen — Molly and Sophie

At my next visit to see Dr. Berg, I told him I wanted to cut down on my drugs. Doug was totally against all drugs, and wanted me off all of them, but Dr. Berg said he would have to wean me off them gradually, or I would have a bad reaction. Also, he talked me into staying on Wellbutran for the immediate future. I agreed to that because, actually, I was afraid to be without some drug.

Doug kept cutting down his visits to me, I guess he was also trying to wean me off of him, but I spoke to him five times a day, repeating everything the Destroyer had said to me, and telling him all my fears, just spewing them out one after the other until I ran out of them. And then he'd say, "Talk to you in awhile," and we'd hang up the phone.

He also got me started on jogging every morning. At first he went with me, but again, he wanted me to do it on my own. He told me to try to stay in the present, not think about the past or future, but only the now. The past was in the past. It was over and there was no way to change it. The future was unpredictable, so what was the sense in thinking about it. All we had was this moment, now, the present. That's all there is and all there is to think about.

He also talked a lot about Truth. Truth was who we are when we are free of fear. He kept telling me to go with Truth, to trust my instincts and especially not to engage my thoughts. Just let them pass though. If I didn't pay attention to them, they wouldn't have any power. Yes, easier said than done.

On one of his visits, he brought me some books to read: The *Way of Zen, The Tao Te Ching, The Relaxation Response* and *The Tao of Pooh.* I read all of them over and over. He also fixed me up with a new therapist, a psychologist named Marcy Jacobs, who espoused all his philosophies. I began seeing her every week, having his ideas reinforced, and it was good, just talking to her.

With each passing day, the fuzziness was leaving me. I was now talking to Doug only three times a week, still doing my breathing twice a day, still jogging every morning, seeing my shrink every week, attending Doug's yoga class on Wednesday nights, and practicing the piano every day.

Even cutting down on my drugs, or perhaps because of it, I was feeling better and better every day, until one day I awoke, and it was gone. I looked around my room and there was my dresser, my desk, my jeans thrown over my desk chair, and everything was real.

I got out of bed and looked in the mirror. It was my face I saw. I licked my lips and they were mine. I ran my hands up my arms and squeezed my skin until it hurt. I took a shower and turned the hot water up so high that it nearly scalded me and I screamed. Not because it had burned me, but because I had felt it.

After my shower, I knelt on my knees beside my bed, feeling a little silly because I didn't really believe in God, and I put my hands together and I said aloud, "Thank you, God. Thank you," and the tears crept out of my eyes.

It had been three months since I had left the world, and though I was still feeling a bit insecure, I decided it was time to get my girls back and go back to teaching.

Going back to teaching was not a problem. I was good friends with my principal and she had hired a long term sub to take my place until I came back.

Getting my girls back was the problem. Although I had signed the paper giving Eric temporary custody, he now informed me, on my third telephone call to his office, that he would not give the girls back to me without a court hearing. "I just want to do what's best for the girls," he said.

"But Eric, you know me. You know I have these cycles and then I get over them. You know I always get through the school year without a problem."

"In the past, yes. But who can predict the future."

"Eric, my daughters need me. If you want to do what's best for them, then you'll let me have them back."

"All I'm asking is that you prove it to a judge. If you prove it to a judge, then I'll go along with it."

I wanted to slam down the phone in anger, but I held back. I didn't want to do anything to antagonize him, even though at this moment I hated his guts. "It's going to cost a lot of money; we're both going to have to hire lawyers."

"Sorry," he said, "that's my deal."

What choice did I have? "All right," I said, "but can I have them this weekend?"

He hesitated. "You're sure you're all right?"

"Yes. Completely normal."

"All right. I'll drop them off at ten on Saturday morning, and I'll pick them up at seven on Sunday."

I held back my tears, but my heart was bursting with joy. I was going to see my girls. Even if it was only for two days, it was a start. "Thank you, Eric," I said.

After I hung up the phone, I went to the piano and played the Brahms A Minor Intermezzo, a few Chopin Nocturnes and Etudes, and then the entire Beethoven Tempest Sonata. I played for hours, until I was exhausted. My girls were coming home.

On Saturday morning at ten, my daughters arrived.

Oooooh, what a homecoming!

I was standing outside the house waiting for them as nervous as the day of my wedding, and when they emerged from Eric's new silver Mercedes, I was stunned. How much they'd grown, how much older they looked. We ran into each other's arms, and stood on that sidewalk hugging and kissing, and hugging and kissing some more. I couldn't get enough of them; they couldn't get enough of me.

Finally, we went into the house, and they told me all about school, and how camp had been, and how it was living with daddy, and yes, a word or two about his girlfriend, whose name was Gloria, but whom they called Glory. I only wanted to know one thing about Glory, "Is she nice to you?"

"Very nice," they both said. And speaking of glory, what a glorious two days we had. We spent the weekend shopping at the mall—they especially loved an accessory store named *Claire's*, and going to the movies, and to the ice skating rink. Because of all the ice skating birthday parties they'd been to, they'd both become pretty good skaters. I watched as they whirled around the rink, feeling so much heat towards them that I thought the ice would melt.

Molly was now 11 and reminded me very much of her father. She was tall, with curly brownish-blonde hair, hazel eyes, and obsessed with doing well in school...which also reminded me of myself. But I think she was quieter than I was, and more serious.

Sophie, on the other hand, looked more like me, with black straight hair and green eyes, but her personality was all Claire... very upbeat, fun-loving, out-going, sociable.

Still, the two of them got along really well, perhaps because they needed each other with all the ups and downs in their home-life. I think that my illness may have affected Molly more than Sophie, and I couldn't help but blame myself for her somewhat withdrawn personality. But I don't want to paint too black a picture of Molly...she was still fun to be with, and both girls had a great sense of humor, and we had a totally wonderful two days together.

And then on Sunday at seven, Eric arrived to take them to his house. My stomach was in turmoil as I walked them out to his car. He got out and walked around to where we were standing.

"Hi, Zoe," he said. "You're looking good."

"Thanks," I said, "So are you." I was trying to sound normal, chatty, friendly, because my only goal at that moment was to get him to let me see my girls again as soon as possible. "So Eric," I said, "when can I see the girls again?"

"I'm not sure," he said.

"What about next weekend?"

"I'm not sure," he said again. "We'll see." And then turning to Molly and Sophie, "C'mon, girls, we have to go."

My body was tingling, not my depersonalization tingling, but because I was so nervous. I had to hold steady, to look normal. "When will you let me know?"

"Sometime during the week."

"Why? What's going to happen during the week?"

"Zoe, I really don't want to discuss this now."

"Well, when can we discuss it?"

"I don't know," he said.

I felt I was losing control, but I couldn't help it. "Eric," I said, "why are you doing this to me?"

He paused. "Because you're ill."

I thought of saying, you left them with me for years when I was ill. But instead I said, "No, I am not ill anymore. I'm fine."

"That's for the court to decide," he said. And then to our daughters, "C'mon, girls, it's time to go."

Still not willing to give up, I said, "If I can't have them next weekend, can I have them the weekend, after?"

"I already told you. We'll see."

I could see it would be fruitless to go on arguing with him, and even more fruitless if I appeared angry or upset, so I took both my girls in my arms, and held them as if I would never let go. They held tightly to me, too, and began crying, "I don't want to leave you, mommy," and I told them I didn't want them to leave either, but they had to go now, but I would do everything in my power to see them again as soon as possible. Finally, I had to let go.

I held my tears in check as they got into Eric's silver Mercedes, but as soon as it turned the corner, I began to sob, relentlessly, non-stoppably. How could he take my girls from me?

On Monday when I got home from school, there was that same process server who had served me with the divorce papers waiting at my front door. "Are you Zoe Simoneau?" he asked, as if he didn't know.

"Yes," I said.

He handed me a large tan envelope, "You are served," he said, and walked down the cement walkway to his car.

As soon as I got into the house, I tore open the envelope and shuffled through the papers. As I read them, I felt as if I'd been stabbed in my gut. My first reaction was to call Eric and scream at him, but my second reaction was more sensible. I called Claire at her office. "Claire, I need your help again," I said. "I've just been served with papers from Eric. They're about the girls. He wants full physical and legal custody of them. I can't let that happen. We've got to stop him. We've got to."

"And we will," Claire said. "You need to make an appointment with Steve Fein as soon as possible."

I hesitated. I didn't mind going to Steve about my divorce, which had been in limbo all this time, but a custody battle, where he'd find out all about me? I didn't think that was a good idea. My parents still hadn't told any of their friends about my malady, and if he found out, mightn't he tell someone, like his wife, and then everyone would find out? "Maybe we should go to someone who's not a friend of our parents."

"Don't worry about it.," Claire told me. "There's such a thing as attorney/client privilege and if he's an ethical guy, and I believe he is, he won't tell anyone anything, not even his wife."

I still hesitated. I'd done enough harm to my parents, I didn't want to do anymore. "Are you sure?"

"Yes, I'm sure. You just don't know how many incompetent lawyers there are out there. I think Steve is the best....and that's what you need....the best."

"Okay, then," I said reluctantly, "I'll make an appointment. Will you come with me?"

"Of course," she said. "I'll check my schedule to see what times I'm available."

"Great," I said, full of gratitude.

We went on a Wednesday at 3:30, after school for me.

Steve's office was pretty intimidating. To me, he'd always been just a friend of my parents, a nice-looking middle-aged guy, with a head of brown hair and rimless glasses. I had never seen him in a suit and tie, or in such a formal setting as his office, with its huge black desk, black leather pull up chairs, black leather sofa, and a floor to ceiling glass window that looked out on the hills of Encino.

"Nice office," I said, handing him the package of documents.

"Would you like anything to drink?" he asked, taking them.

"No," we both answered, "we're fine."

After we were seated, he leaned forward. "I spoke to Eric's attorney this morning and we agreed to put the divorce on hold until after the custody hearing."

"Sounds good to me," I said.

"Now let's take a look at these," he said, pulling the papers out of the tan envelope and reading through them. "I see he's asking for full custody of your daughters, alleging that you're an unfit mother. Can you tell me about that?"

I looked at Claire and she looked at me. *Well here goes*, both our looks said.

Then I began to talk. I told him about my illness, and how it seemed to happen every summer, and what had transpired between Eric and me the last few months. He didn't seem disturbed by anything I told him, just listened intently, and when I was finished, he leaned back in his black judge's chair, folded his hands on his big black desk, and said, "We may have a problem here."

I felt the blackness of his office invade the cells of my brain, shutting out all light and hope.

Claire stepped in, "But can it be fixed?"

"I hope it can," he said, "but it's going to depend on a few people. The court will appoint an evaluator who will interview Eric, Zoe, and the girls, and probably Zoe's psychiatrist to determine if Zoe is capable of caring for her children." Then looking at Zoe. "He will testify to that, won't he?"

I was amazed to discover that I didn't know the answer to that question. "I don't know," I said.

"Well, unless he will," Steve said, "we're going to have to find a therapist who will. Only problem is, if we don't call your therapist to testify, the other side surely will."

My heart dropped to my toes. "Oh God, this is terrible."

"Well, don't lose hope," Steve said. "We're going to do our best to at least get you joint custody."

"That's all I ask for," I said. "It's not what I want, but if that's all I can get, then I'll be thrilled."

"Give me the name and phone number of your psychiatrist and I'll contact him as soon as you leave."

"The thing is, Steve," I said, "I actually have two therapists: my psychiatrist and my psychologist."

"Then I'll need both numbers. Now, if you have some time, I'd like to go over these papers."

"Yes, I have time," I said.

"Well, you don't need me for that," Claire said, standing up, "so I'm going back to work." She kissed me, and Steve stood up and they hugged each other, and she said to him, "Take good care of my big sister."

"I will," he said.

After Claire left, Steve and I went over the papers and the more I read, the more depressed I got, but also the more determined to win.

The court date for the custody hearing was set for October 11, 1991, just one month after the horrendous attack on 9/11. I think all of us who passed through the metal detector at the courthouse that morning couldn't help but think about that day. It had been a devastating event in my life...like the loss of innocence. I had always taken my safety from foreign attack for granted, and now that illusion had been shattered. I mourned for my daughters who would grow up with all these fears that hadn't existed before; that they would never feel as safe as all the past generations of Americans, and I worried that it was only a matter of time before something like this happened again. Who knew what or when it would happen? But I felt that it would. If only I could lock my girls in my house forever. But as of this moment, they didn't even belong to me.

At nine o'clock, the four of us appeared in the courtroom: Eric and his attorney, Mr. McCormack (a stocky man with bristly white hair), me, and my attorney, Steve Fein. Claire didn't come because she knew nothing important was going to happen that day, and sure enough all that happened was that the two attorneys went out into the hall and agreed on an evaluator and then came back into the courtroom, told the judge (an elderly man with a kind face) who it was, and he appointed a Ms. Eftie Partamian, to be the evaluator.

"What happens next?" I asked Steve, as soon as the two of us were back out in the hall.

"The evaluator will contact you and set up an interview with you. She's also going to interview your psychiatrist."

"And what about Eric and the children?"

"Yes, she's going to interview them, too."

I was already feeling goose-bumps. "I just hope Eric's half as nervous as I am," I said.

"I'm sure he is," Steve said, as we exited the building just ahead of Eric and his attorney.

Eric and I had said nothing to each other, not even 'hello.' I just couldn't bring myself to even look at him, I hated him so much.

The evaluator, Ms. Partaminian, called me the next day and I made an appointment to go see her on a Thursday afternoon after school. I was a nervous wreck as I parked in the underground parking facility of her building. This was life or death. This was will I get my daughters back for half the time, one week a month, one weekend a month, or not at all.

I was shaking as I entered the elevator. Why hadn't I asked Mom or Claire to come with me? Or maybe even Andrew. He was so lighthearted, he would have kept me calm. As I approached the door of Ms. Partamian's office, I thought of Doug. I thought how odd it was that I hadn't thought of Doug first. It was then, I realized an amazing fact: I wasn't depersonalized. All this tension, pressure, worry, and I was nervous, yes, shaking, yes, but I was not depersonalized. I was just suffering like any normal person.

There was just a tiny waiting room outside Ms. Partamian's office. No receptionist and no one else waiting. As I was about to take a seat, she came out to get me. She was a small, dark woman, neatly dressed in a black and white pin-striped suit, who held out her hand to shake mine. "I'm Ms. Partamian," she said. "And you must be Zoe Simoneau."

"Yes," I said.

"Nice to meet you," she said, and led me into her office. There was a small wood desk, a brown leather sofa, an easy chair, and a coffee table in front of the sofa with a box of tissues sitting on it—I already felt I needed one. The room was cozy, fresh flowers and framed photos on her desk, several green plants scattered about the room, and books and knick-knacks in a walnut wood bookcase.

I felt as comfortable and at ease as I could under the circumstances.

"Have a seat," she said, and motioned me to the sofa as she sat on the easy chair with a yellow pad of paper and a well-sharpened yellow pencil in her hand. "So," she said, "tell me about your disease."

I settled back and began my story. I had told it so many times to so many therapists that the words came easily. It didn't matter that this was a life and death situation, the story was still the same. Steve had warned me to tell the truth, because everything was going to come out one way or another in court.

"You know," she said, "I'm really not familiar with the term 'depersonalization', but I am familiar with the term dissociative behavior, so I'm assuming it's very similar. Now tell me more about this voice."

You would have to fasten on that, I thought. "It basically tries to sabotage me by telling me that I'm going to get depersonalized, and that could create enough fear in me so that I would become depersonalized."

"Well is it a separate entity, or part of you?"

"No," I said. "I know it's just my alter-ego. I don't have a split personality if that's what you mean."

"And does it ever tell you terrible things. Things you may never have shared with anyone before."

I thought carefully before answering. I knew what she was looking for. "It only tries to destroy my confidence," and then hesitantly, "to destroy me."

"What about your daughters? Does it ever talk to you about your daughters?"

"No, only to tell me that Eric is going to take them away from me and I'm never going to get them back."

"What about physical harm?"

"Not to my daughters. Absolutely not. Or to anyone else."

"What about you?"

I wanted to lie. I wanted so badly to lie. "Only when I've been so totally out-of-it, it has told me to commit suicide."

The words sounded shocking even to me, and I could see the disappointment in Ms. Partamian's face.

I couldn't let this happen, I couldn't. "Ms. Partamian," I said. "I want you to know that even in my deepest depression, my girls have always meant the most to me of anything in the world. I would never hurt them. In fact, if I thought there was the slightest chance I could ever hurt them, I would give them to Eric in an instant. But my disease doesn't make me violent or irrational. In fact, my problem is I'm too rational, I think of too many problems.

"All these years, I've managed to take care of my girls, good care of them. I've done what I've had to do. Of course, I've had help. My family's been wonderful, and I have a wonderful caretaker for them, who's been like a second mother to them. They've never missed out on anything. They go to school every day, to camp every summer, they've had ballet lessons, and swimming lessons, and they both play soccer, and we go to the library every two weeks to get books, and I'm teaching them to play the piano, and now Molly is going to Hebrew school. Through everything I've been through, I have always been a good mother. Even Eric will tell you that. Please Ms. Partamian, don't take my girls from me. They need me."

Ms. Partamian had sat quietly listening to every word I said.

"Zoe," she said, "if I may call you that, I sympathize with your plight, and I would like to do everything I can to see that you have some time with your daughters. Let me ask you, as far as the disease, what point are you at today, this moment?"

"Right now, at this moment, I am perfectly normal."

"And what are the chances that you will be cured someday?"

"I actually feel that I will be cured some day. Perhaps I already am. I've been seeing a new psychologist and also an expert in Eastern philosophy who's using a different approach and this approach seems to be working."

"Who is this person?"

"His name is Doug Ladea."

"And what are his credentials?"

What was he really? I felt a little embarrassed. "He's a certified yoga instructor," I said, "but he knows a lot about Eastern philosophy."

Ms. Partamian's eyelids closed for an instant. "And what is his approach?"

"He has me meditating twice a day, every day, and when I have a negative thought, I don't dwell on it, or try to fight it. I just let it pass through like the wind in the trees. I'm also jogging, and trying to stay in the present, and I've also cut down on my medication, and I'm still not getting depersonalized. I mean, if I was ever going to get depersonalized, it would have been coming here today. But I'm not."

"And your voice?"

"I haven't heard my voice for two months now."

Ms. Partamian looked at her watch. "Well, time's up, but I do want to come for a home visit and I want your daughters to be there. Is tomorrow at 3:30 convenient for you?"

"Yes," I said, "anytime after school is convenient for me."

"Good. Then I'll call Eric and make sure that he can have the girls there by 3:45. If there's a problem, I'll call you, but otherwise, I'll see you tomorrow at 3:30."

"Great," I said, focusing on only one thing, I would get to see my girls tomorrow...no matter for how short a time.

We both stood and she held out her hand. "It's been nice meeting you," she said, and we shook hands.

"Nice meeting you, too," I said.

She walked me to the waiting room, and waited until I was out in the hall, before closing the door behind me.

After my initial elation at getting to see my girls the next day, all the way to my car, I began to worry about all I had said to Ms. Partamian. I didn't know if I had done well or not. I had told the truth, and said what I wanted to say. There was nothing more I could do. Just go home and make sure my house was as neat as it could be. Everything depended on Ms. Partamian.

The next afternoon, I was again feeling pretty nervous—partially because of Ms. Partamian and partially because I would get to see my daughters. Ms. Partamian arrived promptly at 3:30. I showed her through the house with my flowery prints and dried and fresh flowers, papers still piled high in the den—there was no way to neaten that room, the yard with the last roses of the fall still blooming, then upstairs to the children's bedrooms, both spic and span with ruffled bedspreads, desks, stuffed animals, and bookcases filled with books, games and art supplies, then back downstairs where I offered her tea or coffee, just as the doorbell rang.

I hurried to open it with her right behind me, and there were my two beautiful daughters. They both ran into my arms and we stood hugging and kissing each other and me telling them how much I missed them and them telling me how much they missed me. I noticed Eric sitting in his Mercedes, apparently going to wait for them.

After the girls and I finally broke apart, and I introduced them to Ms. Partamian, whom they said they had already met, Ms. Partamian asked if I would mind waiting in the den while she talked to my daughters in the kitchen.

I said, "No, of course not."

I waited in the den for what seemed an hour, trying to concentrate on correcting papers, or going over my plans for the next day. But it didn't matter how hard I tried, I could concentrate on nothing, I could think about nothing, except what must be going on in the kitchen. What was she asking my daughters, and how were they responding? I knew they loved me and wanted to be with me, but would that be enough for Ms. Partamian?

Finally, finally, they came running into the den. "Don't worry, mommy," Molly said. "I know she's going to let us come back to you."

They both had their arms around me, and I noticed Ms. Partamian in the hallway watching.

It seemed a minute later that Ms. Partamian said it was time for the girls to go. I walked them to the door and it took a few minutes for the three of us to let go of each other. Molly and Sophie were crying and I was crying, and Ms. Partamian was watching. Eric got out of his car and began walking up the pathway.

"Time to go, girls," Eric called.

They pulled away from me and went to meet their father.

Ms. Partamian held out her hand to me. "Thank you," she said. And then, "You have two wonderful daughters. You should be proud."

"I am," I said, praying that was a good sign.

"Well then," she said, "I'll see you in court."

"Yes," I said, "see you in court." And she was out the door.

I felt up, then down, full, then empty. If ever I needed to spew out my thoughts, it was at this moment. I called Doug.

Our next court date was November 15. This time, there were eight of us attending: Eric and his attorney, Mr. McCormack, Steve and I, Ms. Partamian, Dr. Berg, and my mom and Claire.

It was the perfect setting for me to become depersonalized, in this strange environment, on the most important day of my life, and while I felt jittery, tense, frightened, they were all normal feelings that any person in my predicament would feel.

I watched as each person took the stand.

In response to Steve's questioning, Dr. Berg testified that while I had this illness, which he didn't know the cause of or the cure for, in his opinion, there was no risk that I would harm my children.

Then it was Eric's attorney's turn to question him. "How can you be so certain that Mrs. Simoneau won't harm the children?" Eric's attorney asked. "Isn't it true, doctor, that you don't really know much about this disease?"

"I know as much as anyone else," Dr. Berg said, a bit defensive.

"Yes, but you don't know what causes it, you don't know what cures it, and you don't know all the ramifications of it. Isn't that true?"

Dr. Berg cleared his throat. "On the basis of what we do know, however, we know that no violence has been attached to this disease."

"How about suicide? Has that ever happened to someone who suffers from depersonalization?"

"The statistics are mainly anecdotal," Dr. Berg answered, "and depersonalization disorder is very closely related to many other disorders."

"Well then, anecdotally, has anyone who suffers from depersonalization disorder and/or these other closely related disorders ever committed suicide?"

Dr. Berg, reluctantly, "Well, of course there have been suicides and suicide attempts from these other disorders, but as far as I know, I can't specifically say that a person suffering from depersonalization disorder has ever committed suicide. And furthermore, there is no evidence, even anecdotally, that a depersonalized person has ever harmed another person."

"But it could happen, couldn't it, doctor?"

"And you could walk outside and get hit by a car," the doctor said. "We have to go by what we know, and to my knowledge, there are no studies and no statistics for attempted suicide, suicide or homicide committed by a person suffering from depersonalization disorder."

Eric's attorney thought for a moment. "We don't even know how to define a depersonalized person, isn't that correct, doctor?"

"No, but we do have behaviors that fit into that category."

"But couldn't Mrs. Simoneau have some other disease, like depression, or schizophrenia?"

"She could have some symptoms in common with those disorders," my doctor said, "but her symptoms are best described as depersonalization disorder."

The attorney looked over his notes. "No more questions for this witness."

Steve stood, "Redirect, your honor."

The judge nodded his approval.

"Doctor, how would you describe my client's present condition?"

He thought a moment, then cleared his throat, "I'd say she's doing better than ever. We've cut down her meds, and as of this moment, she is a perfectly well, functional human being."

"Thank you," Steve said, "no more questions."

When Dr. Berg left the witness box, he smiled at me. I'm not sure I ever saw him smile before.

The next person to testify was Ms. Partamian. "I have interviewed all of the parties involved in this proceeding, per my report. I find that Eric Simoneau is an excellent father, that both Molly and Sophie are well adjusted, loving children who don't feel neglected or unloved in any way. They know that their mother gets sick at times, but they still love her and want to live with her." She locked eyes with mine as she said, "I believe that Zoe Simoneau is a responsible, loving, and fit mother and should have joint custody of her children, on the condition that if and when she does become depersonalized, she hands over full custody to Eric Simoneau until she is well again. I also request the court to revisit the situation every six months to be sure Mrs. Simoneau's condition is stable."

I only heard one phrase in all she said, "should have joint custody." When she came down from the witness stand, I wanted to run to her, to hug her, to kiss her, to thank her, but I could not.

I heard my name called, and for a moment I turned numb, as if a dentist had just injected me with Novocain. There was no feeling in my arms, legs, or feet, but I forced myself up, and began walking to the witness stand, my legs so wobbly, I didn't know if I could make it, except I had to.

Then I was seated. I took my deep breaths, and Steve took me through every question we had prepared for.

Then it was Eric's attorney's turn. "So, Mrs. Simoneau, you testified that you want to do everything possible for your daughters. Isn't that right?

"Yes," I said, feeling slightly more confident.

"Well, don't you think the best thing you could do for your daughters is let your husband take care of them?"

"No," I said.

"But your disease..." he said. "It's unpredictable. What if you're at the movies and you have an attack, or at the mall and you have an attack? Or driving and you have an attack?"

"It isn't like that," I said. "I can still behave normally, rationally."

"You mean, while you're depersonalized?"

"Yes," I said. "Even though I don't feel that I'm in reality, I can pretend to others that I am."

He thought a moment, "So are you pretending now?"

"No," I said, calmly. "I am not depersonalized now."

"Well how are we to know?"

Steve stood up, "Objection your honor, badgering the witness."

"Move on, Mr. McCormack," the judge said.

"Yes, your honor," and then back to me. "Is it true you hear voices?"

"Only one voice, a voice within my head."

"And do you do whatever this voice tells you to do?"

"It doesn't really tell me what to do. It mainly undermines my confidence."

"Has it ever told you to commit suicide?"

I knew this was killing me, but I had to answer, "Yes."

"Has it ever told you to kill your children?"

"Never," I said, hating this man as much as I hated Eric.

"No more questions," Mr. McCormack said.

I walked down from the witness box in a daze. It had been horrible. More horrible than I could have imagined.

Next, Mr. McCormack called Eric to the stand, and after he was sworn in, Eric answered several questions intended to demonstrate that he was an exemplary father and most capable of taking care of the girls.

When Mr. McCormack was finished, Steve stood and approached the witness stand.

"Mr. Simoneau, you have lived with Zoe as man and wife for 13 years. Is that correct?"

"Yes," Eric answered.

"And in all that time was there ever a day, one single day when you did not trust your children to Zoe's care?"

"Well I wasn't comfortable when she was ill."

"Well, did you stay home from work to look after them?"

He paused, and then reluctantly, "No."

Tears came to my eyes and I thought, God Bless You, Steve Fein.

"And did you often leave them alone with Zoe when you knew she was depersonalized?"

Reluctantly, "Yes, but..".

Steve interrupted, "A simple yes or no, please."

Eric lowered his voice and spoke so softly, it was almost a whisper. "Yes."

"I have no further questions," Steve said.

The judge said, "I will hear closing arguments now. Mr. McCormack."

Mr. McCormack stood, "Your honor, I believe the facts have proven Mrs. Sinoneau is a good and competent mother when she is healthy. But there's the rub. She is not healthy a lot of the time. She has a disease...a disease that no one really understands. No one knows what brings it on, or how long it will last, or what makes it go away. She hears voices, your honor. A voice that tells her to commit suicide. Might this voice also one day tell her to kill her children...to relieve their suffering? I have sympathy for Mrs. Simoneau. She seems like a fine, loving person. But this hearing is not about Mrs. Simoneau, it is about two innocent, helpless little girls. Are you really willing to take the risk of giving these children over to this woman, who may at any moment, unpredictably, become ill and do harm to them?"

I cannot describe the feelings within me when I listened to this man...the churning inside my stomach, the aching in my heart, the anger, the fury, the sadness, because even if I looked deeply into every dark corner of my soul, I knew I could never harm my children.

It was Steve's turn to talk.

"Your honor, I believe we have proven that not only is Zoe Simoneau fit to have custody of her daughters, but that she is a kind, loving, and competent mother. It's true that she does have a disease; it's true that she has heard a voice on occasion, but she has never acted on that voice's advice. She has always done the right thing for herself and her children. She is not a threat to her children. Even her own husband, the Petitioner, has agreed that he has trusted her all these years with the care of her children; he did not even miss one day of work when she was depersonalized, and he left her alone with them when she was depersonalized. That's how much he trusted his wife to care properly for her children. Her psychiatrist testified that she has no violent tendencies, that she has had this condition since childhood, and has found a way to live a viable life with it. The court-appointed evaluator has testified that Zoe's daughters love her and want to go back to her, and the evaluator's recommendation is that Zoe have joint custody of the children. Your honor, please don't take Molly and Sophie away from this loving and deserving mother."

The judge said, "We'll take a ten minute recess and then I will make my ruling."

We all got up and went into the hall. My stomach was doing flip-flops, but the first thing I did was hug Steve. "Thank you," I said. "Thank you so much." I could not let go of him.

"You were awesome," Claire said to Steve.

"I hope the judge agrees with you," Steve said.

"You were terrific," Mom said. And then, "So what do you think the judge is going to do?"

"I have no way of knowing," Steve said, "but I think we did the best we could."

"I think we're going to win," Claire said.

"From your lips to God's ear," Steve said.

I looked at Eric down the hall with his attorney, and knew they were having the same conversation we were having. Who was going to win; who was going to lose.

"I can't stand this waiting," I said.

"I know," Steve said. "But it'll all be over soon."

It seemed like an hour before the judge summoned us back into the courtroom, and when we were all seated and quiet, he said, "This has been a difficult decision for me because of this unique set of circumstances and my sympathy for the Respondent, but on the sole issue of what is in the best interest of the children, I award sole legal custody to the father, Eric Simoneau, and award temporary joint physical custody to the Petitioner, Eric Simoneau and Respondent, Zoe Simoneau, provided that if the Petitioner at any time feels that the Respondent is mentally or physically incapable of taking proper care of the children, he shall have the right to remove the children from the Respondent's home immediately and deny visitation to her without a further court order.

"Temporary joint custody is to be divided equally between the Petitioner and Respondent in any manner agreed to by the Petitioner and Respondent. I am also setting a date in six months for a re-hearing on this matter, at which time, I will also want a report from Ms. Partamian. He turned to his clerk and she gave him the date of May 9, 2002, at 9 a.m. He then said, "Mr. McCormack, please prepare the order."

With a final look at us all, he banged his gavel, "Court is adjourned."

We all rose, and as the judge left the courtroom, I turned to Steve, "What does it mean?"

"It means we won," he said with a broad smile.

Jubilation burst from every pore of my body. I wanted to sing, to dance, to shout from the rooftops. "We won," I repeated, tears filling my eyes, and immediately felt my mom's and sister's arms around me.

"When do I get my girls?" I asked Steve.

"We're going out in the hallway right now to work that out with Eric and his attorney. Of course, you realize that he does have full legal custody of the girls for now, but as long as you're healthy, you get them half the time."

"That's all I want," I said, the tears now streaming down my cheeks. And then the three of us encircled Steve, all of us hugging him and each other.

Out in the hallway, the four of us, Eric and I and our attorneys, got together and began talking. Eric and I decided that we would each have the girls every two weeks, beginning Saturday mornings at 10, and ending Saturday mornings at 10. We thought that would be less disruptive for them. This was Thursday. "So does that mean I get them this Saturday morning?" I asked.

"Yes," Eric said. "I'll drop them off."

I didn't want to sound too excited because then he might think I had been worried about losing, so I just said, "That works for me. And should I return them to you the second Saturday morning?"

"No," he said. "I think I'll always just pick them up and drop them off."

"Fine," I said.

All of a sudden, the hallway became quiet. It was an awkward moment. Everything was settled, or at least for the next six months, and Eric and I didn't know what to do or say. Were we enemies or friends?

It was Eric who broke the silence. "I'm sorry about all this, Zoe...it was nothing against you...it was just that if something happened...I wanted to be able to get the girls without having to go to a judge."

My first reaction was anger. All this torture he had put me through, and now he was apologizing? I studied him for a moment. He was Eric, this nice curly-headed guy I had married. But he was also the man who had cheated on me, taken my daughters away from me. The man I had hated for the past several months. How could I forgive him just like that? And yet, a part of me did want to forgive him, and perhaps in time I could forgive him for the cheating. But I didn't know if I could ever forgive him for taking my daughters from me, even if he thought it was what was best for them.

I didn't know what to say, so I said, "I understand."

"Well then, see you on Saturday morning," he said, very matter-of-factly.

"Yes," I said, trying to sound as casual as he had sounded.

Walking back to where Mom and Claire were waiting, Steve said, "We're going to have to get on with the divorce now."

"The divorce should be a piece of cake after this," I said.

"It should be pretty cut and dried," Steve said. "He's a salaried employee and so are you."

"Good," I said. "The simpler, the better."

"Call my office and make an appointment to come in and fill out the forms," he said.

"I will," I said.

By now, we had reached Mom and Claire. He kissed and hugged each of us and then walked off, briefcase in hand.

"I love that man," I said to Mom.

"I know," Mom said. "He's a great guy."

"And a great attorney," Claire said, because she was the one who would know.

The three of us decided to stop for a drink on the way home to celebrate. We chose a small Italian restaurant near the courthouse, and sat in the bar. Mom and I ordered a glass of white wine; Claire ordered a Margarita.

"What a glorious day," Mom said, as the drinks arrived.

"Yes," I said and we all touched glasses. "To getting my children back," I toasted.

"To good health," Mom said.

"To both," Claire said.

After Mom left to go make dinner for Dad, Claire and I sat talking. I felt that the last two months had been all about me, and I wanted to hear about her.

"So how're things going?" I asked.

"I don't want to dampen your day," she said.

"Nothing could dampen my day," I said. "I want to hear about you."

"Well, it's just the same old, same old. I don't know what to do about Phil." I knew all about Phil, the lawyer who worked in her office, a married man with three children, whom she'd been seeing for about two years.

I didn't really approve of Claire having an affair with a married man after what I'd been through with Eric. But Claire, in some way, seemed fragile when it came to men, so I didn't want to give her a guilt trip—especially today. "What's going on?" I asked.

"He keeps telling me how much he loves me, how much he wants to be with me, how much he hates his wife, but he just can't leave his children."

"How long have you been going with him?" I asked.

"It'll be two and a half years in January."

Even longer than I thought. "You know, Claire, I'm the last one to give anyone advice, but maybe it's time to move on."

"I know, I know. I knew from the minute I started up with him that it was a losing proposition. But I was just so crazy about him; and him about me. There was this magical connection between us, to say nothing of the sex. God, but the sex is incredible."

I looked down at my wineglass. "I wouldn't know about that," I said.

She stared at me for a moment. We had never discussed my sex life, although she had talked about hers frequently. "So, does that mean you're still a virgin?"

I laughed. "No, I have two kids."

"Then what?"

I was a little embarrassed to tell her the truth, but so happy to be getting my girls back that I didn't care what I said. "I just never enjoyed it," I said.

"Believe me, there were plenty times I didn't enjoy it either," she said, shocking me. "It has to be with the right man, and he has to know what he's doing. This whole thing about just coming together in a burst of passion is just a bunch of bull. A woman needs more than that."

"Well, I wouldn't know. Maybe neither of the men I slept with knew what he was doing. Or maybe it's the drugs. There's never been a time I wasn't on drugs except when I was pregnant, and I know for sure that some of them kill the libido. Or it could be my disease, or it could be just something wrong with me."

"So you've never had an orgasm?"

"An orgasm? What's that?" I said sarcastically.

"How sad," she said. And then she put her hand on mine. "Someday it'll happen. Someday the right man will come along, and it'll happen."

"I think the right man has come along, but unfortunately, he doesn't like me that way."

"You mean, Doug?"

"Yes, Doug. If a man could ever get me aroused, I think it would be Doug."

"Why?"

"You've seen him. He's just so darn appealing. And he's so sweet and gentle."

"I know what you mean. He is one good looking dude. In fact, if he wasn't your friend, and if I wasn't involved with Phil, I'd go after him myself."

"Would you really?"

"Yes, I would. But of course, not if you're interested in him."

"I am interested in him. Very interested in him, but as I said, he doesn't seem to be interested in me. As anything more than a friend, that is."

"Well then, why don't you try seducing him?"

"Seducing him," I said aghast.

"Yes, seducing him."

"You're kidding, of course."

"No, I'm serious."

"I wouldn't know where to begin."

"It's easy. Just invite him over for dinner, wear something sexy, like a black see-through teddy," (I had to laugh at that) "and after he's had a drink or two, put your arms around him, kiss him, rub up against him, and maybe he'll come around." She laughed, "No pun intended."

"You make it sound so easy, but I don't know if I could do it."

"Well, you'll never know if you don't try. You know men can sense it. They know who's available and who isn't."

"I don't know," I said again. "I think he's got this idea that it would be unethical for him to have sex with me."

"Then you've tried?"

"No, but I did tell him I was in love with him."

"You did?"

"Yes, when I was on my way out of my last incident. He'd been coming over every day and the day he told me was going to stop coming over every day, it just came out."

"So what'd he say?"

"What I told you, that it was just a doctor-patient kind of thing. That it wasn't real love."

Claire seemed lost in her thoughts, then took a sip of her Margarita. "Do you still talk to him? I mean outside of yoga class."

"Yes, but less and less."

"Well then, why not take give it a try? Invite him to dinner and see what happens."

Now it was my turn to think. Did I have the guts? "Maybe I will. Maybe after Eric picks up the girls in two weeks. Maybe I'll do it then."

"I hope it works out for you," Claire said, picking up her purse, "Now, I've got to dash."

"Oh, Claire," I said. "I feel so bad. I wanted to talk about you, and instead we ended up talking about me."

"It's okay," she said. "I'm just a broken record. Your life is much more exciting."

"Today, yes. As exciting as it gets."

We walked out the door together, hugged, and she kissed me on the cheek. "I'm so happy for you," she said.

"I love you so much," I said. "You're the best sister anyone could have."

"No," she said, "you are. We'll talk soon." And she headed to her car, and I to mine.

Chapter Seventeen – Taking a Risk

On Saturday morning, my daughters returned to me.

Again, I was waiting outside of the house when they drove up in Eric's silver Mercedes, and the minute they stepped out of the car, we ran to each other. I couldn't stop hugging and kissing them, and they clutched at me and wouldn't let go. I couldn't keep the tears from flowing, not because I loved them so much, but because they loved me so much.

The next two weeks were heaven for me, just seeing them at breakfast, driving them to school, picking them up from school, hearing their footsteps upstairs while I was making dinner, hearing the sound of their voices as they talked or laughed or even sniped at one another, seeing their faces across the dinner table, or when they were reading or doing their homework, or just watching TV. I didn't think I needed anything else in my life... just them, and that I continue to be healthy.

I had a negative thought for a moment here and there, like this is too good to be true, or how could I be so lucky, and there was a hint of fear hovering like a shadow I could not see somewhere inside me, but I just let my thoughts and feelings come and go. I did not try to stop them, or dwell on them, or encounter them. I just let them be.

And then on the second Saturday morning, after two weeks of bliss with my daughters, Eric picked them up. Suddenly, the house felt emptier than it had ever felt. I missed them more than

I had ever missed them. But at least I could console myself with the fact they would be back again in two weeks.

I turned on the radio to the Metropolitan opera, cut up some fresh fruit, piled some cottage cheese on top, sat down at my butcher block table to eat my lunch, and thought about the weekend. That night, I was going to dinner and a movie with Renee Demsky, a teacher friend from school who was also divorced, (it was amazing how since Eric had left, I had moved from the world of couples to the world of singles), but Sunday I had nothing to do. I then thought about my conversation with Claire. Did I have the nerve? The nerve to call Doug and try to seduce him? I still wasn't sure how I would do that. And what if I succeeded? What if he had sex with me and I still felt nothing? Perhaps it was better to leave things as they were. But then again, maybe it was better to take a chance. Doug had always told me to go with my feelings, to not think, to go with truth.

I walked over to the phone and called Doug at the studio. "Hey, Doug, it's Zoe. Are you busy?"

"I've got a class about to start," he said. "What's up?"

"I was just wondering if you'd like to come to dinner tomorrow night."

"Just a second," he said.

In a minute or two, he was back. "Yeah, tomorrow's good. What time?"

"Seven o'clock?"

"Sounds good," he said. "See you then."

I had the same kind of shorthand with Doug as I had with my mom. We never said, "How are you?" but always got right to the point. I think he could tell by my voice when I said, "Hi Doug" or "Hey Doug," just where I was at. (And I know about ending a sentence with a preposition.) When I had called him after court and told him the good news, he knew something good was coming just from my, "Doug."

Now that I had invited him to dinner and he had said 'yes', it was time to think about what I was going to serve.

I came up with: a big salad, no tomatoes, (he didn't like tomatoes, but loved cucumbers), La Brea Bakery Rosemary bread, (we both loved that) and rigatoni with marinara sauce. For dessert I'd get him some Haagen Daz coffee ice cream, his favorite.

Now it was time to think about what I would do after dinner.... the grand seduction scene. I could dress sexy, like Claire had suggested, or just go up and kiss him and hope he kissed back. This wasn't a game I was used to playing; it was a game I had always tried to avoid. I decided I would not dress sexy—no see-through black teddy for me—just wear my usual jeans and a pink sweater, to match the color of my eyes, as Frankie used to say, and then do what Doug had always told me to do, not think, just go with the flow.

Doug brought over a bottle of wine, a Cabernet Sauvignon. I had gone through a large part of my life not drinking anything alcoholic because of some pill I was on, but since I'd cut down on my meds, I often had a glass of wine with dinner.

He opened the wine while I got the food on the table, and I wondered if I could eat anything, considering how nervous I was feeling. I picked at the salad, poked at the rigatoni, didn't even consider the Haagen Daz, but did drink a 2nd glass of wine. It filled me with warmth and made me feel lighthearted.

With glass in hand, I looked at Doug sitting across from me, and imagined him holding me, kissing me, and I felt a rush of excitement running through my body: something purely physical, something I may never have felt before. Perhaps this was it, the moment I'd been waiting for. Perhaps I could feel something, and if ever I was going to feel something, it would be with Doug.

From then on, each time my eyes fastened on him, I was afraid to look in his eyes, afraid he would notice it, see something different about me. I'm sure he sensed something was different during dinner, but he could have no clue as to what it was. Or maybe he did. I hoped he did.

He finished his ice cream, the dishes were rinsed and put in the dishwasher, the table was sponged off by Doug, and standing close to each other at the sink, I put my arms around his waist, and lifted my face, hoping he would to kiss me. He put his arms around me, but did not kiss me, "Zoe, I can't do this."

"But why?"

"I've already explained why."

"But I'm better now and I'm still in love with you."

"No, you're not."

"Please, kiss me, kiss me just this once."

He kissed me on the cheek and said, "I'm sorry, Zoe. You know I love you, but there can never be anything romantic between us." And then pulling back. "Thanks for the wonderful dinner, but I think I better go now."

"No," I said. I couldn't let the evening end this way. I couldn't let him go. "Is it all right if we do our breathing together?" I asked.

He gave a little sigh. "Of course," he said.

And then a gulp of air before my next question. "Is it all right if we do it in my bedroom?"

He looked at me with some uncertainty. "Why in your bedroom?"

"Because you told me it's important to do it in the same place at the same time every day."

"Is everything okay?" he asked, apparently realizing that tonight was different from all other nights, even though he wasn't Jewish.

"Everything's perfect," I said.

He smiled. "You don't have any ulterior motives, do you, Miss Zoe?"

"Me? How could you think such a thing?"

"Okay," he said.

Once upstairs, I took off my shoes, pulled down my comforter, placed two pillows under my head and one under my knees and lay down on my bed, while Doug carried over my desk chair and sat beside me.

It was cold in the room, so I pulled up the comforter and covered myself with it. I closed my eyes and Doug and I began to breathe, Doug's gentle voice saying, "inhale deeply" then counting, "one, two, three," and then saying, "exhale slowly," and then starting over.

When 20 minutes had gone by, he ended with "Just let yourself go. Stay in this place of peace for as long as you wish." A few minutes later, he stood up, and in a voice, soft and wispy as a white cloud, he said. "Thanks again for the wonderful dinner. See you on Wednesday."

"No," I said, turning to look at him, my insides aquiver. "Please don't go. I'm feeling so cold and alone…please come under the covers with me."

"Zoe, I've told you, nothing can happen between us."

"Nothing will," I said. "It's only that I'm cold and I need you to warm me."

"That's a good line," he said. "One I never heard before."

I smiled and lifted the covers, waiting for him.

He sat back on the chair, took off his shoes, and fully clothed climbed in beside me.

I moved into his body, pressing hard against him, trying to have our bodies meld together, to become part of his body, part of his warmth, and then I lifted my lips to kiss his, and he pulled away.

"Zoe, we can't do this."

"But why not? I love you so much, and I want you so much."

"Zoe, I love you, too. But not in a sexual way. You're my friend, but you can never be anything else."

"Then make love to me anyway. I've never wanted sex in my life before, but I want it now, with you. Please. I promise I won't expect anything. You don't have to marry me, or love me, or even take me out on a date. You don't have to call me in the morning, or call me ever. I just want you now, this moment. I want you to make love to me."

"Zoe, you're so beautiful in every way, but I can't do this."

"But why?"

"Because as I told you before, what you're feeling toward me isn't love; it's gratitude from a patient to her doctor."

"Doctors have sex with their patients all the time, and anyway, you're not a doctor."

He gave a little laugh. "You're so cute," he said.

"Does that mean you're not going to have sex with me?"

"That's what it means," he said.

I lay there feeling petulant, let down, upset with him, upset with myself. "Then will you just lie with me and hold me in your arms? I feel so alone."

He thought a moment, obviously torn between staying and leaving. "Yes, I can do that," he said, and held me until I fell asleep.

In the morning, I was up at six, showered, dressed, and came back into the bedroom to find him already up and putting on his shoes.

"Hi," he said.

"Hi," I said and came and sat beside him on the bed. "Thanks for staying with me last night. I would have been so depressed if you had left."

"I know," he said, taking my hand. "That's why I stayed."

"I wish you could feel about me the way I feel about you."

"I don't know," he said. "I don't think I'll ever love anyone again the way I loved Nicole."

"Maybe you're afraid you'll be hurt again."

"Did I ever tell you, you should be a therapist?" he asked.

I smiled. "No, but I bet I'd do a better job than most of the ones I've been to."

"I think you're right about that," he said. Then standing up, he leaned over, kissed me on the cheek and said, "Thanks again for the wonderful dinner, but now I gotta go."

I looked up at him. "Will you come again?"

"Sure," he said. "Anytime."

Later, drinking down my orange juice with my vitamin and my xanax, I thought about Doug. "That's not ever going to happen," I said aloud. I would have to find some other person to be the great love of my life. And if I never found him, I would have my daughters, my teaching, my music, and that would be enough.

Chapter Eighteen – Kiska

2002 started well for me.

First and foremost, I had my daughters back, at least two weeks a month, and my Destroyer was silent.

I no longer needed to make phone calls to Doug except as a friend. I still had feelings for him, but had pretty much given up on anything romantic happening between us. He was always kind and loving, but obviously not ever going to be in love with me.

I was devoted to meditating twice a day; jogging every day, now up to three miles a day (except if I had my girls, I might skip a day or two); seeing my therapist, Marcy Jacobs, every Thursday after school; and going to Doug's Wednesday night yoga class with Caitlin and also Renee Demsky, my divorced friend from school, who had joined the yoga class in December and now also had a crush on Doug. Didn't everyone?

And I was back to having a lesson with Ms. Hockensmith every two weeks and practicing the piano every day. What for, I didn't know. Except that I could not bear to see my technique go downhill, and of course, being at one with the music was as thrilling as it had always been.

At my piano lesson with Ms. Hockensmith the third week in February, I walked into the living room and immediately knew something was wrong. Ms. Hockensmith had left the front door unlocked for me, but there was no Ms. Hockensmith. I set my music on the piano, and walked through the house, calling, "Ms. Hockensmith, are you here?"

Finally I reached the windows facing the yard, and there was Ms. Hockensmith sitting on the grass and lying on the grass in front of her was Kiska.

I ran into the yard. "Ms. Hockensmith, are you okay?"

Ms. Hockensmith looked up me, looking more pale than usual. "I don't know what to do," she said.

It was so unlike Ms. Hockensmith to be unnerved; she was always in perfect control.

"It's Kiska," she continued. "He can't walk."

I looked from one to the other and I didn't know who I felt worse for: Kiska or Ms. Hockensmith.

Kiska looked so pathetic, lying there on his back legs, his front legs forward as if he was trying to stand up but couldn't. I hadn't realized how much I cared for Kiska; how much I enjoyed seeing him each visit. He had crept into my feelings unnoticed. Tears came to my eyes. I felt a tightening in my chest. Poor Kiska.

I sat down beside him and began stroking his grizzly fur. He began purring. I know a dog can't purr, but he was. "We'll have to get him to a vet," I said.

"My vet's number is in the house. It's under 'vet' in my little black book. Can you call him?"

"Of course," I said, and hurried inside, found Ms. Hockensmith's little black book and found the vet's phone number. When I got him on the line, he said, he'd be at the clinic until nine, and that we should bring Kiska right over.

Yes, but how, I thought. This was a big dog.

When I got back outside, I told Ms. Hockensmith that we had to get Kiska to the vet. She looked at me blankly, and then echoed my thought, "But, how are we going to get him there?"

"I'm thinking that if you take the front half and I take the back half, maybe we can carry him," I said.

"Maybe we should put him on a blanket," Ms. Hockensmith said.

"Yes," I agreed, and she went in the house, got a blanket and brought it back out.

"I'll open the back of my car before we try to pick him up," I said. Fortunately, I had purchased a Ford Bronco the previous year.

"And we can take him through the side gate," Ms. Hockensmith said.

Within the next ten minutes, after the most harrowing purely physical experience I'd ever had, lifting that dog onto the blanket and carrying him to the car, we were on our way to the vet's.

"I left the front door unlocked," Ms. Hockensmith realized halfway there.

"Shall I go back?" I asked.

"No," she said from the back of the van where she was semi-lying next to Kiska and stroking his head. "The only thing that's of any value is my piano. I don't think I have to worry about that."

When we got the vet's, the vet, and his white coated assistant, carried Kiska from the car to the examining room, and within a few minutes, the doctor looked at Ms. Hockensmith, and said, "I'm sorry. I have bad news. He has arthritis in his hips. There's really nothing we can do for him."

"But there must be something," Ms. Hockensmith said. I'd never seen her look so bewildered and helpless, and my heart was breaking for her.

"I'm sorry," the doctor said.

She heaved a deep sigh. "So what does it mean?"

"If he can't walk," the doctor said, "he can't do anything. He's fourteen years-old. That's old for a dog of his size. It's time to put him to sleep."

I thought she would scream, or cry, but she was stoic. "All right, then. That's what we'll have to do."

I felt so bad for her, I wanted to go to her, put my arms around her, have her cry on my shoulder, but there was still this barrier between us: "Don't touch."

"You're doing the right thing, Ms. Hockensmith," the doctor said.

I wondered how long he'd known her, and he still called her Ms. Hockensmith. But then so did I.

The doctor spoke again. "I'll get everything ready, and you can stay in the room with us, and pet Kiska so that he won't be afraid. He won't feel anything."

"Thank you, doctor," Ms. Hockensmith said.

When it was over and we were driving home, she, hugging the blanket to her chest, said, "I don't think we'll have a lesson tonight."

"Of course not," I said, and then asked her questions about Kiska, and she kept talking about him, until I pulled up in front of her house.

I got out of the car and helped her and her blanket out, and we walked through her unlocked door to the living room so that I could get my music.

"I see the piano's still here," she said.

"Yes," I said, "but you better check your jewelry."

"I only have one thing of value and I keep it in a safe place," she said. And then, "So, maybe you should come next week, the same time?"

I told her that would be fine, and she walked me to the front door.

"Thank you," she said, "for all your help with Kiska. I don't know what I would have done without you."

"I'm glad I was here and could help," I said. I wanted so much to put my arms around her, to give her a hug, to let her know how sorry I was, and that I understood how she was feeling, but I had that damn music in my arms. I stood there, feeling like a fool, and then without thinking, I bent over, set the music down on her hardwood floor, and did put my arms around her and give her a big hug. She lifted her arms and hugged me back. We stood holding each other for a minute and then she pulled back.

I looked to see if there were tears in her eyes, but I saw none.

"Thank you again," she said. "You really are a remarkable woman."

"No," I said, "You're the one who's remarkable." And I picked up my music, and headed for my car.

Chapter Nineteen – Glory

In March, four months after I got my girls back, I met my husband's beloved, the woman he had cheated with, the woman who had broken up my home, the woman who had broken me: Glory Sandoval. Her name was Gloria, but since Molly and Sophie called her Glory, I thought of her as Glory.

Eric and she were going to be married in April, and Molly and Sophie were going to be bridesmaids at the wedding. Apparently, Glory had never been married before and wanted the whole she-bang: the big church wedding (Catholic), and the reception after at the Spanish Hills County Club. I knew that would make Heather very happy because now her only son was going to get the wedding she had always wanted him to have.

I couldn't blame Molly and Sophie for being excited about the upcoming event and wanting to tell me everything about it: the dresses they were going to wear, how beautiful the church was, and the country club, and how excited they were about the party the morning of the wedding, when all the bridesmaids, including my girls, were going to gather at a beauty shop to get their hair, nails and makeup done.

Well, that would be exciting for an eleven and nine-year-old. And I was happy for them. I didn't begrudge them all the fun. But all this talk about the wedding was upsetting to me. Very upsetting. I told myself over and over again, that I shouldn't still be angry with Eric and Glory, that it wasn't healthy for me, that

I should forgive them. But much as I wanted to, much as I tried, something deep inside me would not let go. I could not forgive them for all they'd done to me.

We met at Molly's first soccer game of the season.

Sophie and I were sitting on our folding chairs waiting for the game to begin, when Eric walked up with his arm around a young dark-haired woman. She had a pretty face, but kind of an hour glass figure: big bust and hips, but a slim waist. I was surprised that Eric would be attracted to her, since he had seemed to love my slim body. But then I supposed men notoriously like big breasts, and he was a man.

I knew that Glory had been a secretary in Eric's office, and an old saying popped into my mind, "If you want to marry a doctor, become a nurse; if you want to marry a lawyer, become his secretary." I wondered how long their affair had been going on before Eric told me about it.

Sophie immediately got up, ran to Glory, and put her arms around her, "Hi, Glory."

"Hi, sweetie," Glory said.

My heart leapt. Who was this strange woman my daughter seemed to love? It was a tough moment for me. Of course I had been hearing about Glory for the past few months, even before the wedding plans. The girls often talked about her, where she'd taken them, what she said, what she cooked for dinner and how nice she was to them.

But now, actually seeing her in person, actually seeing Eric with another woman, the woman he adored, the woman he was going to marry, was a little hard to take. Even though I no longer loved him, even though I had once hated him, still, it hurt.

Eric introduced Glory to me, and she held out her hand. What was I supposed to do? Turn my back on her, slap her in the face like they did in the movies, tell her how much she'd hurt me? Or forgive her on the spot? I couldn't do any of those things, so I shook hands with her.

"I'm so happy to finally meet you," Glory said. "The girls are always talking about you."

"I hope they're not saying anything bad," I said, as I would normally say.

"No," Glory said, "All good."

And then Glory opened her folding chair and plunked it down right next to my chair, and grabbed hold of Sophie and pulled her onto her lap. "Come here little sweetheart," she said, enfolding Sophie in her arms and kissing her on the cheek.

I couldn't help being upset about that. That was going a little too far. Grabbing my own daughter from me; I wasn't ready for that.

"Sophie's such a little sweetheart," Glory said, stroking her hair. "You've really done a great job of raising her and Molly."

I did not appreciate that remark either, coming from her. Who was she to pass judgment on whether I was a good mother or not?

At this moment, Sophie pulled away from Glory and came and sat on my lap. I hugged her tightly, so thankful that she had chosen to sit with me instead of Glory. (I was glad that Glory was nice to my girls, but I didn't want them to like her more than they liked me.) I felt I had to say something to Glory's last remark, so I said, "Thank you for being so nice to the girls."

"Oh I adore them both. They're both so sweet."

"Yes, they are," I said, giving Sophie an extra squeeze.

"You know," Glory said, "there's something I want to say to you."

I immediately panicked. I didn't want to hear anything that started with, 'there's something I want to say to you.'

Glory took a breath, "I just want you to know that I really feel bad about all that's happened, and I hope you can find it in your heart to forgive me."

I was completely stunned by that. I hadn't expected that. I didn't know what to say, so I said nothing and Glory continued on in her upbeat breezy style. "I think it would be good for the girls if we could be..." thinking about the right word...."friendly."

That word made me feel even more uncomfortable. She stole my husband and now she wants to be my friend? I wasn't ready for this, not any of it, but I had to say something. "Yes," I heard myself say aloud. "We could be friendly."

And then Molly was running down the field, the ball on her foot, and I stood up cheering, "Go, go, go," and Molly took aim, kicked as hard as she could, and the ball was in the net. We were all standing and cheering now, Glory yelling the loudest.

Chapter Twenty — Going with Truth

At the court hearing in May, after my meeting with Ms. Partamian, the judge ruled to continue custody as per his previous order, and scheduled another hearing in six months to the following November. I was ecstatic.

After, in the hallway, Eric and I decided to split the upcoming summer: the girls would spend the first half with Eric who was going to take them and Glory on a cruise to Alaska; and the second half with me. I was floating as I exited the courthouse; I would have five straight weeks with my daughters!

By the time I got home, I had already planned three things to do with them: 1) anything they wanted to do; 2) anything else they wanted to do; 3) go to the mall, the beach, the theatre, the Hollywood Bowl, the Skirball Museum, the Getty Museum, a tour of the L.A. County Museum with my mother as their guide, the movies, lunches and/or dinners with my mom and Claire, get their hair and nails done at Andrew and Amy's salon, and finally, go on a trip to San Diego for a week.

I wanted to take them to Vacation Village, a resort where my parents had taken our family when I was a child, but when I called, Vacation Village was no longer in existence. So I booked another hotel on Mission Bay, with a beach and a swimming pool, and while in San Diego, we would go to Sea World, Legoland, the San Diego Zoo, Wild Animal Park, and spend a lot of time just lounging around the pool or on the beach.

Now that I had planned what I was going to do with the second five weeks of the summer, I had to start thinking about what I would do for the first five weeks that Eric would have them. I actually didn't have anything to do. Of course, I could always spend more time practicing the piano, but that would still leave me with a lot of free time, and that was the one thing I didn't want to have, especially the first few weeks after school ended.

I needed to find an activity. I thought about becoming a docent at the new Getty Museum, or the new Skirball Museum, but I wouldn't be able to continue on with either once school started. I thought about taking classes in art, music, literature and/or drama, and that seemed a good option, but not compelling.

Then one afternoon, I was talking to Missy about the school that her son, Timmy, was going to. It was a private school for children with special needs and not too far from my house. Of course, Missy had mentioned the school before, but it hadn't clicked into my brain that it might be a place I would want to teach. But now, Missy said, they needed teachers desperately. That hit me as the exact thing I wanted to do. I immediately called the Morrison Academy, made an appointment, went for an interview, told them I could only work the first five weeks of summer vacation, and was hired.

On Friday, June 21st, school ended at Porter Valley Elementary School, and I did not get depersonalized.

During those last three weeks of school, I did have some glimmers of anxiety, some moments of disquiet, unease, concern, but I didn't fight them, just took my deep breaths and let them pass through.

So now, instead of spending the summer, hiding in my closet, I would be teaching at the Morrison Academy and then spending five glorious weeks with my precious daughters.

From the moment I walked into the classroom at the Morrison Academy, I knew this was where I was meant to be. Much as I loved the sweet, adorable, bright children I had been teaching, I immediately felt an affinity for these children. They didn't have the same handicap I had as a child, but they were still suffering as I had suffered.

There were eight youngsters in my class, including Timmy, ranging in age from eight to ten, all with varying degrees of processing difficulties. Some were quiet, some loquacious, but all were off in their own worlds, their own universes, isolated from all of the people around them. I could empathize with how they were feeling, and was overwhelmed with the desire to help them as Doug had helped me...to bring them back to this world, to teach them to interact, to have a friend, to learn something...no matter how small. That was my job and my challenge. In a way I felt ill-equipped to do it—I'd had no training in dealing with these children, but I'd had my own experiences, and surely that would help.

I spent each day trying to make little inroads. Two of the children had been main-streamed, but hadn't done well enough scholastically or socially to remain in a public school. But all of the children had been teased, ridiculed, and ostracized their whole lives, especially by other children.

Of the eight children in the class, I could only communicate with the two who had been main-streamed. The others would be difficult to reach.

Timmy might be the biggest challenge. He had to be in constant motion and refused to make eye contact.

David was a non-stop talker; he knew everything there was to know about baseball players: their batting averages, their ERA's. He was amazing. He'd just spout out all these facts, but no one was listening to him, and he seemed incapable of listening to anyone else, even me.

Elena talked a bit and seemed to understand what I was saying to her, but had difficulty communicating her thoughts to me. Fortunately, the school had a computer and Elena could sit down and type sentences on it. She couldn't say the sentence, but she could type it.

I felt I needed a way to bring these children together, to have them develop friendships. Each one was so alone in his or her own world. I felt *that* was more important than reading, math, or any other subject I could teach them. Once they were socialized, I thought, anything would be possible.

I thought about bringing a piano into my room. Perhaps the children could communicate with music. Of course, the school didn't have a piano. But then, aha, I did have a piano: my old upright. But what was the point of bringing it over if I was leaving in five weeks?

But then, what if I didn't leave?

The more I thought about it, the more I was convinced that I didn't want to go back to my other school; I wanted to stay here with these children. I felt I needed them as much as they needed me. Even if the work was draining—no matter how much patience I had or how much energy, most nights I went home utterly exhausted—there was nothing in life I wanted to do more than help these children.

I spoke to Mrs. Hudson, the administrator, a lovely, soft-spoken black woman (who reminded me of Anita Hill of Clarence Thomas fame), who told me, yes, they wanted me, and I could begin permanently in September, but I would have to get started on obtaining a credential in Special Education.

I happily agreed, and immediately called my friend, the principal at Porter Ranch Elementary School and gave her notice that I would not be returning in September. I then met with a counselor at CSUN who informed me I needed an additional 30 hours. That was disappointing, but I figured it would only take two years of night school and one session of summer school, and I could do it, so I enrolled in two night classes that would start in September.

The five weeks with my class at the Morrison Academy passed quickly, with little inroads here, a little progress there, and my growing determination to do everything possible to help these children.

And then it was time for my five fabulous weeks with my precious daughters. They couldn't have gone better. Both girls loved the trip to San Diego, and all the other things we had planned to do, and all the things we hadn't planned, like going to the market together, cooking dinner together, playing Boggle, Scrabble and Monopoly, or just sitting in the family room watching TV together. Just being a family.

Both girls seemed to be getting taller by the day, and more grown up. Molly, at twelve, was already five-feet-five, just about as tall as me. She was going to be a tall one, but beautiful, with that curly blonde-brown hair, and hazel eyes. She was quiet, reserved, but so intelligent. She wanted to become a doctor, like all my uncles, and I was thrilled about that. Even if it didn't happen, I wanted my girls to aim high.

Molly was also a natural athlete, probably taking after my mom, dad, and Claire. She excelled at both tennis and soccer; she was my dad's dream come true. He took her out to play tennis every week, even the weeks Eric had her, and came to almost every tennis match and soccer game.

As if she wasn't busy enough, Molly, now in her third year of Hebrew school, was going to be a Bat Mitzvah next summer. Unlike me, she was looking forward to the event, especially the service. The Rabbi was training her to conduct the entire service on her own. Like me, however, she didn't want the big party afterward. She wanted a small party, with just a few of her friends and the immediate family. But my mom was already working on her to invite my friends, my mom's friends, and the hordes of relatives we had in Michigan.

Fortunately, Eric had gone along with the kids getting a Jewish education, even driving the girls to Hebrew School on the weeks he had them, but he refused to pay for any part of it, including the upcoming Bat Mitzvah.

Sophie, at ten, may not have been as book-smart as Molly, or as gifted athletically, but she was a darling girl. Like Claire, she had a ton of friends, and was more affectionate and more adventuresome than Molly. She wanted to be an actress and was taking singing and dancing lessons, and also guitar lessons from Andrew. Last semester she'd had the lead role in the school play, and this semester she was going to play Peter Pan, and perhaps fly on stage, if the school could arrange it.

Both girls were slim and healthy eaters. Like Doug, they tried to stay away from sugar and fat, which was exactly how I tried to eat. But they weren't fanatic about it. Every now and then, the three of us would go to Baskin Robbins and indulge in a hot fudge sundae with chocolate ice cream, nuts, whipped cream and a cherry, giggling the whole time about how bad we were.

In September, I went back to teaching at the Morrison Academy and began my night classes at CSUN.

The first thing I did when the semester started was get my upright piano moved from my dining room into the school auditorium. I felt it would be good for all the children in the school to learn to play the piano, or at least fiddle around with it. While most of them only banged away at the keys, a few kids seemed fascinated by the sounds, going up and down the keys from the lowest tones to the highest tones, and back again. Little strides, I told myself, little strides.

At this time of my life, I felt that I was now the happiest and luckiest person in the world. I had my girls back, my teaching, my family, my friends, my savior, Doug, finally a great therapist, Marcy Jacobs, and I was healthy. As for love....I could only hope that one day that too, would happen.

Three weeks before Christmas, Mrs. Hudson approached me in the hallway. "You may or may not know that every Christmas, we have a fund-raiser for the school. Missy tells me that you're quite the pianist. I was hoping that maybe you'd like to participate in our program."

Immediate reaction, panic. "No," I said, "I don't play in public."

Mrs. Hudson stared at me for a moment with her velvety all-knowing eyes, and I saw her thought waves percolating. To disturb the universe or to let it lie. "All right," Mrs. Hudson said, apparently not wanting to embarrass me or invade my privacy. "But, maybe think about it," and she turned and left.

That night, I got a call from Missy. "I hope I haven't embarrassed you."

I had told both Missy and Teri about my affliction shortly after I started seeing Marcy Jacobs. "It's nothing to be ashamed of," Marcy had said. "It's just an illness like any other, and you should tell your friends; you should tell everybody. No one's going to think less of you, and you'll see...it'll be like a great burden lifted from your shoulders." Marcy had been right.

"No, of course not," I said.

"It's just that you're such a great pianist and it'd be so good for the kids to hear you play."

"But then, there will also be their parents."

"So what do you care? They've all been through the worst. So if you make a mistake or have to leave the stage, or can't get up on the stage, they'll understand. They've all lived through it."

Yes, I thought. It made a lot of sense. If I was ever going to play before an audience...what better audience than this one? There was nothing at stake here. Even if I just played, "Mary Had a Little Lamb," it would be appreciated. "Okay," I said aloud, "I think I'll do it."

In spite of being bright and breezy on the phone with Missy, I didn't sleep well that night. What the hell had I done? I was doing so well, everything was perfect, then why was I going to jeopardize everything...for this, a little fundraiser for a little school? I must be nuts.

The next morning, I called Doug and told him what I was thinking of doing.

"I'll think you'll do okay. Just stay in the moment, do your deep breathing, and I think you can get through this."

"But is it worth taking the chance?"

"How do you feel about that?"

"I want to do it. I want to do it so badly...just to prove that I can. But I'm so afraid."

"When is the program?"

"December 21st."

"Okay, I'm coming over to your house on December 21st, to hear you play some pieces. How do you feel?"

"Fine."

"Then that's it. You'll just be playing for me and for all the little kids who won't know or won't care what you're doing."

"And what about the parents?"

"What parents?" he asked.

"I gotcha," I said.

After I hung up the phone, I thought, if I just play for Doug and the little kids, I shouldn't have a problem.

That day, I told Mrs. Hudson that I would probably play, but it would have to be a last minute kind of thing. "So don't put me on the program."

"That's fine," Mrs. Hudson said, and started to walk away.

"You see, I have this problem…" I hesitated.

"We all have a problem," Mrs. Hudson said, again starting to walk away.

But I continued talking. "I just get this stage fright to the extreme."

Mrs. Hudson turned to face me. "I understand," she said. "Don't worry about it. We'll just go with the flow…if you feel like playing, I'll just get up and announce you. Okay?"

"Okay," I said, feeling relieved, no pressure. If I felt like playing that night, I would. And if I didn't, I wouldn't. In the meantime, if I had any bad thoughts, I would just let them pass through.

The night of the program, it was raining….an ominous sign, I thought, but I showed up, my umbrella dripping, my daughters in their yellow raincoats holding my hands, the auditorium smelling musty and damp, and I sat down with all the other teachers, moms, dads, and kids.

The first performer was a juggler. In spite of the fact that he was doing amazing tricks with balls and bowling pins, there was a lot of rustling in the audience, a lot of children calling out, a lot of moms and dads trying to keep their kids sitting and quiet. But I liked it…I liked the informality of it. It was kind of a free-for-all. I liked that nothing had to be perfect; that whatever happened would happen.

Next up was a ventriloquist, and the same kind of fussing took place during his performance, although he had three different hand puppets which you would think would keep the kids quiet and interested, but they didn't. It all reminded me of a bawdy café in Victorian England; or during the French Revolution, with everyone drinking and eating, singing and fighting.

Then Mrs. Hudson stood on the stage and said, "Perhaps one of our teachers, Ms. Simoneau, would like to play something on the piano?"

I kept my focus on Mrs. Hudson. There was no one in the room but the two of us, and Mrs. Hudson wanted me to come up on the stage and play a piece for her. No big deal. As I approached the stage, I kept my eyes on the piano, my piano, the one that had been in my house for fourteen years. I was just going to play a nice little Chopin waltz before starting dinner. The TV was on loud, but that wouldn't bother me. I pulled out the bench, sat down, and just played that sweet little Chopin waltz amid the chattering and jostling of the adults and kids in the audience, and the children's voices calling out to me.

When I finished, I stood and looked at the audience. I hadn't even been aware they were there.

I bowed and smiled amid the applause as if it was nothing, but a torrent of joy was rushing through my veins. I had done it. I had played in public.

"Would you like another piece?" I called from the stage, not believing that I was doing such a thing. But it had been so easy.

There was a smattering of applause and calls of "yes" and "please", and a few parents still standing and clapping, and I just sat down at the piano and played *The Flight of the Bumblebee*.

After the show, several parents came up to me to tell me how beautifully I had played, and one of them asked if I would be interested in playing for a fund-raiser for the City of Hope, a private hospital, specializing in the treatment of cancer.

I told her I would think about it.

Chapter Twenty-One— Ms. Hockensmith

I was really looking forward to my next lesson with Ms. Hockensmith, so I could tell her all hope was not lost, that I had performed, albeit with a bunch of screaming kids in the audience, but I had done it!

I was now back to seeing Ms. Hockensmith every month or two because of my busy schedule, and while I was thinking about giving her a call to make an appointment, I got a call from her sister, Carolyn Mayberry.

"I'm sorry to inform you, Zoe, if I may call you that, that my sister has died."

Oh no, I thought. Oh no. I was completely devastated. How could she have died without me having a chance to say goodbye to her? I could not conceive of it, fathom it, the world without Ms. Hockensmith. I thought she would always be there for me. I had taken her for granted, like my mom, my dad. They had always been there for me; they would always be there for me. And so would she. My skin turned to ice. I felt this vast emptiness, this gap in the universe, this hollow in my stomach. Ms. Hockensmith was gone.

"But she wasn't that old." I said. "And I never noticed that she'd been ill."

"No, it was quite sudden."

"How sad," I said. Then wondering if it was proper to ask, "What did she die of, if I may ask?"

"It was heart failure."

Somehow that made it even sadder, I thought. I thought of her life...no husband to love her, no children, Kiska dying, and perhaps, even I had in some way broken her heart.

"She was a wonderful person," I said.

"She often talked about you," Carolyn said. "You were one of her favorite pupils."

"I'm glad," I said. "But I'm afraid I let her down. I couldn't play in public, you see. And I'm sure that was her dream."

"She never mentioned that," Carolyn said. "She only spoke about what a dedicated pupil you were, and what a nice person. And she so much appreciated your being there when Kiska died."

Tears came to my eyes. "I was glad I could help," I said.

"The funeral will be on Sunday at 2 at St. Bedes Episcopal Church in Santa Monica. Can you make it?"

"Yes," I said.

She gave me the particulars and hung up.

For some reason, I called Doug immediately. "Ms. Hockensmith died," I told him.

"Your piano teacher?" he asked.

"Yes. My piano teacher."

"I know you're going to miss her," he said.

"Yes, so much."

But I didn't know how much until I realized that there would no more visits to her house, no more sitting at the piano going over pieces, no more playing concertos and duets. She was like a best friend to me, even though I knew almost nothing about her personal life. I wished I had spoken to her more, gotten to know her better, gotten to have her know me. There was so much I wanted to tell her. How much I appreciated her. How sorry I was that I could not be the pianist she wanted me to be, and how much I cared for her. She was a unique person in my life....like no other, and now she was gone.

On Sunday, I was at the church a little before 2, surprised at how many people had come to pay their respects. For some reason, I didn't expect very many. She seemed to live such a reclusive life.

A woman, whom I was told was Carolyn, was standing at the door greeting people. She reminded me so much of her sister, same grayish straight hair, same calm look and gentle demeanor. I introduced myself and told her what a wonderful person her sister was and how much I would miss her.

"Thank you," Carolyn said, "and thanks for coming."

"It's wonderful to see so many people here," I said.

"We do have a pretty big family, and then there are a lot of Joan's pupils here with their families. There are also two of her former students here from New York. Perhaps you can meet them at the reception."

"That would be wonderful," I said, feeling sad that I didn't know anything about any of these people.

As some point in the service, the minister asked if anyone would like to say a few words about Joan.

I watched as person after person stood up and spoke about their sister, their cousin, their aunt, their friend, their teacher, and I wished I had the courage to stand up and say something. They talked about what a kind person she was, that if anyone needed someone for any reason, she was there for them. They spoke about the tragic death of her fiancé from pancreatic cancer when she was only twenty-eight years old, and how she had stayed loyal to him all these years; they talked about Kiska and how devoted she was to her dog: he was the child she never had; and her two nieces and three nephews talked about what a great aunt she was. That they could go to her with any problem and she never judged them, but always tried to help.

And then there was silence. Everyone was waiting for the next person to stand and say something. And then somehow my body rose up, as if propelled by its own motor. I didn't even know what I was going to say, but there I was standing in front of all these people.

I said, "Hello everyone. I'm Zoe Simoneau, and Ms. Hockensmith was my piano teacher for 25 years." I took a breath. "She wanted so badly for me to be a concert pianist. But I couldn't do it." Another breath. "I know I disappointed her." Another breath. "But I only want to say what a wonderful piano teacher she was; she knew everything about every piece ever written for the piano." A little laughter in the audience. "But what I really want to say is that she was a wonderful person, a true lady, kind, and deep." And I took another breath. "And I loved her. I wish I had told her that when she was alive." And I sat down and began to cry.

The week after Ms. Hockensmith's funeral, I received a call from the lady who had come up to me at the Christmas program. Her name was Gillian Rothenberg, and she wanted to know if she could put me down to play the piano on February 12th at the Hilton Hotel in Woodland Hills.

"What time?" I asked.

"The program's from 1 to 3, so whatever's convenient for you."

"All right," I said. "Put me down for 2, but I should tell you that I have this stage fright problem, so if I can't make it at the last moment, you'll have to have someone else ready to go."

"No problem, if you can't play, we have an opera singer who will be delighted to sing another aria or two."

"Good enough then. I hope to see you on February 12th."

"Me, too," Gillian said, and hung up.

I decided the best way to handle this would be to not think about it at all, but I had to think about what piece or pieces I would play, if I played. What would ladies at a luncheon like to hear? Probably something short and snazzy. I thought about the Brahms' Rhapsody, a few Chopin pieces, and maybe the Liszt Sonata in B minor. I decided I would practice each piece to perfection, and then worry about which one it would be at some later date.

I asked Mrs. Hudson, if I could leave two hours early on February 12th, and she said no problem. My aide could handle the class for two hours without me.

For the next three weeks, I focused exclusively on my class, on the piano lessons I was giving at school, on my girls, and on my practicing.

As to my piano lessons at school, they were going pretty well. I had uncovered seven children, who could actually learn to read notes, two who could not read the notes, but liked playing on the keys and could play some semblance of a melody, and then there were several who just liked banging on the piano. And that was all right, too. I felt in some way, that even those who only banged were getting something out of it, and in some way all of them were making some kind of connection with one another.

On February 12th, I left my classroom at 1:15, went into the teacher's bathroom, changed from my jeans into a skirt, from my tennis shoes to black pumps, powdered my face, put on fresh lipstick and walked outside to meet Doug. I had arranged with him to pick me up at 1:30, and when I emerged from the school, there he was, waiting for me.

"Where to?" he asked, as I got into the car.

"The Hilton on Canoga Avenue."

At ten minutes past two, Gillian opened the door to the banquet room, and Doug and I walked inside. I saw a stage and a lovely black baby-grand on the stage. I saw no one else inside the room. As I climbed the few steps to the stage and approached the piano, I noticed it was a Yamaha. Somewhere in the distance I heard my name, Zoe Simoneau.

I had decided on the way over that I would play Chopin's Fantasy Impromptu, if I actually made it to the piano. I thought the name was fitting, and that the ladies would enjoy the theme of "I'm Always Chasing Rainbows."

I sat down on the piano bench, my fingers touched the keys, and I was immediately transported to a place where the conscious did not exist. I did not have to think about my fingers or the notes. I did not have to think at all; just pour every emotion I was feeling into the sounds emanating from the keyboard. I was completely and utterly immersed in the beauty of the melodies surrounding me.

When I was finished, I felt exhilarated, as I always did when I finished any piece I played well. And I had played this piece as well as I could.

It was then, I heard the applause and turned to set eyes on a sea of women, perhaps 200, all standing, applauding and calling out, "Encore, encore."

I stood, bowed and smiled at them. How wonderful they looked in their elegant suits, and lovely hair-dos.

And then, an unfamiliar sensation came over me. I wanted to play more for them; I wanted to please them. I thought of what to play. How about something light and quick? I sat back down at the piano, and rattled off Chopin's Black Key Etude. Again when I finished, there was this great applause and they were all standing again, and I didn't feel frightened, I didn't feel depersonalized, I felt great!

That afternoon, when I picked up my girls from school, I told them that I had just come from playing the piano at a women's luncheon. Of course, they knew about my illness and my fears of playing the piano in public.

"How did you do it?" Molly asked.

"Well, I had my best friend and guru with me, Doug."

"But still, weren't you nervous, Mom?" Sophie asked. She was the opposite of me. She loved performing in public.

"Not consciously, no. Because I put myself in a frame of mind where I didn't even know I was playing in front of an audience."

I'm so proud of you," Molly said. And then, "Do you think you'll do it again?"

"I don't know," I said. "Maybe I will. Maybe if someone asks me."

Later that evening, somewhere between cutting up the lettuce for a salad and seasoning the salmon for dinner, I felt this explosion of joy throughout my body. I had done it. I had performed in public. And actually enjoyed it.

Then I was overtaken with sadness. If only Ms. Hockensmith were still alive so I could share this with her.

Chapter Twenty-Two— Fate

Three months later, on a rainy evening in May, after her fourth court hearing where the judge continued his original order, Zoe was at the gym. She had joined the gym six months earlier because she felt her "almost" daily jog and weekly yoga class with Doug weren't enough exercise. She was going to be 37 at the end of the month, and was intent on making her body as strong and healthy as it could be. She liked using weights and feeling she was in control of her body, in control of her life. Each week she was making progress. Each week she could do more than last week. Her mantra was "Healthy body; healthy mind." Now where had she come up with that?

She had just gotten off the treadmill after running four miles uphill, when she heard a voice behind her say, "Zoe, is that you?"

She turned around, and there standing before her was Frankie. She felt a myriad of conflicting emotions: shock, embarrassment, excitement and curiosity. "Frankie," she said, "what are you doing here?"

"I belong to this gym."

"I've never seen you here before."

"I guess we're on different schedules," he said.

He looked great...older, his black hair still long and shaggy, with a few streaks of grey in it, his eyes black as ever. He was wearing un-pressed shorts and a worn grey t-shirt that said "TO

Baseball" but he was just as appealing as he had been 19 years ago.

"How've you been?" she asked.

"Good," he said. "And you?"

She considered all the things she could tell him and settled on, "Good."

"Now tell me the truth," he said.

"Why, do I look that bad?"

"No," he said, "you look that good."

"Thanks," she said, actually feeling young, slim and strong in her black tights and top.

"Say," he said, hesitating, "you wouldn't have time for a cup of coffee, would you?"

"Sure," she said. It was Eric's week to have the girls and she was all caught up on her classes at CSUN, so she had no reason to rush home.

There was a small café in the gym, and they walked over and sat at a tiny round glass table.

After they ordered, decaf tea for her; decaf coffee for him, he looked at her ring finger on which there was no ring, and asked, "Are you married?"

"Divorced," she said.

"Me too," he said. And then as they were served their beverages and he poured some cream into his coffee, he said, "You know, not marrying you was the biggest mistake I ever made in my life."

She smiled, "Maybe marrying me would have a bigger one."

"Why do you say that?"

"I've been through some pretty bad stuff," she said, "and dragged my husband through it with me."

"Yes," he said, "but if you had married me maybe there wouldn't have been any bad stuff."

"Maybe," she said. "We'll never know."

"So did you become a teacher?"

"Yes, I did. I taught 3rd grade for 14 years, but now I'm teaching kids with special needs at a private school, and I've gone back to CSUN to get my credential in Special Ed. What about you? Did you end up working for your dad?"

"Yes, I did, for a while. But it wasn't for me. My dad wanted me to be something I wasn't…a business man in a suit. I couldn't handle it."

"So what did you do?"

"Promise you won't laugh?"

"Promise."

"You won't believe this. I went back to school and became a teacher, a P.E. teacher."

She was surprised, considering how much he had disliked school. "Really."

"And now, I'm the baseball coach at Thousand Oaks Community College."

"Ah," she said, "that explains the t-shirt. Thousand Oaks Baseball."

He looked down as if he didn't remember which t-shirt he was wearing. "Yes," he said.

"Amazing," she said. "So you're living your dream."

"Not quite the dream I wanted, but the dream I could have."

His words touched a nerve in her. Should she say it or not? Then she said it, "I guess I could say the same thing about my life."

"In what way?" he asked.

"I wanted to be a concert pianist, and ended up being a school teacher."

"Yes," he said, "but being a school teacher is a worthy profession."

"Does that mean you're liking it?" she asked.

"I love the kids, I love being outdoors, and I love baseball. So what could be bad?"

"Nothing," she said. "By the way, do you have any kids?"

"No, unfortunately. My wife didn't want to ruin her figure. She only married me because she wanted to be an actress and thought my dad would put her in a movie. But when that didn't happen, she dumped me." He paused. "I should never have married her."

"So why did you?"

"She was pretty and it was time."

"Not a good reason."

"No, but my life's been good other than that." Sipping his coffee, "How about your husband?"

She had to think about that. "I guess I have to say he's basically a good guy, but he did some pretty awful things."

"Like?"

"Like cheating on me, and trying to take my daughters away from me."

"That doesn't sound like a basically good guy."

"Well I did hate him for quite awhile, but being totally objective, I can understand why he did what he did."

"Does that mean you don't hate him anymore?"

She had to think about that one. "Maybe a part of me still hasn't forgiven him, but no, I don't hate him anymore. Things are actually pretty good between us now."

"You're pretty forgiving."

"Yes, it's part of my .." She hesitated: therapy, philosophy, weltanschauung? And settled on, "philosophy."

"Not to hate anyone?"

"Yes. I think it hurts the person who hates, not the person who's hated."

His black eyes focused on hers. "And did you hate me, too?"

She thought back to that day, so many years ago, Frankie at her bedroom door saying, *I think we shouldn't be engaged anymore.* Aloud she said, "I think I was too out-of-it to hate you."

"Does that mean you've forgiven me, also?"

She tried to look at him as the man he was now, but all she could see was that boy of 19, who had plunked his tray next to hers so long ago at Pierce College. "Of course," she said.

"How long did it take?"

"I don't know, but I do know I forgave you."

"Well, I'm happy about that."

They both sipped their beverages, and then he said, "So, tell me about your daughters."

"I thought you'd never ask," she said, glad the conversation was taking a lighter turn. "I have two adorable girls: Molly, 12, and Sophie, 10. They're both very sweet and very smart. And I love every minute I get to spend with them. Eric, my ex, and I share joint custody, so I only have them two weeks a month, sometimes three, if Eric will let me have them an extra week."

Frankie drained what was left in his Styrofoam cup, and then focusing back on her. "Did you love him? Your husband. I mean when you were first married, before he cheated on you."

She thought about it. "I'm not sure," she said. "I'm not sure I know what love is."

"Did you love me?"

"I think I did. I thought I did. Maybe not."

"But you were going to marry me."

"Yes, but I was a kid. And anyway, it wasn't as if we were really going to get married. We were just going to get engaged, remember?"

"How could I forget?" And then a far away look in his eyes. "I'm so sorry I walked out on you. I've thought about it all these years."

"You shouldn't have. You were so young, and depressed about being cut from the team."

"I know all that, but still I should have stuck by you. I wish there was some way I could make it up to you."

"You don't have to make it up to me. It's in the past. It doesn't matter anymore."

"I know," he said, and then as if struck by a great idea, "How about if I take you out for a big fat dinner, and then to a Dodger game?"

She laughed. "You haven't changed a bit."

"Yes, I have. But for the better, I hope."

"You were such a nice kid."

"But I did a shitty thing."

"I know it was all your parents' fault," she said with a bit of sarcasm.

"Of course," he said. "Isn't it always? But still, I should have been stronger; I should have done what I wanted to do."

"I think it's time you forgave yourself," she said.

"I don't know if I'll ever be able to. But at least I can do what I want to do now. And that's take you out to dinner and a ball game."

She smiled, "That does sound like fun."

"So, do we have a date?"

"I don't know," she said.

"Why not?"

It was tempting. She liked being with him. He had lost none of his charm or good looks. And she was attracted to him. But she was doing so well. Should she take a chance of opening up her feelings for him again, of having her heart broken by him again?

He interrupted her thoughts. "It's only dinner and a ball game." He paused, and then in a persuasive tone, "I want to hear about you…about everything that's happened to you in the last…18 years?"

"Seventeen," she said. And then abandoning all rationality and going with her emotions, going with truth, "All right, let's do it," she said.

She gave him her phone number and they agreed to go out to dinner that Saturday night. She was just as curious about him as he seemed to be about her.

Eric dropped the girls off at 10 that Saturday morning, and after lunch Zoe took them to the Mall. They still loved the jewelry at *Claire's*, and they spent at least an hour picking out clip-on earrings and necklaces and bracelets.

They both wanted their ears pierced, but since Zoe had waited until she was in college to do hers; she thought they should wait at least until high school.

Andrew disagreed with her. "What's the big deal? In some cultures they do it when the girls are babies. And sometimes the men, too." Andrew would think like that since he had his ear pierced at 16.

It was a little moral dilemma. Claire agreed with Andrew; Mom and Dad agreed with her. Finally, she decided she'd just wait until their begging became too difficult for her to bear, and then she'd let them do it no matter how old they were.

On this Saturday, they didn't even bring up the subject…just looked at this earring and that, asking each other's opinion, and hers, and finally each one choosing three pairs of earrings, a bracelet, and a necklace. After shopping, the girls wanted to see the movie, *Holes*, so they bought pizzas and Cokes in the theatre and happily watched a pretty darn good movie.

By five-thirty, Hortensia had arrived to babysit and since Zoe didn't know what time she'd be home, Hortensia was happy to sleep over. Hortensia was, after all, part of the family.

At six, the doorbell rang. It was Frankie. Zoe brought him in and introduced him to the girls and Hortensia, and then the two of them left for dinner.

"We'll probably get to the Dodger game late," Frankie told her, "because I have this special restaurant I'd like to take you to."

Remembering his penchant for fast food places, Zoe said, "Don't tell me it's Burger King."

"No, it's a little nicer than that."

He had a black Acura SUV, and she noticed that the back was filled with baseball bats, balls, and other sports paraphernalia. "It'd be pretty easy to guess what kind of work you do," she said as they were driving along Ventura Boulevard.

"My cars always looked like this...except everything was in the trunk...out of sight."

"Aren't you afraid of theft?'

"Nothing's back there that can't be replaced. I keep my valuable stuff at home."

The words 'valuable stuff' reminded her, "Are you still collecting baseball cards?"

"Not so much, but what I do have is pretty valuable. I keep them in a safe deposit box at the bank."

"So someday you'll be a rich man."

"I'll never be rich," he said, "but I do okay. Besides coaching, I also run a baseball camp in the summer, which is more fun than profitable, but every little bit helps."

After a short drive, they arrived at the restaurant which she wouldn't have known was there if he hadn't parked in front of it. Inside, it was tiny, dark and quiet. "How did you find this place?" she asked.

"A friend of mine told me about it. He knows I like little mom and pop places...I hate big noisy restaurants."

"Me, too," she said.

There were only 12 tables in the place, all covered with white tablecloths and cloth napkins, and the husband was the chef and his wife was the waitress. "This is really quaint," Zoe said, happy that it was small and quiet. She really did hate big noisy restaurants.

The menu was limited. Some fish, some pasta, short ribs of beef, and steak.

"What do you like?" he asked.

"I think the grilled salmon with capers," she said.

"Sounds good to me. I'll have the same."

After they gave their orders, and a bottle of red wine arrived, Frankie asked, "So tell me what have you been doing the last 17 years?"

She sipped at her wine. "Teaching, being a mom to my two girls..."

He interrupted her. "They're really beautiful. Just like their mom."

"Thanks," she said. "They're not just beautiful, they're also good people. I can't believe how kind and caring they are. I suppose I'm prejudiced, but since I deal with children all the time, I guess I do have some credentials."

"I'm sure you're completely objective."

"Only sometimes I worry that they're too grown-up. Probably because of what I put them through."

"And what's that?"

"My illness. It has a name, you know."

"No. I don't really know anything about it. I left before I could find out."

She glowered at him in a friendly way. "I told you to forget the past."

"Sorry," he said, "but it's not so easy. The guilt runs pretty deep."

She put her hand on his. "You didn't do anything most men wouldn't have done."

"I hate to think of myself as most men. But go on. I want to hear about your illness."

"It's called 'depersonalization disorder'."

"Meaning?"

"Exactly what it says. You lose the person you are."

Taking another sip of wine. "Sorry, but I still don't understand."

"I tried to explain it to you that day. That day you came to see me."

"But I didn't understand it then, and I still don't."

She had been through this so many times, she should have been able to define it easily, but at this moment, it still seemed difficult. "It's as if I'm in a dream. I can see everything, the people, the place, even myself, but nothing seems real to me, not even myself."

"Sounds pretty awful."

"It is," she said.

"So how often does this happen to you?"

"It's unpredictable," she said. He was looking at her, waiting for her to continue. Should she tell it all, or not tell it all, and she then plunged forward. "It happened several times when I was a child, and then it seemed to happen every summer. In fact, I spent many summers completely out-of-it."

"How terrible for you."

"And everyone around me. Fortunately, my mother, and sister and brother, and sister-in-law pitched in to help, and my mother-in-law while I was married, and of course, Hortensia, whom you just met. She was a lifesaver. In fact, I don't know how I would have survived without all of them."

She took a breath. "So you see how lucky you were not to have gotten tied to me."

Frankie, looking at her with his black syrupy eyes said, "I don't see it that way. I see how sorry I am that I couldn't have been there for you."

Zoe felt the tears forming in her eyes.

Then their salmon arrived.

Zoe and Frankie both dug in. "Ummm, this is delicious," Zoe said.

"That's why I come here," he said. "And of course, for the ambiance."

"So enough about me," Zoe said between mouthfuls of salmon. "Tell me about you."

"No," he said, "I want to hear more about you. Are you still playing the piano?"

"Funny you should ask," she said. "As a matter of fact, I just played in public for the first time in my life."

"No kidding."

"Yes, it was part of my illness...not being able to play in public. But then at Christmas time, I played for a fundraiser at my school, and amazingly, played again for another fundraiser for the City of Hope."

"Fantastic," he said.

"Yes, it was fantastic. I never knew how good it would feel. Connecting to other people in that way." Zoe reminisced for a moment, thinking back to standing before all those people, the applause, the admiration on their faces. Then she came back to Frankie. "Now that really is enough about me. It's your turn to talk."

"Well, as you know, I went to NYU Film School, lived with my sister, her husband, and their two kids, for a year, and really hated New York."

"I've never heard anyone say that."

"It wasn't my kind of place...too noisy, too busy, everyone rushing about, knocking you over in the subway. I think I became a lot more belligerent there, and as you know I'm usually a pretty peaceful guy."

"Did you go to any plays?"

"Yes, a lot. But more movies. I was a film major."

"And how did you like the school?"

"The school was pretty cool. But most of the people there really wanted to be there. Really wanted to be actors, writers, directors, or producers. I wanted to be a baseball player, so I didn't really fit in, although I did make some good friends."

"How was it living with your sister?"

"No problem. She has a boy, he was seven then, and that was the best part of my day, playing catch with him."

She laughed. "You are a dyed-in-the-wool baseball player." And then more pensive, "It's sad you never a son of your own."

"Yes," he said, "the greatest regret of my life, except for leaving you, of course." She gave him a smiling look of reprimand, and he continued, "But now I've got 28 boys a year, so I'm a happy camper, in that respect."

She took the last bite of salmon. "So, tell me about your marriage."

"As I said, she was a great actress. She conned me into thinking she loved me, but all she wanted to do was get into my dad's pictures. Unfortunately, my dad didn't think she was such a great actress and never cast her...so she dumped me."

"Oh, Frankie, how sad."

"It's all right. Looking back, I wasn't really in love with her. More flattered that such a beautiful girl could really love me."

Zoe reflected for a moment. "I guess it was the same with me and Eric. I was so flattered that such a brilliant and handsome man could love me."

"Then you weren't in love with him, either?"

"I don't know. I don't know what love is. Maybe I was at the time."

"And what about me?"

"I don't know about you, either."

"Thanks a lot," he said.

And trying to make him feel better. "But I was crazy about you."

"Except sexually," he said.

She felt a little embarrassed. "Then you noticed."

"I did and I didn't. I was a young kid then and all I wanted to do was get my rocks off. I didn't really understand that it was my responsibility to make you happy, too."

"And now you do."

"I've been with a lot of women since then, although no one I wanted to be with for the rest of my life, but I've learned a lot."

"So now you're an expert."

"Absolutely." Finished with his salmon, he wiped his mouth with his napkin. "Why don't we go back to my place and let me prove it?"

She laughed, "I see you haven't changed a bit."

"Not in my feelings for you," he said. "So what about it?"

She looked at him. He was Frankie. The same Frankie he had been 17 years ago, his black shaggy hair, his black eyebrows over those intense black eyes, the infectious smile on his face. She had been attracted to him then and she was attracted to him now.

But going to his place? Having sex with him? Was she really ready for that? Would she be letting herself in for another let-down, another disappointment? Not just from him, but from herself. Perhaps she should wait awhile, get to know him better. But it was nagging at her—the big question. Was she capable of enjoying sex? She was the healthiest she'd ever been. She had felt sexually attracted to Doug, and now she was feeling it for Frankie. That same desire rising from deep within her...to be close to him, to feel his body close to hers, and for whatever else might happen.

"So?" he asked.

"I'm thinking about it," she said, still considering all the ramifications. She wasn't on the pill...she could get pregnant, and then there were all the sexually transmitted diseases including Aids. The whole thing was crazy, and yet, there was an excitement about Frankie. Nothing logical or intellectual...something visceral. What would Doug say? Go with truth. And the truth was, she wanted to be with Frankie. "I *would* like to see where you live," she said.

"Great," he said, reaching into his back pocket for his wallet. The wife/waitress had left the check on the table. Then looking up at her, "Nothing's going to happen that you don't want to happen."

"I'm counting on that," she said.

Driving to his place, she asked, "What about the Dodger game?"

"We'll go tomorrow night," he said.

He lived in a small two-story house in Calabasas. It had no yard to speak of, but what did he need a yard for with no children? She liked it. It was cozily furnished in browns and beiges, the same as his parents' Tarzana house. There was an oak bookcase on one side of the living room filled with his trophies, and the walls were covered with photographs of him in different baseball uniforms with different teams, and him alone with different people who must have been important to him, and a few pictures of, she assumed, famous baseball players.

"Who's this?" she asked, pointing to a man in a San Diego Padres uniform.

"That's Tony Gwynn," he said. "He was the kind of hitter I wanted to be. Not power, just consistency."

"And that?" she asked pointing to another photo.

"That's Bob Feller, you must of heard of him, one of the greatest pitchers of all time, and that's me with Roberto Alomar, one of the greatest 2nd basemen of all time. And this," he said with pride, "is my team at Thousand Oaks Community College, the greatest guys in the world." She looked at their young faces, and Frankie's face beside them, beaming.

"I bet you're a good coach," she said.

"I hope I am," he said, putting his arms around her. "But I didn't bring you over here to look at my photos." He pulled her to him and he kissed her lips gently, oh so gently, but still she felt a shiver run through her body. Was it nervousness or excitement?

"I'm feeling nervous," she said.

"I understand," he said. "I'm going to go really slow and anytime you want to stop, just tell me."

"And what if I don't want to stop?" she said in a teasing voice.

"All the better," he said.

"One other thing," she was embarrassed to say it, but it had to be said, "I'm not on the pill...do you have..." she couldn't say the word condom, "something?"

"I have the best," he said. "I think it's called, 'tickle me Elmo'."

She laughed. "You always could make me laugh."

"You're my girl," he said, kissing her again, lightly on the lips, kind of teasing her, pressing gently, then a little harder, then more gently, and suddenly she relaxed. He was 19, she was 18, and she was crazy about him.

As he led her up the stairs, he said, "How about if we take a shower?"

"You mean, now?"

"Yes, now. I always find that a nice hot shower relaxes me. How about you?"

Yes, a nice hot shower did relax her, but under these circumstances? "Can we keep the lights off?" she asked.

"You have nothing to hide. You've always had a beautiful body."

"Thanks, but still...."

"Sure," he said, "we'll keep the lights off."

He led her to his bedroom, did not turn on the light, but she could see from the moonlight that the room was large and neat, and there was a brown comforter on the bed. She wondered if it was the same one he'd had 17 years ago.

He undressed her slowly, deliberately, pulling off her lime green sweater that did bring out the green of her eyes, pulling off her jeans, unhooking her bra, kissing and caressing her each step of the way, and then he turned on the water in the adjacent bathroom and led her in, and standing there naked, their two bodies entwined, she lost herself in the hot water, the steam, his caresses. He was washing her with soap, massaging her back, holding her back to his front, so that she felt his erection as he washed her breasts.

Then they were back in his bed and she was feeling his lips on hers, his tongue in her mouth, the urgency of his body pressing against hers. She remembered his kisses, the feel of his arms about her, the touch of his skin, his body. He was caressing her everywhere, his hands, his mouth, his tongue, and she was letting go, letting everything go, and just feeling, feeling, feeling. Feeling places she didn't know existed; feeling sensations she had never felt before. Where did it come from? All this passion, all this need, wanting it to go on forever, not wanting to stop, "Don't stop," she said aloud, and was groaning, wanting to scream, wanting to yell, "I don't believe it, I don't believe it, I don't believe it."

Finally when it was over, she collapsed on his body in a stream of sweat, unable to believe that it had happened, that it had finally happened, that she was not a freak but a real woman, capable of orgasms, full of tingling nerve endings that were still vibrating. He continued to caress her, and unbelievably, she reached another peak, and he held her tight and said, "Go, go, go," and finally she was spent, totally and utterly at peace.

She clung to him, kissed him all over his chest and arms, and face and lips.

"I guess I don't have to ask, how it was," he said, pulling her on top of him, and holding her close, so that their bodies felt fused together.

"It was awful," she said. "Terrible. I didn't feel a thing."

"I could tell," he said. "Maybe we'll do better next time."

"I don't think that's possible."

"Maybe not, but it'll be fun trying."

She was quiet for a moment. "Should I tell you what I'm thinking?"

"You can tell me anything," he said.

"I'm wondering if there ever was anything wrong with me. I mean, sexually. Was it that you and Eric were poor lovers, or that I was on drugs, or is it that I've changed?"

"I don't think we'll ever know the answer to that...but I can tell you that right now you are one wild woman."

"You did it to me."

He began stroking her buttocks and the back of her legs. "Do you want to try again?" he asked.

She said, "You mean now?"

"Yes, now. This very minute."

"Are you up to it?"

"I don't have to be up to it."

"Well then, yes. I have a lot of making up to do."

Later that night, lying in her bed back home, with her children asleep in the rooms next to hers, Hortensia asleep in the guest room, she thought about Frankie and all that had transpired that night. Finally, finally, she felt like a woman. Finally she had experienced what every normal woman experiences, if she's lucky; what Claire had experienced a thousand times. Finally, she understood what all the fuss was about. Why people would kill for it, or ruin their lives for it, or give up everything for it. And finally, she understood why Eric left her, and why Claire stayed with Phil all those years.

How sorry she felt for all the women who hadn't experienced what she had tonight, and how sorry she felt for herself...all those years of suffering through sex, when she could have felt the ecstasy she felt tonight. Frankie had brought it all out of her, and for that, she would always be grateful. But did she love him? She thought about Eric and Doug. Frankie was so different from both of them. Eric was security; Doug was peace; but Frankie was excitement.

She turned on her side. She was totally physically and mentally exhausted. What a wonderful feeling. She wouldn't think about anything else tonight. Tonight she would just relive all that had happened with Frankie, and tomorrow, in the light of day, she would sort it all out.

Chapter Twenty-Three — Visiting the Past

A month later, on a Sunday afternoon, Zoe, Molly and Sophie were driving with Frankie out to the Malibu house. As they were winding through the canyon, Frankie put his hand on Zoe's. "How are you feeling?" he asked.

"I'm a little nervous," she said.

"Should we call Doug?" he asked in a teasing tone. He knew all about Doug, her feelings for him, and how much he had helped her.

She smiled. "No. I'm not that nervous."

Soon the ocean came into view. "Look girls," Zoe said. "Look. There's the ocean."

It appeared just as they made their way around a curve on the mountainous road. All of a sudden, there it was, this huge expanse of blue grey water, going on to infinity. It never ceased to enthrall her, every time it came into view. And even sitting on the beach, or driving along the ocean highway, it was an amazing sight.

"When can we go swimming, Mom?" Sophie asked.

"Right after lunch," Zoe answered. She had brought their swim suits and boogie boards. Her plan was that right after lunch, the four of them, Frankie, Zoe and the girls would climb down the narrow wooden steps to the beach and spend the afternoon in the sun and the water.

In a few minutes, Frankie drove through the open iron gate that fronted the Felder's house, and parked in front of the garage.

The Felders always kept their cars in the garage so the salt sea air and moisture wouldn't rust the exterior or interior.

"Well, here we go," Frankie said to Zoe and the girls, as they ambled out of Frankie's black SUV.

He opened the front door with his key, and they entered the massive blue-cushioned living room with its 180 degree view of the beautiful blue Pacific. Zoe remembered the last time she'd been here, and shuddered. What a nightmare that had been. What a nightmare it might be again. She let the thought pass through.

The girls ran to the window. "This is really awesome," Molly said.

"Yes, isn't it beautiful," Zoe said, following them, again struck with amazement at the fantastic view.

In a minute, Sheila appeared from the kitchen, just as thin, but looking a little older, her hair a little blonder, her makeup a little more noticeable. "You're here," she said approaching Frankie and giving him a kiss on the cheek, and then holding out her hand to Zoe. "So glad to see you again."

"Thank you…" Zoe hesitated, what to call her? And decided on, "Sheila."

"And these must be your daughters," Sheila said, looking at Molly and Sophie.

Both girls moved closer to their mother's side, as if to protect her, or perhaps themselves. "Yes, this is Molly, and this is Sophie," Zoe said.

"They're beautiful," Sheila said.

"You have an awesome house," Molly said, always the polite and well-mannered child.

"Thank you," Sheila said.

Sophie turned to her mother, "Can we go down to the beach now?"

"I think we better wait until after lunch," Zoe told her.

"Well then, can we eat lunch now?" Sophie, the uninhibited child, asked. Sheila laughed as Molly nudged her sister as if in a reprimand.

"I'll tell you what," Sheila said to Sophie, "We'll eat just as soon as Sheldon shows up."

At that very moment, as if on cue, Sheldon appeared, winding his way up the staircase from his office.

"Well, well, well," he said, "the gang's all here." He went directly to Zoe and took her hand with his left hand, patting it with his right, "How nice to see you again." Then looking at the girls, "And these must be your daughters." He was all charm, but he, too, was looking older. His paunch was now a belly, and he was completely bald except for a fringe of grey-black hair that circled the back and sides of his head.

"Yes," Zoe said. "This is Molly and this is Sophie."

He held out his hand to each of them. "Well, what pretty girls. So tell me, how old are you?"

"Twelve," said Molly.

"Ten," said Sophie.

"Well, I thought you were older than that. You both look so grown up. And you're both so pretty."

Both girls seemed to relax. Zoe could tell they liked him.

"Now, let's have lunch," Sheila said, smiling at Sophie, and they all followed her into the kitchen.

Sheila had set a lovely table, flowered china plates and crisp cloth napkins sitting on blue lace place-mats, with a centerpiece of fresh flowers. She served a large mixed green salad, tuna salad, egg salad, a basket of various kinds of breads: egg, whole wheat, and French rolls, and after they were seated, brought to the table a steaming casserole of macaroni and cheese. "I know young people love macaroni and cheese," she said to Molly and Sophie. "Both my grandchildren in New York love it."

Sheila was right about the macaroni and cheese; Molly and Sophie did love it. They actually loved everything that was served, as did Zoe.

After the pleasant lunch with the magnificent view, Sheila and Sheldon both directing most of their conversation to Molly and Sophie, but also asking Zoe about her job, Sheila shooed them all out of the kitchen. "I'll clean up. You all just have fun."

Nevertheless, Zoe did help clear the table.

Then she, Frankie, and the girls changed into their swim suits, got one of Sheila's beach blankets and some towels, took their boogie boards and net bag carrying bottles of water, sun screen, and a nerf ball so that Frankie could play catch with the girls, and headed for the living room.

As they were walking out to the patio leading to the steps, Sheila appeared and said to Frankie, "You go ahead with the girls. I want to talk to Zoe for a minute."

Frankie looked at Zoe, and she looked at him. "Go ahead," Zoe said, "I'll be down in a few minutes."

He hesitated for a moment, "Okay, see you on the sand."

As Zoe watched the three of them make their way down the steep wooden steps, a feeling of dread was building in her stomach…was this going to be it? Was this going to be the confrontation she had been worrying about for the past two days? The end of another beautiful dream, a repeat of the last time she was here?

Sheila took both Zoe's hands in hers, "Zoe, I just wanted to apologize." Zoe let out her breath. "I just want to tell you how sorry I am for what happened all those years ago. I acted so badly. I just want to say I'm sorry, and I hope you'll forgive me."

Tears were forming in Zoe's eyes, as she said, "Oh, Sheila, how kind of you and how courageous. Of course I forgive you. I forgave you years ago."

The two women put their arms around each other and hugged, and when they let go, Sheila said, "If only I'd known then, what I know now…."

"It's all in the past," Zoe said, "it's time to move on to the future."

"Yes, the future," Sheila said. "I'm so happy that you're doing so well and that you and Frankie have found each other again."

"Me, too," Zoe said.

And with a little pat on Zoe's arm, "Now go on and join your family."

"Yes, I will," Zoe said, and then as she was about to walk out the patio door, she turned to Sheila and said, "Thank you, Sheila."

The tears were spilling out of her eyes as she made her way down the steep wooden steps. There were so many steps, maybe a hundred, but there at the bottom, playing nerf ball on the sand and running in and out of the waves breaking against the shore, were the three people Zoe loved most in the world.

Chapter Twenty-Four — Thanksgiving Day, 2008

Gail was rushing about, putting the finishing touches on the tables before the company arrived. She set out, as she did every year, paper turkeys she saved from year to year, vary-colored gourds and corncobs, and fresh flowers. She had set two tables: one in the dining room for the adults, and a folding table in the adjacent living room for the children. There was no way she could get everyone around one table, although she would have preferred that they all sit together. But thank God there were too many of them to sit at one table.

At 4 p.m., as she was putting out the appetizers on the kitchen table, the doorbell rang.

She took a sip of the white wine she had just poured for herself—she always felt she needed a sip of wine before the first person arrived at a big party—and hurried to the front door. It was Doug with a bottle of red wine in his hand. Gail greeted him with a hug. "I'm so happy to see you," she said.

"I'm so happy to be here," he said, handing her the bottle.

As she closed the door behind him, she said, "Are you up to doing a little work?"

"Whatever you need," Doug said.

"Could you put out a few bridge chairs for me?" she asked in her, 'I hate to ask, but you'd be doing me such a big favor' voice.

"No problem."

Doug set to work and when he was just about finished, Gail walked over to him. "I can't thank you enough," she said.

"For putting out a few chairs?"

"Yes, for that," she hesitated a moment, "and for saving Zoe's life. What would we have done without you?" she asked.

"Zoe saved her own life," he said, unfolding the last bridge chair and setting it at the kids' table.

"No," Gail said, "she couldn't have done it without you."

"But I couldn't have done it without her."

"Oh, you," Gail chided, "you just won't take credit for anything."

And then the doorbell rang.

It was Andrew arriving with his brood...his wife, Amy, and his two kids, Aaron and Jessica. He was carrying his guitar and looked quite presentable for him, wearing jeans and a real shirt with buttons and a collar, only one earring, and none of his tattoos visible.

His hair and Amy's both looked great, shaggy with several shades of blonde in them, only Amy had thrown in some red as well, but then what would one expect from two successful hairdressers? And they were successful. Their shop had done so well, in fact, that they had recently purchased a very expensive home in Calabasas.

Amy was not only a pretty girl, but a smart one, and Gail gave her most of the credit for the success of their salon. Several of Gail's friends and acquaintances went to them, and of course everyone in the family went to them, not because they wouldn't take any money from family, but because they were great. Andrew was still playing an occasional gig, and the whole family, including Gail and Dan, went to see him play whenever they could.

Now, Gail hugged each of them, especially the little ones. "There's appetizers on the kitchen table," she said, "and drinks on the bar."

Doug came to the door and embraced Andrew and his family. "Good to see you, dude," the guys said to each other.

The doorbell rang again.

Gail hurried to it. Claire was standing at the door with her new boyfriend, Alex. Alex was 42, two years older than Claire, and worked at the Jet Propulsion Lab with Caitlin's husband, which was how they met – Caitlin had fixed them up. Alex was tall, had played basketball in high school, and loved to go camping, which Claire now also loved. Every weekend the two of them could get away, they would drive his camper to the mountains, the desert, the beach, and would go hiking, biking, swimming, or all three. Imagine that, Claire in a Winnebago. Who would have believed it?

Gail liked Alex and would be thrilled to pieces if Claire married him. She prayed for it daily. How sad that Claire was 40 and still not married. It might already be too late for her to have a baby. But what could one do? Life was a throw of the dice. Some people were lucky; others weren't. It was no more complex than that.

Dan finally came into the living room. He'd been watching football all day—starting with his Lions being trounced by the Tennessee Titans first thing in the morning, and ending with the Dallas-Seattle game—and was a little late getting ready. "Drinks and wine are on the bar," he said. Then he circled the room, hugging each person he came to, except Alex. When he came to Alex, he shook his hand. "Nice to see you again," he said.

"Thanks for having me," Alex said. He had his arm around Claire, and Gail thought, *This looks serious. Please, dear God.*

Everyone got a drink and then gathered around the kitchen table dipping vegetables into spinach dip, tortilla chips into guacamole, and shrimp into cocktail sauce. "Umm, delicious guacamole," Claire said. She was so slim that Gail was happy to see her eating.

"I got it at Trader Joe's," Gail told her.

"And did Dad get the wine there, too?" Claire teased. "Two-buck Chuck?" She was referring to a Trader Joe wine that sold for two dollars. "Of course," Gail said. "We only serve the best."

The front door opened, and in came the last guests: Sheila and Sheldon Felder, and Zoe, Frankie, and their three kids, Molly, Sophie, and Jack. All of them were surrounded by the rest of the family and there were hugs and kisses, shaking of hands, and then Frankie took Jack, Aaron and Jessica out to the back yard to hit and catch balls.

Frankie was hoping that Jack would love baseball as much as he did, but if he didn't that would be all right too. Actually, it was Andrew's son, Aaron, who was the baseball star. Ironic, Gail thought, that Andrew who had hated baseball would have a son who loved it. Perhaps the love of sports was inherited, after all, except in her family it had skipped a generation.

It wasn't long before Dan was out in the backyard with the kids, sitting on a patio chair, not participating, just watching, elated at how good the young ones were. Even Jessica liked to play ball. Maybe she would join a softball team in the spring. All thanks to Uncle Frankie.

Gail joined the group eating appetizers. How beautiful Molly and Sophie looked. She had worried about them. Worried that their mother being sick for such a lot of time would affect them adversely, but they seemed to be perfectly well-adjusted. Molly'd always been such a quiet girl, a lot like her father, and in a way, Gail had to give Frankie credit for bringing her out of her shell. His being so lively and outgoing had rubbed off on Molly.

Molly had gotten her father and mother's brilliance, and at 17 had already been accepted to UC Berkeley where she was going to major in pre-med. Another doctor in the family...what a wonderful thing.

Sophie, who'd always been vivacious, at 15, still wanted to be an actress. Speaking of vivacious, how different she was from Zoe at that age. All Zoe had cared about was her piano and her school work. Sophie loved being the center of attention. She thrived on it....maybe a bit like Claire, except that she'd always been thin like her mom. Her mom, Zoe, still so slender and pretty, and how well she looked today.

It had been a great five years for Zoe. She had gotten through her wedding with Frankie, albeit a small affair, just the immediate family at the synagogue, and then out to dinner at a lovely restaurant on the lake in Westlake, without a problem. Then gone through the pregnancy and birth of the new baby, Jack, what a doll, with only a murmur of her disease. And then, of course, there was her piano career, nine or ten appearances in the last five years: two recitals, six or seven times accompanying a violinist, singer, or cellist, and the crowning glory: her appearance as guest soloist playing Beethoven's 2nd Piano Concerto with the Cal State University Symphony. It wasn't the L.A. Philharmonic, but for Zoe, to play in front of any audience....Gail never thought she'd live to see the day.

Of course, there had been dips along the way, but dips Zoe came out of in a few days, or a few weeks at most. She had a good support group now with Frankie, who adored her, and Doug still on call, and her therapist, Marcy Jacobs. Between the three of them, Zoe was leading a mostly normal life. Thank God, Gail thought. Thank God.

Gail looked at her watch; it was time for dinner.

She was going to serve buffet style. Everything was ready to go: either warming in the oven: turkey, stuffing, mashed potatoes, sweet potatoes, green bean casserole, and rolls; or staying cool in the refrigerator: a mixed green salad of baby lettuces and veggies, cranberry sauce, and a relish tray of black and green olives and kosher dill pickles. For dessert there would be apple, cherry, pumpkin, and boysenberry pies with whipped cream, an assortment of cookies, and various flavors of ice cream. No one would go hungry today.

Before serving dinner, after the cocktail hour, which was really the wine hour, Gail called everyone to gather around the dining room table, and announced, "As you all know, it's a tradition in our family for us to go around the table and everyone say what he or she is thankful for. Who wants to start?"

"I will," Jessica, Andrew's nine-year-old said. "I'm thankful for my mom and my dad, and that we get to go to grandma's house every Thanksgiving for dinner, and for my new I-Pod."

Everyone chuckled.

"I'd like to say," Sheldon said, "that I'm thankful for Gail, who brings us all together on these wonderful occasions. And I'm thankful for all my grandchildren, even the ones in New York whom I seldom get to see. But thank God I get to see Molly, Sophie, and Jack. You are the lights of my life."

"Thanks, grandpa," Molly said.

"I love you, grandpa," Sophie said.

Sheila spoke, "I'll ditto that," raising her glass and looking at Molly and Sophie. "But I also want to say how thankful I am that Zoe is part of our family." She seemed choked-up. "She's made all of us so happy. Where would we be without her?"

"Home alone," Sheldon interjected, and everyone laughed as Zoe said, "Thank you, mom," and Andrew raised his wine glass, and said, "Here, here, to Zoe."

"To Zoe," everyone said, several raising their glasses.

After a brief hesitation, Claire, holding hands with Alex, spoke, "I'm thankful for my wonderful family, and that Alex is in my life." A little blush.

Alex went next, "I'm thankful that Claire is in my life and that she has such a wonderful family." They turned to each other and sent looks of love.

Molly, who was holding Jack, said, "I'm thankful for my mom and dad, and Frankie, and my grandparents and aunts, uncles, and cousins, and my sister, Sophie, the drama queen, and my little brother, Jack, the cutest little boy in the whole wide world." And she gave Jack a big kiss on the cheek.

"Let's hear it for Jack," Andrew said, and everyone called out, "Jack, Jack, Jack."

When they quieted down, Sophie said, "I'm thankful for my mom and dad, and Frankie, and my sister and brother and everyone here today, and that I get to play Maria in *The Sound of Music*. And you all better be there. December 17, 18 and 19."

Another chuckle among them, as several called out, "Of course, we're coming," and, "We wouldn't miss it."

Then Frankie turned to Jack, who was still in Molly's arms. "Hey, big guy, do you want to say anything?"

"Yes, I want to say," Jack said, thinking as he went, "I love my mommy.... and my daddy..... and my Molly and my Sophie.... and everyone."

Frankie said to his son, "That was so good, Jack." Then putting his arm around Zoe's shoulders, "I'm thankful that I married my beautiful 18-year-old sweetheart and that we have three great kids, Molly, Sophie and Jack," looking at each as he spoke his or her name, "and that I have a father-in-law who loves baseball as much as I do."

Dan laughed and then said, "As you all know, I'm not a man of many words," (a few snickers in the group) "but I just want to say" (looking directly at Andrew) "how proud I am of all my children and how happy you've made me by giving me the best grandchildren in the world." Then, as if remembering something, "And to Doug...you know I love you like a son...so where are my grandchildren?"

Everyone laughed and Doug said, "I have to find a wife first."

"Well then, Doug, why don't you go next," Gail said.

He thought a moment, "For all of you who know me so well, I'm just thankful to be here, now, at this moment."

Andrew said, "I'll ditto what Doug said, but basically, I'm just happy I'm going to get a good meal tonight 'cause Amy doesn't cook for me anymore. Anyway, I wrote a song about that, *Amy don't cook for me no more*, which I will sing for you later."

Aaron said, "I'm thankful for my mom and dad and my Uncle Frankie who's going to make me into the greatest baseball player who ever lived."

"Here, here," Andrew said. "Let's hear it for Uncle Frankie."

And everyone joined in, "Uncle Frankie, Uncle Frankie."

There were only two people left, Zoe and Gail.

Gail, wanting to save the best for last, spoke up, "I guess it's my turn. Well, I just want to say, looking around the table at all of you, all of the people who mean the most to me in this world, I am bursting with joy. I wish you all good health, and may we all be together next year at this same time." She raised her glass and everyone clicked glasses and said, "Good health" or "Next Year," or both.

Now it was Zoe's turn, "I guess I'm up. Well, I am thankful for my beautiful daughters, Molly and Sophie, for my handsome son, Jack, for my wonderful husband, Frankie, for my dearest friend, Doug, for my family who stood by me through my darkest days, and for every minute that I am in the real world. I know that life does not stay in the same place for very long, and that at any moment, everything can change, but for today, for this

Thursday afternoon in November, 2008, everything is as good as it gets."

Everyone was quiet for a moment, and then Frankie pulled Zoe close to him and said, "Amen."

Glasses clicked as "Amen" echoed throughout the room.

"And now," Gail said, "let's eat."

The End

About the Author

Rosalee Jaeger grew up in Detroit, Michigan, graduated from the University of Michigan where she won the prestigious top Hopwood Award for fiction; acquired her teaching credential from UCLA, studied creative writing with, among others, Robert Kirsch and Megan Crane at UCLA; taught piano, high school English and social studies; managed a law office; and won several Valley Writer's Club awards.

She has edited several published books, short stories, and the movie, *Jinn*; and has published one previous novel: *Love and Other Passions.*

She now resides in Los Angeles with her husband, Martin Jaeger.

Questions for Discussion

1. What are Zoe's strengths and what are her weaknesses?

2. How do Zoe's parents affect her early life, and then her later life?

3. Do you consider her parents, good parents? If so, why; if not, why not?

4. How does Claire affect Zoe's life; and how does Zoe affect Claire's life? Did they love each other?

5. How does Andrew affect Zoe's life, and how does Zoe affect Andrew's life?

6. Who is the stronger person in Gail and Dan's relationship?

7. What effect do Gail and Dan's parents have on the people they become?

8. Do Gail and Dan love their children equally?

9. Do you like the young Frankie? If so, why; if not, why not?

10. Do you think the young Frankie was good for Zoe?

11. How did Frankie's parents affect the lives of Zoe and Frankie?

12. In what ways did Frankie change from the young man to the man who later enters Zoe's life?

13. Do you think you Zoe's illness was caused by heredity or environment? Give reasons to support your view.

14. What kind of person was Eric? Was he justified in leaving Zoe? Was he justified in taking the children? Did he change throughout the course of the novel?

15. Have you ever met anyone like Doug? What makes Doug so likable?

16. Do you believe Doug's techniques were totally responsible for Zoe's improvement?

17. What are your feelings about Ms. Hockensmith and her relationship with Zoe?

18. Did you like or dislike Gloria? Why?

19. What were the most touching moments of the novel?

20. Why did Zoe's illness often reappear in June?

21. Why did the author change "Point of View" in the last chapters?

22. Were you satisfied with the ending? Why or why not?

8011146R0

Made in the USA
Charleston, SC
30 April 2011